D0105813

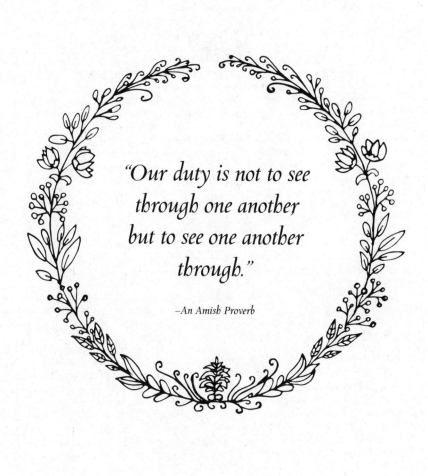

"Our duty is not to see through one another but to see one another through."

–An Amish Proverb

MYSTERIES *of* LANCASTER COUNTY

Another's Treasure
Garage Sale Secret
An Unbroken Circle
Mixed Signals
Stamp of Approval
Plain Beauty

PLAIN BEAUTY

MYSTERIES *of* LANCASTER COUNTY

Leslie Gould

Guideposts

New York

Mysteries of Lancaster County is a trademark of Guideposts.

Published by Guideposts Books & Inspirational Media
39 Old Ridgebury Road
Danbury, CT 06810
Guideposts.org

Copyright © 2019 by Guideposts. All rights reserved.

This book, or parts thereof, may not be reproduced, stored in a retrieval
system, or transmitted in any form or by any means, electronic, mechanical,
photocopying, recording, or otherwise, without the written permission of
the publisher.

This is a work of fiction. The village of Bird-in-Hand, and Lancaster County,
Pennsylvania, actually exist, and some places and characters are based on
actual places and people whose identities have been used with permission
or fictionalized to protect their privacy. All other names, characters,
businesses, and events are the creation of the author's imagination, and any
resemblance to actual persons or events is coincidental.

Every attempt has been made to credit the sources of copyrighted material
used in this book. If any such acknowledgment has been inadvertently
omitted or miscredited, receipt of such information would be appreciated.

Scripture references are from the following sources: *The Holy Bible, King
James Version (KJV)*. *The Holy Bible, New International Version (NIV)*. Copyright
©1973, 1978, 1984, 2011 by Biblica, Inc. Used by permission of Zondervan.
All rights reserved worldwide. www.zondervan.com

Cover and interior design by Müllerhaus
Cover illustration by Bob Kayganich, represented by Deborah Wolfe, LTD.
Typeset by Aptara, Inc.

Printed and bound in the United States of America
10 9 8 7 6 5 4 3 2 1

PLAIN
BEAUTY

CHAPTER ONE

The breeze inspired Martha Watts to turn her face heavenward on a perfect early September morning. The baby blue sky shimmered as the sun warmed the day, and the leaves of the maple tree held a hint of gold, signaling that autumn was on its way.

Holding a basket of warm apple-caramel muffins, Martha couldn't help but smile. She was ready for the change of seasons.

And ready for the day ahead. Thursday mornings had come to be one of her favorite times of the week at Secondhand Blessings, the business she ran with her two sisters, Elizabeth and Mary. Rachel Fischer, their Amish neighbor and friend, led a quilting circle in the store from ten o'clock to noon that attracted both Plain and *Englisch* women alike.

This was the first circle since Labor Day. Martha had feared business at the shop might slow after the holiday, but there had been as many tourists as the week before zipping around the village. Hopefully that would bode well for their secondhand shop, which was a combination thrift store and gift shop, selling used and new items outright or on consignment.

Mary, Martha's younger sister, worked in a flower bed to the left of the door. She wore jeans rolled halfway up her calf, an orange T-shirt, and sneakers. Her blond hair was pulled back in a high ponytail, making her look much younger than her fifty years. But it wasn't just the ponytail, Martha thought. Mary always appeared younger than she was. Her carefree, happy-go-lucky personality added to that, along with her knack for living in the present. Martha did her best to appreciate Mary's personality for the positive aspects and not expect her sister to be more responsible than she was capable of.

"What do you think?" Mary held up a pot of deep purple mums. "Should I plant these here? Or in the backyard?"

"Here." Martha nodded toward the flower bed. "That way everyone can enjoy them. They'll look so pretty against the bright red planks." Years ago, their grandmother and grandfather had turned the family barn into a secondhand store and then, later, Mama had run the business. When she was ill the business had closed for five years, but then their older sister, Elizabeth, had the idea to revive the shop after Mama passed away. Martha, whose husband had also recently passed on, and Mary, whose husband had divorced her, both moved home to help.

Mary gave a thumbs-up with her free hand held high and then placed the pot of flowers down. With a dramatic flair, she plunged her trowel into the soft soil.

Martha couldn't help but grin. Her sister's impassioned approach to life sometimes annoyed her, but she had to admit she was entertained by Mary too.

She turned toward the front door and stepped inside, squinting until her eyes adjusted to the light. The building would always have a rustic feel, but it also felt cozy and cheerful with the racks of clothes, jewelry, old furniture, decorative items, tools, and shelves of household products. The gift items, which included Amish-made pot holders, kitchen towels, soaps, baskets, toy horses, and tins of fudge, filled the shelves to the right of the cash register. Sturdy pieces of furniture, both old and new, were gathered in another section. The charm of the shop, combined with the beautiful keepsakes, blessed Martha every time she stepped inside.

"Ready for the quilting circle?" she called out to Elizabeth, who, at fifty-seven, was two years older than Martha.

"Just about." Elizabeth wore a denim skirt, a brown blouse, her apron, and her signature practical shoes. She had pulled some chairs to the middle of the open area, around the quilting frame. The group was working on a simple nine-patch pattern made out of burgundy, forest green, and royal blue squares.

Martha set the muffins on the table next to the coffeemaker and then slipped her apron over her neck. Hosting the quilting circle took them away from their usual tasks, but it also brought women into Secondhand Blessings who shopped before and after the circle and talked up the business too. Word of mouth was still the best advertisement, especially in their village of Bird-in-Hand, located in the heart of Lancaster County.

The *clippety-clop* of a horse pulled Martha's attention back to the front doors. Rachel always arrived at least fifteen minutes early. Martha pulled her phone from her pocket. *9:45.* Rachel was right on time.

Elizabeth completed the circle of chairs as Martha stepped out to greet Rachel. A horse and buggy, driven by a woman, had turned into the parking lot. But it wasn't Rachel. It was Betty Yoder. A car turned in too, driven by Anne Hostetler.

The two had been at odds a few months ago but were now friends and members of the quilting circle.

Mary stood and brushed her hands on her jeans. "I'd better go get cleaned up." She grabbed the trowel and empty flowerpot and headed to the garden shed. Soon, Rachel's sisters, Marietta and Leora, arrived. Both had gray hair and laugh lines, while Leora was a couple of years older than Marietta, who was a few inches taller. Both of the women were widows, and they lived together in a *dawdy haus* on Leora's family land, which her youngest son now farmed. They were older than Rachel and just as sweet.

Speaking of Rachel, it wasn't like her not to be early. She lived on the farm next door and often walked over with her daughter Phoebe, who had Down syndrome, unless they were running errands before or after the quilting circle. Rachel had seven children at home, besides a grown son. Not only was she an amazing mother, but she was also a good aunt to her brother Alvin's daughters, whose mother had passed away several years before.

Martha greeted the women and told them to help themselves to muffins and coffee. "Rachel will be here soon." She hoped she was right.

Perhaps she'd been detained at home by one of her children. Martha could only imagine the trouble Rachel's twin eight-year-old boys might get into.

At the sound of horse hooves she stepped to the door again, but it was a buggy passing by. Her phone began to buzz, and she pulled it from her pocket. TRISH flashed on her screen. She answered it, ready to tell her only daughter she'd call her back in a couple of hours.

As soon as she said hello, Trish said, "I'm so glad you answered." Her voice sounded exhausted.

"Sweetie, what's going on?"

"It's Celeste." Martha's granddaughter was six and had just started first grade. "You know, I told you she's been sick? That she missed a couple of days of school."

"I remember," Martha said.

"Well, she's sick again. Her fever spiked last night. Do you think I should take her to the doctor? Or wait and see how she is by this afternoon?"

"Take her in," Martha said. "Go to urgent care if you can't get an appointment with her pediatrician. And let me know what you find out."

"Thanks, Mom," Trish said. "She's had some pain, but she can't really describe it. I was up most of the night with her—and I'm not thinking very clearly."

"That's understandable." It was at times like this, even though Martha doubted anything was seriously wrong, that she missed being in Kansas with her kids and grandkids.

After Trish said goodbye, Martha checked the time on her phone. 10:10. This wasn't like Rachel at all. Martha went to her contacts in her phone and pressed Rachel's number as she stepped into the driveway of Secondhand Blessings, looking down the road toward the Fischers' farm. Rachel's family phone was in a shed at the end of their driveway, so it wasn't as if anyone would actually answer the call. She'd have to leave a message.

Just as the call went to voice mail another buggy approached, but this one slowed and then turned. It was Rachel, with Phoebe on the seat beside her.

Martha let out a sigh of relief, but as the buggy neared it was clear that Rachel was distraught. Her movements were flustered, and her ever-present smile was missing. Martha followed the buggy to the hitching post. "What's wrong?" she asked as Rachel jumped down.

Rachel headed to Phoebe's side of the buggy to help her down. As she passed Martha, she said, "Little Davie is in the hospital. He has leukemia."

Martha's hand flew to her mouth. Davie was Rachel's great-nephew, but he was more like a grandson to her. The little one was four years old and absolutely darling with his dark eyes and honey-colored hair. How horrible that he had cancer.

To complicate things, the little boy's father had died in a farming accident a year ago. Trudy, Davie's mother, had already dealt with so much heartache in her young life.

Martha's thoughts went to her own daughter and granddaughter. *Please, Lord...*, she prayed silently. Surely nothing so dire was wrong with Celeste.

Rachel held Phoebe's hand as she climbed down. The young woman was twenty and a good help to her mother. "Davie's been sick for a few weeks and had a round of tests a couple of days ago," Rachel said, "but Trudy just found out the diagnosis." She tied the horse's reins to the hitching post and nodded toward Secondhand Blessings. "By the time I get inside, I'll be fine."

Martha marveled at Rachel's resolve. She wasn't so sure she could be as in control, but then again Rachel clung to Phoebe's arm as they marched toward the red barn.

Rachel didn't share her news with the other quilters, not even her sisters, which didn't surprise Martha. Rachel was the kindest and gentlest person she knew, but she was also very reserved.

It was Martha's turn to wait on customers during the circle time and Mary and Elizabeth's to join the other women. And Martha hovered close by, listening in when she could. It seemed as if the women sensed that Rachel was going through a trying time, because at first they were quiet, but after a few minutes Mary cracked a joke at her own expense.

"You all are doing great," she said, "but my stitches look like those of an eight-year-old who stayed up past her bedtime." The women laughed.

Rachel said drolly, "I believe they look like those of a fifty-year-old woman who needs to invest in a pair of reading glasses."

Everyone laughed again, including Mary.

When the laughter died down, Mary retorted with, "Cheaters? Nah, I'm too young for those." She put her hand on the back of her neck and struck a pose. The seriousness seemed to be broken, and the women began chatting as they continued their quilting.

Martha helped a customer find a pressure cooker in the small appliances section and then plugged in a bedside lamp for another customer so she could see that it actually worked.

The second customer nodded toward the quilting circle. "Is anyone welcome to join?"

Martha nodded. "At this time, yes. I imagine if we end up with too many quilters, we'll have to put a limit on the number." She told the woman that the group met every Thursday morning at ten.

"Thank you," the woman said. "I can't join anytime soon, but I'll keep it in mind. They're all having such a good time. My grandmother taught me to quilt as a child, but I haven't done it for years."

Martha didn't quilt either, except during her turn with the circle. She had so many things on her ever-expanding to-do list that the only time she felt she could dedicate to it was if she was interacting with Rachel and the group.

The two hours sped by, and the quilters started to pack up to go home. Some were working on projects of their own during the week. Others were beginners and only quilted with Rachel, hanging on to her every word of advice.

Rachel said farewell to each of the women except for Marietta and Leora. She asked them to stay then huddled with them, Phoebe still at her side, speaking softly. After a few minutes Leora asked Phoebe if she'd like to spend the afternoon with her aunts.

Phoebe grinned. "*Ja*, I would."

"We will bring her back after supper," Marietta said.

Then the two sisters headed out with Phoebe between them.

Once they'd left, Martha turned to Rachel. "Can you share the news with Elizabeth and Mary? They need to know too."

Rachel nodded and waited for Mary and Elizabeth to return from putting chairs away. When she told them about Davie, both sisters gave her a hug and assured her they'd be praying for Davie and the family before they returned to waiting on customers.

Rachel began to gather her things. "I'm afraid I revealed my lack of faith before," she said to Martha. "The Lord is in control. We must trust Him. Alvin raised his family after his wife passed. Trudy was a teenager and ran wild for a few years, but then she joined the church and married. She stayed strong after her husband died, and I'm praying she'll do the same now. We know *Gott's* ways are not our ways. Trudy will need to grow even more in her faith, and I'm trusting the Lord that she can."

Martha smiled at her. "I know she'll have a lot of support."

"That's true. Our community is already rallying around her."

Martha wished there was something she and her sisters could do to help, but the truth was Trudy wouldn't need anything they could offer. The Amish would do her chores and housework, cook her meals, cover the medical expenses, and do absolutely anything else she needed. It was one of the many beauties of the Plain community.

Rachel finished gathering up her things. As she turned toward the door, an Amish man stepped into the store. The breeze caught his white beard, blew it to the side, and lifted a tuft of white hair from his head at the same time, giving him the appearance of a wild Santa Claus without the mustache. A wild Amish Santa Claus. He squinted and locked eyes with Rachel. "There you are, Sister."

Rachel took a step toward him. "Alvin, is everything all right?"

He exhaled. "Hopefully it will be, but Davie is going to need a bone marrow transplant."

"I'll get tested," Rachel said. "As soon as possible."

Martha would be willing to also, and she guessed Elizabeth and Mary would too, although she knew a family member would be more likely to be a match.

"*Danki*," Alvin said. "But we are also going to have to raise money. The bishop just informed me that the mutual fund is low."

Martha knew that was the fund the Amish community contributed to, to share the cost of medical expenses.

Alvin continued. "You helped with the last school auction. I wondered if you could organize one for Davie."

"Of course," Rachel answered.

"Can you think of a place to have it?" Alvin asked.

"Not off the top of my head."

"At the school?"

Rachel shook her head. "It was big enough for the school auction but not a larger one." She tapped her chin with her finger. "Nothing comes to mind. We certainly do not have the storage space right now."

Alvin rushed on to a new idea. "I thought I would auction off that racing horse I just bought. I have not broken her to pull a buggy yet."

Rachel looked at him in surprise. "Your new horse? Plain Beauty?"

Martha marveled at the name. The horse was destined to be owned by an Amish man.

"Ja, that is the one," he answered.

"No, do not do that. I think we can raise enough money—"

Alvin cut her off. "You do not have any idea how much all of this is going to cost."

"But you were so pleased to buy that horse."

Martha turned toward the counter and busied herself, feeling as if she was eavesdropping.

Alvin ignored his sister's protests. "We will need a place to store the auction items."

Rachel shifted the folded quilt in her arms. "I would like to offer our place, but Silas and I don't have the room right now."

"Neither do I," Alvin answered.

"I will ask around," Rachel said. "And about a place to hold the auction too, although I can't think of anywhere at the moment."

Martha cleared her throat as she looked around the shop. Could the answer to Rachel and Alvin's dilemma be right here, staring her in the face?

CHAPTER TWO

Elizabeth remembered Trudy from when she was a teen-ager and spent time on her aunt Rachel's farm, sometimes for weeks at a time. In fact, Elizabeth had prayed for the girl for years. She had an older sister, Amanda, who seemed to sail through her teen years with no drama. Amanda was now married to a good Amish man and lived nearby.

As Rachel and Alvin headed toward the door, Elizabeth called out, "Do Trudy and Davie need a ride to any appointments? I'd love to help with that."

"Danki." Rachel turned and smiled. "I will let Trudy know."

As they stepped outside, Elizabeth met Martha's bright blue eyes and asked, "What are you thinking?"

"That surely there's more that we can do besides offering rides."

Elizabeth agreed. Of course they'd do whatever they could to help, but before they could discuss the subject more, Martha's phone rang.

She pulled it from her apron pocket. "It's Trish."

"Tell her hello," Elizabeth said. She didn't have any children of her own, which meant she'd always taken a special interest in Martha's and Mary's kids and their grandkids too.

From the tone of Martha's voice, Elizabeth grew concerned.

"I'm so glad you took her to the doctor," Martha said, her delicate features pulled tight.

Celeste must be ill.

After a long pause, Martha said, "I'm praying. Give Celeste a big hug from Grandma and tell her I love her. Love you too."

Martha said goodbye and ended the call.

"What's wrong?" Elizabeth asked.

"Celeste has been running a fever, so Trish took her to the doctor." Martha's face was troubled. "The doctor wants to run tests."

"What are they looking for?"

"Anything right now that explains the fever, her fatigue, and pain, which seems to be mostly in her legs." Martha slipped her phone back into her apron pocket. "Hopefully it's nothing…"

As a young couple came through the door, Elizabeth said, "Perhaps it's just a virus, something she picked up at school."

"That's what I hope," Martha said softly as she turned toward the customers with a smile. "Welcome to Secondhand Blessings."

Elizabeth headed back to the small appliance section to straighten the shelves while Martha directed the couple to the furniture section. The day continued on at a fast pace with the sisters taking turns getting lunch and taking breaks. Late in the afternoon, Elizabeth walked to the house to start the chores while Martha and Mary finished up in the shop.

First, she fed the pets—their border collie, Pal, their dachshund, Tink, and orange tabby, Butterscotch. The pets mostly got along. But one thing was certain—they were always entertaining. Then she took care of the chickens and goats.

Once Elizabeth was in the house, she opened the window over the sink to a slight breeze. Hopefully it would be pleasant enough to eat out in the backyard.

The kitchen was Elizabeth's favorite room of the old Victorian house that had been in their family for generations. The kitchen cabinets had been built by Daddy and painted by Mama. And the window curtains were gingham, made years ago by Mama. They were faded and needed to be replaced, but none of the three sisters would consider such a betrayal of the past.

A lot of love and laughter had filled the room through the years, besides the delicious smells and delectable food. The kitchen was definitely the heart of their home.

As Elizabeth chopped up leftover chicken and then celery, grapes, and pecans for chicken salad, she realized she was humming "Amazing Grace." It had been one of their mother's favorite songs. As she mixed the dressing for the salad, she prayed for Davie and then for Celeste. Two children, one in Lancaster County and one in Kansas, who both needed God's grace.

Her heart skipped a beat. How hard it must be for Martha to be so far away from her children and grandkids at this time.

When little Davie's mother, Trudy, was a teenager, she lived with Rachel and her family for a time. Elizabeth hadn't known the circumstances when she used to pray for Trudy and her sisters, but she did know the girls' mother had died when they were young. Trudy was the youngest of the three girls. The middle daughter, Amanda, had joined the Amish, but the oldest sister had left the order. And, it seemed, Trudy had been running with a wild group of Amish *youngie* during her *rumspringa*.

But, over time, she came around. How tragic to have her husband die and now her little boy be diagnosed with cancer.

Elizabeth offered up a prayer for both Davie and Trudy. And for Rachel, her family, and Alvin too.

Just after five thirty, as Elizabeth finished up the salad, Mary and Martha came in through the back door. "I did not ruin the sale," Mary said. "I simply said we opened at ten tomorrow morning, implying he could think about the purchase and come back."

"But maybe someone else will buy it before then."

Mary rolled her eyes. "Right. There's probably a million in one chance that someone else wants that obscure tool. I don't even know where he dug it up from. On some back shelf, most likely."

Unable to contain her curiosity, Elizabeth asked, "What are you two talking about?"

"An old level that an elderly man was thinking about buying. Mary didn't push the sale—she just let it go."

"Because I'm not as controlling as you are," Mary retorted. "I let people make their own decisions in life."

It was a common argument between the two, who couldn't be more different in personality. Elizabeth, as she'd been doing for years, quickly changed the topic. "How about if we eat outside?"

"What a great idea," Mary said as Martha responded, "No thank you."

Elizabeth laughed. "Well, I'm going to eat outside. I'd be happy to have both of you join me." She pulled three plates from the cupboard. "Let's dish up in here first."

As Elizabeth turned on the bug zapper, Martha did join them on the patio at the picnic table their father had built years ago. Elizabeth restained it every year to keep it in tip-top shape. In the distance, a cow bellowed over on the Fischers' farm.

Buckets full of geraniums and busy Lizzies lined the patio off the back of the Victorian house, and frogs began to croak from a neighbor's pond. The warm scent of freshly cut hay on the property behind them filled the early evening air as the sun lowered in the western sky.

Thankfully, neither Mary nor Martha seemed to carry a grudge when they bickered, which was a relief to Elizabeth. Especially when the three of them needed to work together to help Trudy and little Davie.

After Mary led them all in a blessing, Martha said, "All in all it was a good day, as far as receipts." She spread her napkin in her lap. "So far it doesn't seem we've had much of a decline in tourists even though it's September."

Mary agreed. "We definitely lost the families with school-aged children, which I miss. I love the sounds of kids in the shop…" She sighed. "But it appears more retirees are out now."

"And they tend to spend more," Martha, always the practical one, added.

Elizabeth agreed and then swatted at a mosquito that buzzed by a little too close for comfort. She took a bite of the chicken salad. Not only did more profits in their business mean more of a livelihood for the three of them, but it also allowed them to give more to their church and help others too, which led her to broach the topic she most wanted to discuss. "I've been thinking about little Davie and what we can do to help. I offered to drive them to appointments as needed, which means we might need to juggle our schedules."

Martha nodded, her blue eyes lively. "Of course we'll make that a priority." She picked up her glass of iced tea.

"I'd like to find out more about the bone marrow registry," Elizabeth said. "Who qualifies to be tested and that sort of thing."

"That's a wonderful idea," Mary answered. "There are so many great stories out there about donors saving someone's life. Who knows? Maybe one of us will be a perfect match."

Elizabeth doubted that, but she didn't want to squash Mary's enthusiasm. It definitely was worth it to at least look into being tested. They needed to do everything they could.

Martha switched topics. "Rachel and Alvin will need a place to store auction items and a place to hold the auction. I think we could help with both."

Elizabeth froze. "What do you mean by help?"

"Store the items." Martha took a sip of iced tea. "And host the auction."

Elizabeth wasn't so sure. It sounded problematic—and like a lot of work. "Do we have the space?"

"I think so." Martha put her glass down. "We can get as much of our merchandise out on the floor as soon as possible and use the storage room for the donated items. And then hold the actual auction in the field."

"What if it rains?"

"I doubt that it will, but we should rent tents no matter what—for either shade or rain. And we'll need to rent tables too. I'll talk with Rachel about food. I'm sure she knows people who will take care of all that. Of course, all food items will be for sale, and the proceeds will go toward Davie's care too."

Elizabeth speared a chunk of chicken with her fork. It seemed Martha had everything figured out, but it sounded awfully ambitious to her. It wasn't like Martha to dream so big, but then again they all cared deeply about Rachel and her extended family. Still, it would be a lot of work in a short amount of time. "I hope it won't be too much for us," Elizabeth finally said. "I'd hate to volunteer to do more than we can actually pull off."

Mary had been uncharacteristically quiet, but she spoke up now. "I know we can make it work."

"But," Elizabeth said, surprised her two younger sisters were in agreement, "what if there's someone else who could coordinate and host the auction? Someone who would have more to offer than we do?"

"Rachel couldn't think of anyone," Martha answered.

Elizabeth was sure there was some Amish family who could host the auction—and have more time to devote to it than she, Mary, and Martha could.

Finally, Mary pushed her plate toward the middle of the table. "If we are going to consider hosting the auction, we need to get started on everything tomorrow. Why don't we go over to Rachel's right now and talk with her about it? And see what she thinks?"

"Good idea." Martha took another bite of chicken salad, as if determined to finish eating quickly.

"Only to talk about it though," Elizabeth said. "The three of us need to weigh the pros and cons after talking to Rachel and then decide."

Martha nodded. And so did Mary, although she had a faraway look in her eyes. Was she already thinking ahead to an auction at Secondhand Blessings?

Elizabeth swatted at another mosquito, figuring they only had a few minutes to finish eating before an all-out assault began. She turned her attention to her food too. It wasn't often that Martha and Mary agreed so absolutely on something. Elizabeth hoped they could pull the auction off if needed, but she wasn't as confident. Hopefully Rachel's input would help them make their decision.

As they all drove east along the road toward the Fischer farm, with Martha in the passenger seat beside Elizabeth, and Mary in the back, orange and pink streaks of light appeared on the horizon. There was nothing more beautiful than a Lancaster County sunset.

They'd decided to drive, even though it was within walking distance, so they wouldn't be walking home along the narrow shoulder in the dark.

"I hope we're not arriving too late," Martha said.

"I left a message," Elizabeth countered. "Hopefully someone listened to it and let Rachel know." Perhaps she wasn't even home. Maybe she was over at Alvin's house, where Trudy and little Davie lived. They'd soon find out.

As they turned down the lane toward the Fischers' farm, Rachel's eight-year-old twins appeared in the field. As Elizabeth drove, they began racing on the other side of the fence, alongside the car.

"I'm guessing they got the message," Mary said with a laugh. "It looks as if Matthew and Thomas were expecting us."

As Elizabeth turned into the driveway, six-year-old Dorcas waved from the yard. The girl wore a sky blue dress with no apron around her middle and no *kapp* on her head. She wore her hair in two braids. Rachel appeared at the front door and then stepped onto the porch, waving too. She appeared tired but still happy to see them.

"What a nice welcome," Martha said as Elizabeth parked.

Rachel reached the car by the time they'd all climbed out. "Danki for coming." She turned toward Dorcas. "Go tell your *daed* that our company has arrived."

The little girl took off skipping toward the barn, her braids bouncing behind her.

"Come on into the house," Rachel said. "I have lemonade and cookies and a good breeze flowing through the windows."

The house was painted completely white, with no accenting trim color, but pots of red geraniums lined the porch and added a dramatic splash of color. Rachel opened the screen door and motioned for the sisters to enter first. Elizabeth led the way into the very tidy and sparsely furnished house. Two padded chairs, a rocking chair, three straight-back chairs, and a bookcase furnished the living room.

They followed Rachel into the kitchen, where a large table surrounded by benches was the centerpiece.

Phoebe stood at the kitchen sink. She turned toward the sisters and beamed.

"Did you have a good afternoon with your aunts?" Martha asked.

Phoebe nodded. "A *wunderbar* time," she said. Elizabeth knew the young woman required extra parenting on Rachel's part, but in many ways she was the heart of the family. She adored her younger siblings, along with every member of her family.

The twins banged through the back door and Rachel called out, "Wash up. If you are quiet, you may join us for a snack."

Hannah, who was thirteen, followed her little brothers into the house and said, "Hallo," to Elizabeth, Martha, and Mary. All three women greeted her warmly in return. She was a big help to her mother and the running of the household.

By the time they'd all settled down at the table, Rachel's husband, Silas, and Dorcas came through the back door too, along with Ephraim, who was fifteen, and Luke, who was seventeen. After they'd all washed up, Silas took his place at the head of the table, with Rachel beside him, while Dorcas sat at the end of the table flanked by her twin brothers. The older boys each grabbed a cookie from the plates on the counter and headed into the living room, where they stayed as quiet as mice. Hannah placed the two plates of snickerdoodles on the table while Rachel poured lemonade.

As Elizabeth looked around, she was overwhelmed with gratitude for their neighbors. They'd been so good to Mama and Daddy, and now to Elizabeth and her sisters. She would do anything to help their family, and extended family too.

Elizabeth cleared her throat and said, "We overheard you and Alvin talking about the auction and wondered how we can help."

Rachel smiled. "How nice of all of you." She passed a plate of cookies to Martha. "I haven't put much thought into it yet." She glanced at Silas. "We haven't even had a chance to talk about it, besides me mentioning the idea."

Silas raised his eyebrows. "Rachel, do you have time to take on something like that?"

"We'll see…"

Martha held a cookie in her hand. "Do you have a place to hold it?"

Rachel shook her head. "It will not work for us to have it here, not with the corn harvest coming up. And Alvin cannot hold it at his place." Her expression grew serious. "That really is my biggest concern. Once we have a place, I think the donations will pour in."

"We'd love to host the auction at Secondhand Blessings," Mary blurted out.

Surprised that Mary would make the offer before the three of them had a chance to come to a consensus as they'd talked about, Elizabeth almost clarified that they were considering it. But then tears filled Rachel's eyes, and her voice shook as she said, "This is an answer to prayer. I can't tell you how grateful I am. Silas is right, this is a big task for me to take on right now."

"You won't have to do a thing," Mary said. "Martha is so organized, she can whip it together in no time."

"Mary—" Martha sat with her mouth wide open for a moment but then managed to close it while Elizabeth stared at her youngest sister in disbelief.

Rachel didn't seem to notice. "Alvin and Trudy will be so grateful."

Despite her shock, warmth spread through Elizabeth at Rachel's response. Perhaps Mary and Martha had been correct. They were the right ones to offer a place, and they could probably organize the auction too. Martha seemed to get over her shock because she was smiling at Rachel now too.

"I'll spread the word," Rachel said, "and let people know to take auction items to your place. Would it work for you to meet with Alvin and me soon? We could come up with an auction date then."

Elizabeth glanced at her sisters.

"Yes," Martha said, her voice clear and firm now. "We can do that."

CHAPTER THREE

The next morning, as the sun peeked over the horizon, Martha headed out to the barn with a mug of coffee in her hand, determined to get the shop as organized as possible and ready to collect auction items. The morning air was cool, and as the sun rose, a streak of orange spread above the hillside. Reddy the rooster crowed his announcement of the morning.

Martha juggled her mug as she unlocked the doors and flicked on the lights. Her plan was to consolidate the merchandise on the shelves to make more room for the auction items in the storage room.

The first rays of morning light spilled through the window on the east side of the barn, and the open beams seemed to yawn as if the building were awakening too.

As hard as it was to be so far from her children and grandchildren in Kansas, she relished being back on the property where she grew up. Nowhere else so completely fulfilled the idea of *home* for her. Memories from her entire life were grounded here. Playing in the barn as a child while her mother managed Secondhand Blessings. Helping her father with the outside chores, and learning how to bake and manage a home and grow a garden from her mother. Learning to sew and can and make gifts. All in such a beautiful setting. It really had been an idyllic childhood and a solid foundation for the rest of her life.

She turned toward the small appliance shelves and began rearranging slow cookers, pressure cookers, and coffee makers, creating as much extra space as possible. Her parents' strong work ethic, combined with their faith and the teachings of their church, had launched Martha and her sisters into a life where they used the strength and fortitude instilled in them to serve others.

Not that she and her sisters had been perfect. She remembered plenty of arguments, especially with Mary, and they'd had their rebellious moments too. But by the time she'd had children of her own, she'd hoped she could emulate her mother and father's parenting and instill the same work ethic and faith in her children. For the most part, thankfully, her three had embraced the same values.

Perhaps it was simply a stage of growing older, but she felt—in so many ways—as if her life was coming around full circle as she made a new life for herself where she'd grown up.

Once she'd made more space on the shelves, she stepped into the storage room and retrieved a rice maker and hot pot. She placed those on the shelf, returned for more items, and then repeated the process, over and over. At seven thirty Elizabeth arrived and helped for an hour but then returned to the house. Just as Martha was getting ready to go change out of her sweatshirt, someone called out, "Hallo! Is the shop open?"

Martha stepped toward the door. An Amish man with a long gray beard peeked into the shop. "I have a few items for the auction."

"Oh!" Martha hadn't expected anything so soon. "Great!" She didn't want to sound as if they weren't ready for the items. "What do you have?"

"Tools," he answered. "Come take a look."

Martha followed him out of the barn. In the middle of the parking lot was a wagon filled with hand plows, wheelbarrows, shovels, rakes, watering cans, buckets, lanterns, and buggy and wagon wheels.

"Oh my." Martha's mind scrambled, trying to determine where to stash all of the goods. They wouldn't fit in the storeroom, at least not yet. "Let me get a ledger and pen so I can record what you're donating."

She hurried back into the barn. When she returned, Elizabeth was stepping outside the back door of the house. She wouldn't be pleased with the early delivery. "How did you find out about the auction?" Martha asked as she approached the man.

"Silas Fischer left a message on my machine last night. I listened to it first thing this morning and got to work. I would do anything to help Alvin and his family."

Martha smiled at the man. "What is your name?"

"Jonas Peachy," he answered.

"Would you name off the items so I can write them down?" She was sure she'd get the descriptions wrong without his help.

As Jonas pulled the first rake from the load and simply said, "A garden rake," Elizabeth approached.

"I'll take it," she said. "We can put everything over here by the side of the barn."

"That's a good idea." Martha glanced up from the ledger. They'd need to get everything inside before the end of the day so nothing would be stolen.

Another Amish wagon turned into the driveway, this one with a load of furniture in the back. Perhaps Elizabeth had been right to be wary of volunteering to host the auction. Maybe they didn't have enough room to store—and sell—everything after all.

As Martha darted in and out of Secondhand Blessings all morning, recording donated items, putting what she could in the storeroom, and leaving big items on the west side of the barn, she overheard Mary calling the quilting ladies to tell them about the upcoming auction to raise money for Davie's medical care.

One time, Martha overheard Mary say, "That's a great idea to auction off one of *our* quilts."

Martha shook her head as she hurried by with a stack of handmade dish towels in her arms from an Amish woman who'd gone to school with Alvin over fifty years ago. What was Mary thinking? The group couldn't finish a quilt in two or three weeks. Not when they only met once a week. But that was Mary's *modus operandi*. Dream big—and hope it all works out.

In the early afternoon Alvin stopped by, which surprised Martha since she planned to accompany Rachel to his house that evening. After he parked his buggy and hitched his horse, he pulled a saddle out of the back just as a pickup pulled into a parking space.

The driver of the pickup jumped down and whistled. "That's some saddle," he called out to Alvin. The man wore jeans, a T-shirt, which showed tattoos up and down his arms, and a cowboy hat.

He pushed his hat back on his head and then stuck out his hand as he approached Alvin, who tried to move the saddle to one hand. But it started to slip.

The stranger grabbed it before it hit the ground. "Got it," he said, hiking the saddle up to his chest. "My name's Ty Jones, from the Belmont Racetrack."

Alvin eyed the man. "New York?"

"That's right. Long Island."

"What brings you here?"

"I heard there's going to be an auction. The waitress down at the diner told me."

"We don't know the date yet," Alvin said. He pointed to the saddle in Ty's arms and addressed Martha. "I'd like to put this in the auction. It's Plain Beauty's training saddle."

Ty's eyes went wide as he stared at the saddle in his arms. "Incredible," he said. "Any chance you'd sell this to me now?"

Alvin crossed his arms. "No chance. The auction is to fund my grandson's medical care. I need the highest price possible."

Ty sighed. "Fair enough." He held the saddle a little higher. "Where would you like this?"

Alvin nodded toward Martha. "She is in charge. Let us see where she wants it."

Martha stepped toward the men, not wanting the saddle at the shop at all. "Alvin," she said, "would you mind keeping the saddle with Plain Beauty until the day of the auction? We've already had quite a few items dropped off. If it's valuable, perhaps it would be better to wait to bring it."

"Perhaps you are right." Alvin tugged on his beard. "Would you take a photo of it with your phone? I thought we could talk about publicity ideas this evening. A photo of it would be good. There are some online sites where we, I mean you, could post about it."

Surprised at Alvin, Martha nearly laughed. But instead, she simply said, "Of course. Why don't you hold it, Alvin? I promise not to get your face in the photo."

Ty handed it back to Alvin, who clasped it tightly.

Martha squinted. The breeze blew Alvin's long white beard into the photo as she snapped it. She laughed. "One more, without your beard."

"Oh, it does not matter," Alvin said. "I am guessing my hands are in the photo, so my beard does not matter. As long as my face is not."

Martha assured him it wasn't.

"Is that a silver cap on the horn?" Ty asked as Martha clicked another photo.

"That is correct," Alvin answered.

"And on the dees too?"

Martha glanced from the front of the saddle to the back, along the skirt.

Alvin nodded. "Ja, that is correct too."

Ty whistled. "It's quite the saddle."

Martha agreed. All the more reason to have the saddle stored at Alvin's place. Yes, they had the no-key lock on the barn, but she feared something might happen to it in the storeroom or in moving it from place to place. It was much better for Alvin to be in charge of it.

Ty took his hat off and ran his hand through his hair, which was in need of a cut. "Are you sure you won't sell it to me?"

"Positive," Alvin answered. "But I am grateful for your help." The older man's eyes sparkled, and he handed the saddle back to Ty.

"You want me to lug it back to your wagon?"

Alvin nodded. "If you would."

Ty chuckled. "I'll have to be happy with just touching it," he said.

As Ty headed to the wagon, Alvin said to Martha, "I'll see you this evening. Bring all of your best ideas."

"I will," Martha responded, sounding more confident than she felt. She hoped she'd have some good ideas by then. Maybe she could talk with Mary before she left. Or maybe Mary would go with her.

A few minutes later, Ty returned and looked around. He ended up buying an old horseshoe. As he paid, he said, "I have a collection. I try to pick one up from every state I visit."

That seemed like an appropriate collection for someone who worked at a racetrack. She thanked him for the purchase and handed him his change.

He grinned as he picked the horseshoe up from the counter. "That's great that you're helping with the auction. It sounds like a worthy cause."

"It is," Martha answered. "There's nothing more important than the health of a child."

Ty waved as he headed toward the door.

"Goodbye," Martha called out. "Safe travels."

When she entered the shop, she found Mary consolidating the small furniture section. "Can you watch the counter for ten minutes or so, Mary?" Martha asked. "I'm going to grab something to eat and call Trish."

"Sure," Mary said, straightening her back. "I could use a break from this." She pointed to the storage room. "I've gotten all of the furniture out of the storage room and on the floor, but it's nearly filled with auction items now."

Martha sighed. "I think we're going to have to clean out the shed and put items in there too."

Mary nodded. "I can work on that next."

As Martha headed out the door toward the house, she pulled her phone from her pocket and hit Trish's number. It rang and rang and finally went to her voice mail. "Just checking on Celeste," Martha said. "Call me when you get a chance."

She ended the call and continued on to the house, feeling more and more uneasy with each step. She wished she'd called earlier in the day.

At six thirty Martha picked up Rachel, and the two continued on to Alvin's farm. As Martha turned her car onto Beech Lane, she pulled her visor down against the lowering sun. A flock of starlings swooped toward an oak tree, and a collie ran back and forth along the fence line, barking.

"That is Alvin's dog, Max," Rachel said.

A large white house came into view along with both a barn and an impressive stable.

"Park by the gate." Rachel pointed toward the yard, which was surrounded by a white fence.

The property was immaculate with the dawdy haus behind the big house, a tidy garden, pruned trees, and fenced pastures. There were also three corrals and a tack room attached to the outside of the stable.

Martha parked the car, turned it off, and then climbed out, breathing in the scent of hay and manure and the cooling evening air.

As they started toward the house, Alvin came out of the stable with a young Amish man.

"That's Caleb Yoder," Rachel said. "The farrier. He must have come out to shoe Plain Beauty." She smiled. "Or perhaps visit Trudy."

"Oh?" Martha sensed a budding romance.

Rachel grimaced. "I shouldn't have said anything. He is sweet on her, but she is not interested. At least not yet."

Caleb wore the typical Amish barn pants, suspenders, and handmade shirt, along with a straw hat. He had no beard, indicating that he was single. He carried a large metal box by the handle—most likely his tools for his trade. And he was speaking loudly. "I cannot believe you would auction off such a fine horse. You will have no control over who buys it."

Alvin responded, his voice lower but still audible. "I need to make as much money as possible for Davie's expenses."

"But do you not believe you could get more money selling the horse than auctioning it off? Who will buy it at the auction? Someone in Lancaster. Someone who cannot and will not pay top dollar."

Alvin paused a moment and then said, "But the horse is the biggest draw to the auction. More people will come because of her. Besides, we have already told people she will be part of the auction."

Caleb Yoder shifted his toolbox to his left hand. "I am certain you will come to regret this." He stuck his free hand out. "But I do hope everything works out. For you. The horse. Your daughter. And Davie."

The two men shook hands, and Alvin said, "Safe travels. I trust you will like your new home."

"Danki." Caleb turned toward the horse and buggy hitched to the post next to the tack room.

"I did not know Caleb was leaving Lancaster County," Rachel whispered to Martha. "Perhaps Trudy rejected him."

Alvin followed Caleb to the tack room. They both entered it for a moment. When they came out, Alvin took out a key, locked the door, and then retried it. It was securely locked. Martha couldn't help but wonder if the expensive saddle was in it. But then again, considering Alvin trained horses, there were probably lots of expensive items stored away inside.

Caleb headed to a buggy parked to the side of the stable, and Alvin turned toward the house. "Hallo!" he called out as he noticed Martha and Rachel.

Martha tried to smile, suddenly embarrassed that she'd been eavesdropping.

But as Alvin neared the women, Rachel asked, "What was that all about? With Caleb?"

"He has different ideas is all."

Rachel wrinkled her brow. "But where is he moving?"

"Oh, that." Alvin sighed. "Kentucky."

"Why?"

"His answer?" Alvin looped his thumbs through his suspenders.

"Ja..."

"He has a friend looking for a farrier business partner."

Rachel asked, "Why do you think he is moving?"

"Well, with his parents both dying in the last year, it seems to be a good time for a fresh start. But..." Alvin lowered his voice. "I think our Trudy broke his heart."

Rachel made a *tsk tsk* sound, and then Alvin motioned back toward the stable and addressed Martha. "Want to take a look at Plain Beauty?"

Of course she did. She nodded.

Alvin led the way and opened the door, motioning for the women to go in first. "Caleb's intentions are good, but he does not understand the situation." Alvin didn't sound very convincing. Was he regretting auctioning off Plain Beauty?

On both sides of the stable were individual stalls, all filled with horses. "We board horses too, besides training our own," he said.

Martha marveled at each one. Thoroughbreds, quarter horses, and an Arabian. The stable was as clean as a house. Obviously, the horses were well cared for. Alvin stopped at the very last stall. "Here she is," he said. The horse was a quarter horse and pure black. "She raced as a filly and did really well. But now she is five years old, and it is time for her to retire from the big tracks. She will make a fine buggy horse." The horse turned her head toward them and nodded at Alvin.

All three laughed. "She likes it here," Martha said.

"We are just here to visit." Alvin stepped forward and scratched Plain Beauty's forehead. "I will be back in the morning."

She neighed, and he patted her neck.

"She's beautiful," Martha gushed. She didn't know a lot about horses, but she knew this one was special. She'd never seen anything like Plain Beauty. How could Alvin bear to part with her?

By the look of admiration in his eyes, it would be a difficult process. However, Martha knew the horse couldn't compare to his grandson.

Alvin checked the far door, closest to Plain Beauty's stall, making sure it was securely locked. Then he led the way back through the stable, to the far door. When they exited, he checked it too. Then they headed toward the house.

When they reached it, he opened the screen door for the women. As Martha stepped through the door, Trudy rounded the corner to the stairway with a child in her arms.

"Greet our guest before you put Davie to bed," Alvin called out.

Trudy turned. Davie had his head on his mother's shoulder and wore pajamas. Trudy appeared exhausted, with dark circles under her eyes. She wore a kerchief over her blond hair instead of a kapp, and her feet were bare. Her rose-colored dress was mostly covered with a black apron.

"Hallo, Martha," she said in a soft voice. "Danki for helping *Aenti* Rachel and Daed with planning the auction. We appreciate it." She jostled the boy a little, but he didn't turn his head. "Aenti Rachel said that one of you would be willing to take us to an appointment."

"Yes," Martha answered. "Any of us can, but Elizabeth in particular would like to."

"That would be appreciated," Trudy said. "The appointment is at nine on Monday morning."

"Perfect. I'll let her know. And plan to have her pick you up by eight fifteen." Elizabeth would be thrilled.

"Danki." Trudy turned toward the stairs. "I am going to get Davie to bed. He is all tuckered out."

"Of course." Martha certainly understood. "It's good to see both of you." Her voice caught in her throat. "Good night, Davie. Sweet dreams."

The little boy stirred a little, and Trudy said, "I will come back down after he is settled."

Rachel led the way to the kitchen table, where a pitcher of punch and a plate of sticky buns sat ready for them. "Did Trudy make these?" Rachel asked.

Alvin shook his head. "Some of the ladies have been bringing in meals and things like that." He nodded toward the front door. "Excuse me just a minute. I forgot to make a phone call. I will be right back."

He wasn't gone long. Once he returned, over the snack, they talked about a date for the auction. Rachel had spoken to the auctioneer that morning, and he said he had Saturday, September 21 available. All three agreed on the date. Martha felt a little dizzy at all that needed to be done before then—in just fifteen days.

She pulled the ledger she was using to record all the items from her purse and showed them her system of recording the items so they could easily be shared with the auctioneer when the time came. "We've had a great many items donated already," she said. "We'll put less valuable items in our shed, which has a lock on it. Anything of value we'll store in the barn." She chuckled. "I had one person try to drop off a pair of old chickens today, but I asked them to hold on to them until the day of the auction."

Alvin laughed. "Do not take them the day of the auction either. Someone was trying to see how gullible you might be. Just a joke, I'm sure."

"Oh dear." Martha hadn't thought about that. She knew some of their Amish neighbors had a funny sense of humor. She pointed out some of the smaller items in the list. "I thought we could also hold a silent auction so the event doesn't go into the wee hours of the night."

Just as they were finishing up their discussion, a scream came from the top of the stairs. And then, "Fire!"

Alvin bolted from the table as Trudy came thundering down the stairs.

Martha's heart raced.

"It's the stable!" Trudy yelled.

Alvin rushed to the front door while Martha grabbed her phone from her purse.

As she hit the EMERGENCY CALL button she stammered, "I-I-I'm calling 911!"

CHAPTER FOUR

As Alvin ran toward the stable, Martha hurried out the screen door as if she were Rachel's shadow, asking for the address of the farm as the 911 dispatcher came on the line.

"Twenty-nine-seventeen…"

Martha repeated the numbers and then said, "Beech Lane."

Rachel nodded.

Martha stayed on the line, but as she raised her head she gasped. Flames were shooting out of the far end of the stable where Plain Beauty's stall was, and Alvin was rushing to the front door with the key in his hand. Rachel ran across the lane, holding her dress at knee level. "Alvin," she yelled, "wait for the firefighters!"

Someone yelled from the house. Martha turned. Trudy stood at an open bedroom window. "Daed! I can't lose you too!"

But Alvin had unlocked the door and disappeared into the stable. Rachel kept running and then rushed into the stable too. A minute later, Alvin shooed a horse out the door and then another. Rachel came out, coughing, leading a horse. She handed the rope to Martha and rushed back in as Alvin shooed three more horses out. "Open the far corral!" he yelled to Martha.

She did as she was told and led the first one in, thinking of the Bird-in-Hand fire department. It was completely volunteer.

Their response time was amazing, but it could still be some time before they arrived.

She held the gate open, and three horses ran inside while two trotted toward the house. Trudy came out the front door, her feet still bare, and rushed toward the two. "Go on," she said, her voice firm over the crackling of the fire.

Martha tried to remember how many stalls she'd seen in the stable—and how many horses—but she couldn't, not exactly. Maybe nine. Maybe more. She prayed they were all out.

Rachel came out with one more horse on a lead. Soot covered her face and hands, and she leaned against the corral and coughed. Trudy herded the two rogue horses into the corral, and Alvin ran two more horses out, yelling, "That is all," as he grabbed the hose and turned on the spigot at the outside trough. He began spraying water on the roof of the stable.

The smoke grew thicker and billowed down from the top and over the corral. Martha wasn't sure if they should keep the horses in the corral.

"Wh-where is Plain Beauty?" Rachel stammered.

An expression of panic passed over Alvin's face. "You did not get her?"

"I did not go in that far."

"Her stall was empty and the far door closed, as much as I could see through the smoke…" Alvin turned toward the corral. "She must be loose."

Martha was sure Plain Beauty hadn't come out the near door. But if her stall was empty, she must have.

Trudy stepped forward and tried to take the hose from her daed as Martha worried about the young woman's bare feet. Sparks were falling to the ground all around her.

"No." He held on tight. "You get away from here. Go back to the house. Davie needs you."

Trudy appeared as if she was going to protest, but then a scream came from the house. Davie stood in the open upstairs window, pointing to the stable and crying. Trudy rushed back to the house, holding up her dress as she ran.

Martha's heart raced at the sight of the little boy. It all seemed too much for this family.

Sirens wailed in the distance, pulling Martha's attention back to the fire. "Thank You, Lord!" she said out loud, and realized how fearful she'd been that Alvin and Rachel might be injured.

The horses stamped and snorted around in the corral, obviously frightened. Rachel spoke soothingly between coughing spells, trying to calm them.

The sirens grew louder until a fire truck, followed by a tank truck, turned down the lane, stopping at the end of the stable.

Firefighters started jumping off the back and climbing out of the truck. All wore heavy tan jackets and trousers with BIRD-IN-HAND in neon green on the back along with neon green and white stripes, and black hard hats with neon stripes on them too.

"Is everyone out of the stable?" an older firefighter called out.

"Ja!" Alvin shouted back.

The firefighters grabbed hoses and tools, and two of them coupled hoses together to increase the length.

The same firefighter who spoke before, who appeared to be the chief, yelled, "Are all the horses out?"

"Ja, but one is missing," Alvin responded. "And my dog is also missing. We would have heard him barking if he was here, to alert us to the fire."

"Do you have any idea how it started? A lantern? Fire pit nearby?"

"Ja, I do know." Alvin stepped back as a timber in the middle of the building fell. "Someone wanted my horse. Someone set this fire."

As more firefighters jumped out of the truck, the first one made a call on his radio, requesting police support and another firetruck.

In no time, firefighters were shooting water from the tanker onto the stable.

"You all need to clear out," the first firefighter said. "And the horses need to be at a greater distance from the fire. The smoke is too thick."

"You might as well let it burn," Alvin said. "I have no insurance on it—it will be easier to clean up if it burns out."

"But harder to investigate—clues about the setting of the fire might lead to finding the horse."

"All right. We will take them to the west pasture." Alvin opened the gate.

The sun had just set, and the sky was falling into darkness as the flames licked against the night.

Rachel and Martha each grabbed the leads of two more horses and followed Alvin to the pasture, which was along the lane that Martha had driven up to reach the farm.

When they returned to the corral, Alvin said, "Take care of the remaining four, and then you two should go home."

"Not yet," Rachel said, turning toward Martha. "As long as you are willing to stay a little longer."

"Of course." Martha dragged her forearm across her forehead.

Rachel met Alvin's stride on the way back to the corral. "We should get some flashlights and look for Plain Beauty in case she was not stolen and just ran off."

Before he could answer, one of the firefighters on the far side of the stable yelled, "This door was broken into—someone attempted to force the lock and then rammed the door."

It seemed Alvin might have been right.

Another siren wailed, and a police cruiser came up the lane. Officer John Marks climbed out of the car, nodding toward Martha as he adjusted his hat over his thick, dark hair. His blue eyes were full of concern.

Alvin marched toward him, saying, "The fire is arson, and a valuable horse was stolen."

John stopped when Alvin reached him. "And you are?"

"Alvin Raber. The owner of this farm." He tugged on his white beard with a sooty hand.

"I'm Officer John Marks, from the East Lampeter Township Police Department."

Alvin didn't seem to care where John was from. "Someone tried to force the lock and then bashed the door in. Plain Beauty, who was in the stall closest to that door, is gone."

John pulled a small notebook out of his shirt pocket and jotted a few notes down. "Any chance the horse got loose? Perhaps it ran into the woods."

"Could be," Alvin said. "But I doubt it."

"We were just about to go look for her," said Martha.

John headed over to the fire captain. The two spoke, with the captain gesturing toward the stable.

"Let's go ahead and look around." John turned back to his cruiser, reached through the driver's window, and stood up with a flashlight in his hand.

"I'll get the one out of my car," Martha offered.

Trudy must have been watching from the porch, because she came out with Davie on her hip, and carrying two flashlights. She handed one to Rachel and one to Alvin. Davie reached out for his grandfather, and Alvin patted the boy's cheek, leaving a streak of soot. "Stay with your *maam*," he said. "In the house. Everything is all right. You need to go back to bed and get your rest."

John turned his flashlight on. "We'll go in pairs," he said.

Alvin instructed John to go with Rachel. "She grew up on this property. She knows where to look." He turned toward Martha. "Come with me. Rachel, you two take the south pasture, and look in the woods down that way. We will go up to the north pasture and woods."

The groups separated, and Alvin led Martha past the stable. The area around the back door was soaked in water and foam, and obviously any hoofprints had been erased. But as they shone their flashlights they didn't see any prints farther away either. They passed the barn and reached a band of dirt that separated the grassy area around the house, stable, and barn from the fenced north pasture. Alvin meticulously shone his light up one way and down the other. But there were the imprints of horses' hooves everywhere. It was a horse farm, after all. How could they possibly determine which were Plain Beauty's tracks?

In the distance, Rachel was shining the flashlight over the dirt too.

"If Plain Beauty was on her own, she would have had to jump the fence," he said.

He shone the light into the pasture. "Then again, if she was stolen the thief could have easily chosen where to lead her."

Martha had been thinking about the possible thief. "Why would a thief start the fire? It alerted you to Plain Beauty being gone much sooner than if you'd found out in the morning."

"That's true," Alvin said. "We will have to see what the fire chief finds out. Perhaps the fire was an accident."

He'd been so sure it was arson before. Martha couldn't imagine anyone putting so many beautiful horses at risk.

As they walked through the pasture, Martha remembered Alvin going out to the barn to make a phone call while they were discussing the auction. Perhaps that was information that John needed to know—the police might need to check Alvin's phone records to see whom he'd called—and why.

She shivered, even in the warm air. Alvin wouldn't have stolen his own horse and set his own stable on fire. Would he?

Of course not. She needed to put such a ludicrous thought out of her mind.

They continued on toward the woods, sweeping their flashlights from side to side. When Alvin noticed dog prints in the dirt at the edge of the woods, he stopped and yelled, "Max!"

A whimper came from near an evergreen tree.

Alvin started jogging toward it. Martha followed as he scooped up the collie.

He turned toward her. "I think he's been drugged. I better get him back to the house so I can call the vet."

"I'll keep looking in the woods," she said.

He shook his head. "I will come back later. It is not safe for you to be here alone."

Through the woods, she could see traffic on the highway and businesses on the other side. She believed she'd be fine exploring on her own but acquiesced to Alvin's wishes.

She hoped that when they arrived back at the stable Plain Beauty would be there. Perhaps she ran the other way and hadn't been stolen after all.

They were quiet on their way back except for the dog whimpering. Martha was nearing exhaustion, and she guessed Alvin was too. He stopped at the barn, and she offered to hold the dog while he made the phone call.

"Just sit with him." Alvin lowered the dog to the ground by the bench outside the barn. "I will only be a minute."

Martha petted the dog while she waited. He was definitely impaired. She couldn't fathom who would drug the collie.

When Alvin returned he bent down and scooped the dog up again, but this time he had a hard time straightening his back. When he was finally upright, he groaned.

The firefighters had set up a light near the truck and tanker, and when Alvin and Martha walked into the light, the chief whistled. "Looks like you found the dog. Any sign of the horse?"

"*Ne*," Alvin said. "Is the police officer back yet?"

The fire chief shook his head. "The fire is mostly out—just a lot of hot spots. Of course, we can't investigate anything until tomorrow."

"I understand," Alvin said.

"We saved your tack room."

"Oh?"

"A spark fell on the roof, but we got it out."

Alvin hurried toward the tack room, and Martha followed. The door was wide open.

"Did you break in?" he called back to the chief.

"No. The door was unlocked."

Alvin stepped inside, the dog still in his arms, as the chief called out, "Stay out of there!"

Alvin reappeared, his expression full of anger. "The saddle is missing too."

"What saddle?" the chief asked.

"Plain Beauty's training saddle."

"Why would anyone steal it?" the chief asked.

Alvin stood tall. "Because it is worth *a lot* of money."

CHAPTER FIVE

When Martha and Rachel finally got ready to leave, John asked if he could stop by Secondhand Blessings and speak with Martha the next day about what she remembered as far as the events of the evening.

"Of course," she said.

He turned toward Rachel. "And you too?"

"Ja, my family lives next to Martha and her sisters," Rachel answered, rattling off her address to him. He jotted it down and then turned back to interviewing Alvin.

Rachel put her head back against the seat as Martha drove. "What an ordeal," she said. "I know the Lord will give Trudy and Alvin the strength they need…"

Martha nodded. "And they'll need even more support than before."

"Ja," Rachel said. "I will call the bishop when we get home. But I worry about how much stress Alvin can handle."

"Oh dear." Martha tightened her grip on the steering wheel.

"I believe he was functioning on adrenaline before this evening. Now I do not know what will keep him going."

"Prayers," Martha said. "And the help of his community."

Rachel lifted her head. "Ja. And I cannot tell you how much I appreciate you and your sisters being part of that community."

Martha's eyes filled with tears. Despite her exhaustion, she was grateful she'd been at Alvin's farm. She wasn't sure she'd believe all that had happened if she hadn't witnessed it.

After dropping Rachel off, she hurried on home. She needed to shower, put her clothes in the wash, and get to bed as soon as possible. She and her sisters would have a big day tomorrow, because it was a Saturday. Plus, she'd need to see to more auction details too.

As she pulled into the parking lot of Secondhand Blessings, ready to turn toward the house, her headlights illuminated a collection of tools and furniture in front of the barn.

"What in the world?" she wondered aloud. But then it dawned on her that more auction items had been dropped off after she left. Why hadn't Elizabeth and Mary put the items away?

Martha parked the car and marched into the house. All the lights were off, but the TV screen glowed from the living room.

"Anyone awake?"

No one answered.

She marched into the living room to find Mary sound asleep on the couch. She hardly ever watched TV. Had she been tired? Or lonely?

"Hey." Martha touched her sister's shoulder.

Mary stirred but didn't wake up. Mary and Elizabeth should have put the items away. It was ridiculous that they'd left them out.

"Mary," she said, rather loudly. "Wake up."

First Mary stretched one arm and then the other. Then she opened her eyes. And gasped. "What happened to you?"

"What do you mean?"

"Your face." She sat up straight.

Martha stepped to the mirror by the doorway. By the dim light of the TV she could see that her face was covered in soot, making the whites of her eyes stand out.

"Alvin's stable burned down."

Mary gasped again. "Are the horses all right?"

"Yes. Well, all but one. Plain Beauty is missing. Alvin thinks she was stolen, along with a valuable saddle."

"How awful." Mary leaned her head back against the couch.

"I need to get a shower," Martha said.

"Obviously." Mary yawned.

"But first we need to take care of the stuff by the barn."

"We already did that, remember? Before you left. It's all in the shed."

Martha shook her head. "There's more out there. Tools. Furniture. Other stuff."

"How did that happen?"

"Someone must have dropped it off after we closed. Did you hear a buggy come into the parking lot?"

Mary rolled her eyes. "We hear buggies all the time. Especially on a Friday night with the youngie courting. You can't tell if someone is coming into the parking lot or not."

"Well, did you think to check to see if anyone dropped more off?"

Mary shook her head. "No. Not once. And I doubt you would have either." She was on her feet now. "Go get your shower. I'll take care of the stuff."

Martha headed up the stairs, now bone weary. Before she reached her room, she grumbled, "Yes, Lord, You're right. I shouldn't have jumped to conclusions and thought so badly of Mary. I'll apologize tomorrow." She sighed and stretched. "Again."

The next morning, after feeding the pets and doing the chores, Martha headed out to the barn first thing again, cradling her cup of coffee. As she punched in the code and opened the door, she nearly spilled her coffee. Mary had kept her word about taking care of the "stuff," all right. She'd dragged it all into the entryway of the shop.

Martha groaned. She should have taken care of it last night herself instead of asking Mary to. If she had, she wouldn't have to deal with it now. She'd have to rethink that apology.

Before she had a chance to even put her cup down, she heard hooves in the parking lot. It was six thirty. Surely no one was donating this early. She stepped carefully around the items, placed her coffee on the counter, and then walked back outside, shading her eyes against the rising sun.

A middle-aged Amish woman stopped her wagon right in front of the door. "I have an old treadle sewing machine for the auction," she said.

"How wonderful," Martha said, stepping around to the back of the wagon.

The woman set the brake and jumped down. "I heard about the fire at Alvin Raber's farm last night. I figured they will need more help now than even before."

Martha was surprised that the word was out already about the fire. "Who told you about the fire?"

"Caleb Yoder," she answered. "He is my neighbor."

"How did Caleb find out about it?"

The woman shrugged. "I am not sure. I saw him across the fence this morning. He usually knows what is going on when it comes to horses in the county."

Martha imagined that was so. He seemed to be a caring person.

She helped the woman lift the sewing machine down. "Let's put it inside the door," she said.

When they stepped into the barn, the woman said, "How are you keeping your merchandise separate from the donations?"

"Careful records," Martha answered, remembering that she'd left the ledger in the house. "I'll have this all put away before we open, don't worry."

"Oh, I am not worried. I have helped with auctions before is all—I know what a big job it is." After they put the sewing machine down, the woman said, "My name is Pauline Schmidt. I can help you organize the auction if you need it."

"I'm Martha Watts, and I appreciate that," Martha said, although she wasn't sure if she could incorporate Pauline's help in the project or not.

Pauline opened her purse and took out a piece of paper and a pen. "Call me if needed. I can give you tips and that sort of thing, ideas of what Amish people would be particularly interested in." She jotted down her name, number, and address and handed the paper to Martha. "Call or just stop by. I am almost always home."

"Thank you. I need to go get my ledger to record your donation."

"No need to do it while I'm here. You have my name—and the item."

That was true. Martha walked with Pauline back out to her buggy and told her goodbye. Then she headed to the house, the slip of paper still in her hand. She probably would need help—but at this point she felt too disorganized to know how exactly.

As Martha opened the back door, Elizabeth called out "Good morning" from the kitchen counter, where she poured a cup of coffee. "Mary told me what happened last night." She shook her head. "I can't believe Plain Beauty is gone. What a nightmare."

Before Martha could respond, Mary stumbled into the kitchen in her pajamas. "Coffee!" she cried out. "Bless whoever made it." She staggered playfully to the counter.

Martha continued on to the desk where'd she left the ledger.

"Hey, Martha." Mary pulled a mug from the cupboard. "Have you heard from Trish? How is Celeste doing?"

"It's even earlier there—so, no. I haven't heard from them."

Mary laughed. "I forgot about the time difference. And how early it is here."

Martha didn't respond.

"So." Mary poured her coffee. "Is there a date for the auction?"

"September twenty-first."

"Great!" Mary turned around. "I'll start making posters today and hang them up around town." Her eyes drifted to the clock on the wall. "Wow, it's even earlier than I thought. After what happened last night, you're up early to be dressed and going like you are."

"And it's a good thing," Martha responded. "We've already had a drop-off for the auction." She grabbed the ledger. "Any idea who dropped off the stuff last night that you dragged into the barn?"

Mary sipped her coffee. "Yeah…"

When she didn't say anything more, Martha prompted, "And?"

"There was a note." She took another sip of her coffee and then stared blankly at the floor.

"What did it say?" Martha finally asked.

"I'm trying to remember what I did with it." Mary drummed her fingers along her temple and then grinned. "I remember. I put it by the cash register."

Martha shook her head and headed out the back door. There was no doubt about it. She was feeling stressed.

The day continued with both Amish and Englisch in the area dropping off more and more donations, including cast-iron skillets, quilts and comforters, a pellet stove, a set of china, carnival glassware, more tools, the promise of a cord of wood, a rocking chair, and a burlap bag of daffodil bulbs. The items kept coming all day long. Most of the donors had heard about the missing horse and wanted to know if it had been found.

Martha replied, over and over, that she hadn't heard an update. Most of those talking about the incident had heard that Plain Beauty had been stolen. "Last I heard," she said, several times, "that hasn't been determined for sure."

By the time the shop closed, Martha had managed to record all the items, squeeze the breakable items into the storage room, and put the tools and garden items in the shed. But if the donations continued, they'd need another solution.

The next morning, as Martha sat in the family pew at Mount Zion Mennonite Church between Elizabeth and Mary, her mind kept wandering to the auction—and then to the missing horse and saddle. John hadn't come by the day before to question her. Was a possibly stolen racehorse not a priority? True, Plain Beauty was retired, but she was still worth a lot of money.

Martha tried not to think about who might have stolen the horse, if in fact she had been stolen.

At the end of the service, as the congregation sang, "Blessed Assurance," Martha struggled to turn the situation, including the auction, over to the Lord. For a moment as she sang, "'Perfect submission, all is at rest…,'" she felt a sense of peace.

But as soon as the service was over, Elizabeth turned toward her and said, "I forgot to tell you that John left a voice mail yesterday. He'll stop by this afternoon to question you about Friday night."

Immediately, Martha's thoughts returned to the missing horse and the upcoming auction. She sighed.

"What's wrong?" Elizabeth asked.

"I'm feeling a little overwhelmed," Martha answered.

"About?"

"Everything."

"Have you had bad news from Trish?"

"I need to call her." Martha had been assuming that no news was good news, but in the chaos of the last two days, she'd failed to learn how Celeste was doing.

She made the call once they reached the house in the privacy of her room. But it went straight to voice mail. Hopefully Celeste was feeling fine, and the family had all gone to church.

She sat down on the edge of her mahogany sleigh bed in her childhood room to have a moment to herself. She'd always loved her room. It was her place of safety as a child and then her place of privacy when she was a teenager.

And then all the years she and Chuck were married, they stayed in the room when they visited her folks, sometimes with a baby in the bassinet close by or a toddler on the floor. She sighed as she stood and stepped into the hall to join her sisters. Life had sped by.

Thankfully, Elizabeth had taken charge of getting lunch ready—Caesar salad and turkey sandwiches.

As they finished their meal, a knock fell on the front door. "I'll get it." Elizabeth was on her feet.

"I wonder who it could be," Mary teased.

Martha frowned and started gathering the plates. She wished John had stopped by the day before. Not because her memory was growing cloudy, but because she wished she'd already gone over the details and didn't have that still ahead of her. Perhaps it had all been more traumatic than she was letting on.

Elizabeth led John into the kitchen. "Hello again," he said to Martha. "Sorry I didn't stop by yesterday. Things got a little crazy."

"With the missing horse case?"

He shook his head. "No, I was put on another case. I'll be working on both for a few days."

"How about a cup of coffee?" Elizabeth asked John. "And a piece of apple pie?"

"That would be great." He grinned. "Your apple pie is my favorite."

Mary waved at John from the sink, where she washed the lunch dishes.

"Hello," he said to her and then sat down at the table, taking his notebook out of his pocket.

"Have you had a chance to speak with Rachel?" Martha asked.

He nodded.

"How is she?"

"Worried about Alvin, Trudy, and Davie," he said. "And, of course, Plain Beauty."

"Any leads on the horse?"

He shook his head. "I want to go over the evening, from your perspective."

As Martha spoke, both Elizabeth and Mary joined them at the table and listened attentively. She talked about the dog running along the fence line, and Caleb Yoder's criticism of Alvin for auctioning off the horse instead of selling her. Then she described going into the house and discussing the auction.

"Then Alvin remembered he'd forgotten to make a phone call and went out to the barn to do so."

John stopped taking notes and lifted his head. "What was that?"

"He went out to the barn to make a call."

John quickly returned to his note-taking. "Any idea what time that was?"

"No." Martha hadn't thought about that. "We'd been talking for probably fifteen minutes or so. Maybe seven o'clock."

He took more notes. It appeared that neither Alvin nor Rachel had mentioned the phone call.

Elizabeth poured the coffee while Mary served the pie, and then Martha continued on with the details of the evening—Trudy calling out "fire," Martha calling 911, running out to the stable, and helping to save the horses. "And then the firefighters arrived," she concluded.

John nodded, finished his notes, and said, "Can you think of anything else?"

Martha thought for a long moment and then said, "No."

"I can," Mary said.

"What would that be?" John asked.

"Remember, Martha, you told me we had a customer who saw Plain Beauty's training saddle and wanted to buy it on the spot."

John was definitely interested. "Oh?"

Feeling flustered, Martha nodded. "I didn't think about that." She exhaled sharply. "Alvin wanted to drop the saddle off here for the auction, but I told him it was too expensive for us to be responsible for. This guy—" What was his name? "He arrived at the same time as Alvin and helped him carry the saddle. He knew it was Plain Beauty's training saddle. It turned out he works at a horse racing track …" She racked her brain, trying to remember the details. "On Long Island," she finally said. "Belmont."

"Why did he stop by?" John asked.

"Someone down at the diner told him there was going to be an auction."

"Did he say his name?"

Martha nodded. "Ty…something," she said. "The last name was something fairly common…but I'm not remembering it."

"I'll call the track," John said. "It shouldn't be too difficult to figure it out."

As John finished his pie and coffee, Elizabeth asked him about his children. He was a widower with a son and a daughter. Both were doing fine. Jonathan had left for his second year of college, and Tina had just started her senior year of high school.

Martha glanced from John to Elizabeth, surprised at how calm they seemed in the face of the missing horse. There were clearly two possible suspects. Caleb Yoder and Ty whatever-his-last-name-was.

And, there also was Alvin's mysterious phone call.

"Can you check Alvin's phone records?" Martha asked.

"I'll look into it," John answered.

"Not that I can imagine Alvin staging the theft of his own horse." Martha's face grew warm. "I'm not accusing him of anything."

"Of course not," John replied.

"So," Martha said, "we have Caleb Yoder, Ty something—wait, I just remembered! It's Ty Jones—and Alvin, who may have more information concerning the disappearance of Plain Beauty?"

John nodded. "But don't forget, someone else entirely could be responsible for the fire and theft of the horse." He stood. "And there's still the possibility the fire was started by accident, and the horse ran off. We'll have to wait and see what the fire chief's investigation determines."

Martha understood that John had to explore every angle, but she sincerely doubted any of it was an accident.

CHAPTER SIX

Monday morning, Elizabeth turned down Beech Lane and continued on toward the Raber farm. Trudy and Davie did need a ride to the doctor, and, of course, Elizabeth had been thrilled to be able to serve in that way.

She slowed as a collie walked along the fence line. As she passed him, she noticed a few leaves of the deciduous trees along the far fence line just starting to turn yellow, hinting at the beauty to come. Autumn was Elizabeth's favorite time of year, and she looked forward to the cooler weather and changing colors.

She couldn't help but revel in the beauty of the landscape now though. The lush green field, dotted with horses, warmed her heart.

Then the lane curved. First the farmhouse came into view—a typical large, white home with geraniums in pots on the porch much like Rachel's house. And then a dawdy haus behind it.

But as Elizabeth's eyes fell ahead to the right, to the burnt stable, she gasped. It was so much worse than Martha had described. The slats from the walls were charred and on the ground. Part of the framing still stood, but the roof timbers had collapsed into the middle of the debris.

There were several men, a few Amish and a couple of Englisch, milling around. In the middle of them was Alvin Raber with a straw hat on his head and a shovel in his hand.

Elizabeth pulled her car around by the house. On the porch in a rocking chair sat Trudy with Davie on her lap. The young mother stood, hoisted the boy to her hip as Elizabeth climbed out of the car.

Davie wore a pair of barn pants and a shirt of the same sky blue fabric as his mother's dress.

"How are you two doing?" Elizabeth asked as Trudy stood.

"All right." Trudy reached for a large bag and car seat, both at her feet, as Davie hid his head against his mother's shoulder.

"I'll help," Elizabeth said, climbing the stairs and grabbing both the bag and car seat.

"Let me just tell Daed we're leaving," Trudy said as she started down the steps.

Elizabeth followed and placed both the bag and the car seat in the back seat of her car. Alvin looked up from his place among the group of men and started toward Trudy and Davie. All of the men continued to talk except for one—Bill Richmond. He waved at Elizabeth.

She waved back. Mary would be interested in knowing that Bill was helping Alvin, at least with the demolition. Perhaps he'd be working as a carpenter to rebuild the stable too.

Alvin approached, telling Trudy and Davie goodbye first. "Take notes," he said to Trudy, "so you can tell me exactly what the doctor says."

He stroked Davie's hair, and Davie turned his face toward his grandfather, a hint of a smile on his lips. "*Grossdaddi*," he said.

Alvin rested his hand atop Davie's head. "You be a good boy."

Davie nodded and then, as Alvin turned away, Trudy put Davie down in the back seat of the car and began installing the car seat.

Alvin turned his attention to Elizabeth. "I appreciate you taking Davie to his appointment." He gestured toward the burnt stable. "Life is quite chaotic here at the moment." Then he pointed toward the field, which was full of horses. "Everyone is out of sorts, including the horses." As if on cue one of them, a quarter horse, started bucking in the field, rearing this way and that. Another horse stamped its feet in response.

Alvin sighed. "Anyway, I am very grateful for your help today and what you and your sisters are doing to put on the auction too. Now, I just need to get Plain Beauty and her saddle back."

"Do you have any leads?"

He shook his head. "The police officer…"

"John Marks?"

"That's right. He came back out yesterday afternoon, but I don't think he has any ideas about what is going on."

"Do you?" Elizabeth asked.

Alvin chuckled. "Well, I did tell him who I suspect, although I have no evidence, of course."

"Who would that be?"

"There is a man in Berks County who was interested in Plain Beauty. He could not believe the owner—a man from West Virginia—would sell such a specimen to an old Amish fellow like me."

"Who's the man in Berks County?" Elizabeth asked, even though she knew John already had the details. Still, she was curious.

"Ron Sliter is his name. He trains racehorses. He wanted Plain Beauty just to have her. Said he was disgusted that I would train her to pull a buggy." He shrugged. "But it is a happy life for a horse." He looked toward the field. "Horses want to work."

Elizabeth agreed. All creatures wanted to be useful.

"I know you were planning to train Plain Beauty to pull buggies. But what would an Englischer do with her?"

Alvin wrinkled his nose. "She is only five, so she has lots of breeding years ahead of her. Or she could still race somewhere lesser known. Or train as a ranch horse, to cut cattle. She has lots of good years left."

"Have you thought of breeding her?"

"I have given it some thought—but the stud fee is really high." He shrugged. "I am not sure about that yet."

Elizabeth guessed he could make pretty good money off a foal from Plain Beauty.

The back door of the car swung open. "Daed, we need to get going."

"Of course."

Elizabeth took a step around to the front of the car but then stopped and turned back to Alvin. "What's the name of the previous owner of Plain Beauty?"

"Chambers," Alvin answered. "Boss Chambers. Why?"

Elizabeth shrugged. "Just curious. How long have you owned Plain Beauty?"

"Only a couple of weeks. In fact, I don't actually have the paperwork. Chambers said it was in the mail. I left a message for him again today to say I needed it immediately."

That all sounded odd. Was Boss Chambers trying to deceive Alvin?

"At the time, when he said he needed to get a document notarized and then he would send it along, it all sounded legitimate."

"Now do you think he was trying to pull a fast one on you?" Elizabeth asked.

Alvin shook his head. "No. He does seem pretty disorganized though. He has a good reputation—he will call me back. I am sure the paperwork is on his desk, ready to be mailed."

Elizabeth thought it all sounded suspicious. She nodded toward the stable. "I hope the cleanup goes quickly. I'll get Trudy and Davie back to you as soon as possible."

"Danki." Alvin smiled and headed back toward the stable, where the men, led by Bill, were starting to sort through the debris.

Trudy was quiet at first, but when Elizabeth asked her if Officer Marks had questioned her, Trudy answered, "Ja."

"Was that scary for you?"

"Ne."

When Trudy didn't say anything more, Elizabeth glanced in her rearview mirror. The young woman met her gaze and just as Elizabeth returned her eyes to the road, Trudy said, "I have been questioned by the police before."

"Oh?" Elizabeth wasn't sure how much Trudy would want to say in front of Davie, and was surprised when she continued.

"I ran with a pretty wild crowd during my rumspringa. We had a few run-ins with the law."

Elizabeth nodded to let Trudy know she'd heard. She didn't add that she remembered and had prayed for Trudy during that time.

"Once I was in a car when the driver got pulled over for drinking. Another time, a boy I was with was arrested for selling drugs."

That sounded awfully serious.

"Another time, a girl I was with shoplifted." She sighed. "Ja, I ran with a wild group. I regret every minute of it."

Davie said something in Pennsylvania Dutch that Elizabeth couldn't understand. Trudy laughed and then said to Elizabeth, "He doesn't understand much English yet and wanted to know what we were talking about." She smiled. "I told him I was talking about when I was a girl."

"When did you join the church?"

"Let's see." Trudy paused a minute. "I was twenty-one, so eight years ago. I married Sam when I was twenty-two and had Davie when I was twenty-four. Then Sam was diagnosed with cancer when I was twenty-five." She sighed. "Daed always says that Gott will not give us more than we can handle. But He seems to really be testing me."

"You've had a lot to deal with," Elizabeth said.

They rode the rest of the way in silence until they neared the pediatric oncologist's office north of downtown Lancaster. Trudy gave Elizabeth directions to park in a lot across the street.

Davie had fallen asleep, and Trudy scooped him up and carried him. "He's tired all the time," she said.

Elizabeth held the door, and Trudy led the way into the waiting room, filled with children and adults. Elizabeth found three chairs together and sat down while Trudy continued on to the desk. Some of the kids had bald heads and others wore hats. Several wore face masks. Elizabeth tried not to stare, but her heartstrings grew tighter by the minute as she imagined all the sad stories in the room.

When Trudy returned and sat down, Davie stirred. He turned around on his mother's lap.

"He likes to watch the other kids," Trudy explained. Then she spoke in Pennsylvania Dutch and slipped the face mask she'd picked up at the check-in desk over Davie's nose and mouth.

The little boy protested but then acquiesced.

"What sort of other help do you need?" Elizabeth asked Trudy. "Besides rides to your appointments. Meals? Help around the house?"

"The women in our district are bringing in meals. And Aenti Rachel helped with the laundry last Monday." She wrinkled her nose. "I hope to get that done tomorrow." She sighed. "Of course, it will depend on how this appointment goes. Davie could be hospitalized."

"Oh dear," Elizabeth said.

"If that happens, I will need to stay with him."

"Of course," Elizabeth responded.

They waited quite a while, but finally Davie was called back. Elizabeth grabbed a women's magazine from the rack but couldn't concentrate. She noticed another rack filled with pamphlets, returned the magazine, and began reading the titles on the pamphlets. *Building a Support Community. Caregiving for a Loved One. Coping with Cancer as a Child. Vision Concerns during Treatment. Oral Care during Treatment. Prostheses Resources.* Goodness, there were so many concerns. *Bone Marrow Donors.*

Now that was one Elizabeth needed. She pulled it from the slot. There was information inside about the "Be the match registry" and becoming a potential match. There was no doubt about it—she would definitely get tested. And she was sure Martha and Mary would too.

She continued reading. The procedure was nonsurgical, although the illustration of the large needle going into the patient's back looked awfully painful. She skimmed over the details and landed on the subtitle, *Who can donate?* The text read, *Donors between 18 and 44 are needed.*

Forty-four? Elizabeth's heart sank. She was too old. It wasn't often that she felt *too* old, but staring in front of her was proof that she was.

However, the text continued, *anyone between 18 and 60 can join the registry.*

She clutched the pamphlet and marched up to the receptionist. "Is anyone over forty-four ever considered as a donor?"

"For what?" the young woman asked as she blinked.

"For the bone marrow registry. Do they ever use anyone over forty-four?"

"Not that I've heard of," the woman said.

Elizabeth retreated back to her chair and kept reading. She could still be tested. All it took was to register online and then a cheek swab test would be sent in the mail. She closed the pamphlet. She'd get tested—but probably the most she would be able to do was to drive Trudy and Davie to appointments. She'd have to be content with that.

When Trudy and Davie came out into the waiting room, Elizabeth still clutched the donor pamphlet. "I registered on Friday," Trudy said. "I'm hoping the kit arrives today."

Trudy was young and genetically related. Hopefully she would be a match.

"My daed is too old," she added, "but I left a message for my sisters."

Elizabeth nodded.

Trudy continued. "Amanda is the one you probably know. She's a year older than I am."

"And she lives south of Bird-in-Hand, right?" Elizabeth asked.

"That is right." Trudy led the way to the door, switching Davie to her other hip as she walked. "My other sister, Faye, is five years older than I am and lives in Harrisburg."

As they reached the parking lot, Elizabeth asked, "How did the appointment go?"

"Good. Davie has a lab appointment tomorrow for an infusion and then an appointment on Thursday for more lab work."

"I can take you to both," Elizabeth said.

"That is a lot for you." They reached the car, and Trudy opened the back door. "I can hire a driver."

"I don't mind," Elizabeth said as she climbed into the driver's seat. She didn't have children or grandchildren. She was grateful to help Trudy—although she didn't say that.

"Danki," Trudy replied. "I really appreciate it."

Davie fell asleep again in the back seat. Trudy had buckled his car seat into the middle seat, and he held his mother's hand as he napped. Trudy put her head back and dozed too.

Elizabeth drove silently, not even listening to the radio. She felt protective of the two and truly wished there was more she could do. She thought of Trudy and her sisters going through their teen and young adult years without a mother, while Elizabeth lived close by. Of course, Elizabeth had been busy caring for her elderly parents during that time. It wasn't as if she would have had time to be involved in Trudy's life—or any reason to either—besides praying, as she had done.

Now was the time to do more.

It was nearly noon and the sun shone high overhead. Elizabeth checked the thermometer on her dashboard. Eighty-two. It would be warm for the men working on the stable.

Again, she turned down the lane and slowed as she neared the house. The same collie stalked the fence line. Trudy stirred as Elizabeth turned toward the house. The men had made progress on the stable—most of the debris had been shifted to an organized pile, and a dumpster had been delivered. The foundation of the stable covered the site, and it appeared as if the new building could be built on it.

The men scurried around, working diligently. Bill threw a metal pipe into the dumpster. When he saw Elizabeth, he waved.

Elizabeth waved back and turned the car toward the house. An Englisch woman, wearing jeans and a T-shirt, sat on the front steps. Her long blond hair was pulled back in a ponytail, and she wore flip-flops.

"It's Faye." Trudy spoke so softly Elizabeth could barely hear her. "She came."

Elizabeth parked next to a king cab pickup. Then, as Elizabeth turned off her car, Faye headed toward them. Without even saying hello, she said, "Daed isn't happy I'm here, so I'm going to get going. Call me on my cell phone."

"All right." Trudy climbed out of the car and gave Faye a hug. "Thank you for coming."

Faye nodded. "Call me, as soon as you can."

Without saying anything to Elizabeth, Faye walked around to the driver's side of the pickup, climbed in, and started the engine. Elizabeth waited to climb out of her car until Faye drove away. Then she grabbed the big bag from the back seat while Trudy pulled Davie into her arms and unfastened the car seat.

As they started toward the house, Alvin called out Trudy's name. He clapped his gloved hands together and started toward them.

Bill waved at Elizabeth again and started toward her. "Hey," he called out. "You should tell Mary that Alvin could use some help. I know how much she likes horses—she could come over and help groom and exercise them."

"I'll tell her." Elizabeth tried to listen to Alvin and Trudy's conversation as she spoke with Bill. "Mary would like that."

Bill gestured toward the stable and began talking about their work.

Trudy's voice rose. "Daed, she hasn't been home in four years. Not since Davie was a baby. I'd like to spend some time with her."

"She left," Alvin said. "She cannot come home expecting that she will be welcomed with open arms just because Davie is ill. Our beliefs have not changed. She knows that."

"But she never joined the church. There is no reason we need to shun her."

Alvin looped his thumbs through his suspenders. "I make the rules around here."

Bill must have realized that Elizabeth's attention had shifted because he said, "Anyway, tell Mary hello. If she's interested in helping with the horses, she should stop by and talk to Alvin."

"I will," Elizabeth said.

Trudy turned away from her father and faced Elizabeth. "Danki. For everything."

Elizabeth nodded. "I'll see you tomorrow."

"Pick us up at eight thirty," Trudy said. "We will be ready."

"See you then." Elizabeth walked back to her car. She would have told Alvin goodbye, but he was already back by the stable, consulting with Bill.

And Trudy was headed toward the barn, with Davie still in her arms. Most likely to call her sister.

CHAPTER SEVEN

Martha had fallen behind on keeping the goodies table in the shop stocked and needed to replenish it, so she spent Monday morning baking loaves of lemon poppy-seed bread and cranberry muffins while Mary ran the shop.

Just after noon, once the loaves had cooled and she'd wrapped and labeled them, she headed out to the shop with a tray of the bread. The parking lot was full of a mix of cars, trucks, and buggies, plus a wagon, which was full of furniture and tools. More auction donations, most likely. But she didn't see a possible owner anywhere nearby.

No matter, it was definitely time to call about a storage unit.

Martha stepped inside the shop. Mary stood at the cash register, ringing up a sale, so she didn't interrupt her. Instead she arranged the goodies in the display case and tucked the tray underneath.

Mary finished up the transaction and Martha asked, "Do you know who has the wagonful of stuff out there?"

Her sister nodded toward the Amish man examining a salad spinner on the shelves to their right. "Talk with him."

"All right." Martha grabbed her ledger from underneath the counter. "And then I'm going to call and order a storage unit."

The next hour was a blur of activity. Martha managed to squeeze the tools and furniture into the shed, but it was now officially stuffed. Thankfully, Elizabeth returned and helped with the customers. It wasn't until after three that Martha finally took a lunch break. By closing time, all three of the sisters were exhausted.

Martha and Mary waited on the outside of the barn door while Elizabeth set the code to lock it.

"How about grilled cheese sandwiches for dinner?" Martha asked.

"Sounds good," Mary answered. "Honestly, anything easy sounds perfect. I'm all sweaty—I think I'll take a shower while you get dinner."

Elizabeth joined them, and they started toward the house. "I have a couple of updates," Elizabeth said. She told them about the horse trainer in Berks County who had been interested in buying Plain Beauty and about Faye showing up at the farm.

Then she told them about the bone marrow registry. "We can get tested," she said, "but we won't likely be chosen."

They'd reached the back door of the house, and Mary held it open as she said, "Well, let's definitely get tested anyway. Maybe one of us has super marrow—if we can't help Davie, maybe we can help someone else."

"Speaking of helping," Elizabeth said, "Bill is working out at Alvin's place on the stable." She went on to explain what he'd said about Alvin needing help with the horses.

"I'm all in," Mary said. "I'll drive over soon and see what I can do."

Martha wondered if Mary was really "all in" because of the horses—or because of getting to spend some time with Bill.

As Martha sliced cheese for the sandwiches, Elizabeth logged on to the computer and registered all of them as donors. "The kits should be here in a few days," she said.

Martha pulled out the griddle, turned it on, and then spread butter on thick slices of homemade bread.

"I'm going to see what I can find about the trainer in Berks County. Ron Sliter is his name." After a few minutes of clicking, Elizabeth said, "There's not much. His place is called Triple S Stables. It looks like he works with his son and daughter. Pretty routine. They train and sell horses and ponies. Give lessons. Board horses. The usual enterprise to make a living in the business." She kept clicking. "Alvin said he bought Plain Beauty from a horse dealer by the name of Boss Chambers, in West Virginia. I'll see what I can find on him." She clicked a few more times. "Alvin said the man seems really disorganized. He hasn't sent the bill of sale yet."

"That's odd," Martha said.

"Alvin doesn't seem worried about it." She turned off the monitor. "I can't find anything negative about the guy—but there are several good reviews from people who've worked with him. There's nothing suspicious."

"Speaking of suspicious"—Mary had just returned to the kitchen from cleaning up—"I heard today that Caleb Yoder is having a sale before he moves to Kentucky."

Martha turned toward her. "When?"

"I didn't have time to ask." Mary ran her fingers through her wet hair. "But I imagine it'll be soon."

Martha thought of Pauline being a neighbor of Caleb's. Maybe she could kill two birds with one stone, so to speak. But first she needed to find out when Caleb's sale was.

The storage unit was delivered the next day and, while Elizabeth took Trudy and Davie to an appointment and Mary watched the shop, Martha worked on moving everything she could into it. Mostly small pieces of furniture, kitchen items, and glassware. She left the tools and outside items in the shed.

Once it was all done and Elizabeth had returned, she consulted with her sister about Pauline. "When she offered to help, I felt too overwhelmed. But now that I'm a little more organized, I think it would be a good idea," Martha said. "She could help with pricing and marketing. She knows what items the Amish buyers will be interested in."

"Go for it," Elizabeth said. "And now would be a great time. Mary is going to talk to Alvin tomorrow, and I'll be taking Trudy and Davie to an appointment on Thursday morning."

"Oh!" Martha had forgotten to ask Elizabeth about the appointment earlier in the day. "How did today go?"

"It was just an infusion."

"Any word about Trudy's sister?"

Elizabeth shook her head. "Trudy didn't volunteer any information, and I didn't ask."

Not asking, without a doubt, was best. Still, Martha was curious.

A few minutes later she was on her way to Pauline's, following the directions from her phone's GPS. It wasn't far—just over four miles—but with all of the back roads in the county it was sometimes hard to find places.

The day was overcast with clouds billowing on the horizon. Perhaps late afternoon would bring a thunderstorm, which was all the more reason to be thankful she'd sorted out the donation items and everything was under cover. Nothing would get wet.

She passed under the canopy of a willow tree that reached across the road and then turned right, following the directions from her phone, along a field of corn. The stalks swayed in the breeze, and to the left a windmill spun behind a farmhouse.

Martha always felt such peace driving through the countryside. Although she'd lived in Kansas nearly her entire adult life, Lancaster would always feel like home. Her heart never swelled like this in Kansas.

"Turn left," her phone instructed.

Martha obliged. Ahead was a little cottage and to the right an acreage with another small house and a barn. It was easy to start thinking all the Amish lived in huge houses, but it wasn't true. Many did, but some lived in quite small homes.

She parked and glanced at the property next door, hoping it was Caleb Yoder's. However, there was no sign of a sale.

Martha climbed out of the car, slipped her phone into her purse, and started toward the front door as someone called out, "Over here!"

Shading her eyes as she turned, Martha made out a woman holding a hoe in the garden along the fence line. She wore a bandana over her gray hair, a blue dress, and a black apron.

"Hello! Is that you, Pauline?"

"Ja…"

"It's me, Martha. From Secondhand Blessings."

"Oh, hallo." Pauline made her way to the end of a row.

"I wanted to talk with you about the auction again. About you helping, in particular."

"My offer still stands," Pauline said.

"I don't want this to get out, but I may have agreed to more than I can handle." Martha smiled, hoping she didn't sound as serious as she felt. "I need help with pricing and marketing. Figuring out what Amish buyers would be most interested in."

"I would be happy to help with all of that—and making sure all of the districts in the county know about the auction and that it is for a good cause, for little Davie's medical care."

"Perfect," Martha said. "What is your schedule like?"

"Open." Pauline had reached the edge of the garden. "I can come over to your shop whenever it works for you."

"How about Thursday morning? You can look at the list of items and help me figure out how many tents we'll need. Rachel will be at the shop leading the quilting circle—perhaps we can all talk about food for the auction and how many booths we'll need for that."

"Sounds good. What time?"

"Come over at nine. I'll ask Rachel to come then too." They'd have an hour before the quilting circle started. Martha glanced toward the property next door. "Any chance that Caleb Yoder lives over there?"

Pauline nodded. "He's been staying with his aenti and *onkel* though."

"I heard he's having a sale."

"That's right."

"When?"

"This weekend. Everything is in his barn, including all of his furniture. He doesn't want to move it to Kentucky."

"Is he selling his property?"

Pauline shook her head. "Leasing it."

That was wise. It would be a shame for him to sell his family farm. "Do you think it would be all right if I go over to his aunt and uncle's to speak with him?"

"Oh, that is not necessary. He is in his barn as we speak, cleaning up. Go over now."

Pauline pointed toward a gate in the fence. "Our families have been going back and forth for years. Take the shortcut."

"Thank you," Martha said. "I'll see you on Thursday."

As Martha neared Caleb's barn she scanned the corral for Plain Beauty. She couldn't imagine he'd leave her out in the open, but one never knew. There wasn't a horse in sight though—just a scooter, the kind that was powered by one's foot, that Amish kids and teenagers in Lancaster County used. But perhaps there were horses in the large barn.

"Hello!" Martha called out as she neared the door.

"Come on in," came an answer.

Martha stepped into the barn. It was huge—and apparently empty, except for Caleb, who was pushing a broom in the far corner.

Caleb squinted at her against the light of the open door. "How may I help you?"

"I was over talking with Pauline, and she said you're planning a sale."

"Oh, hallo. You are Martha, ja? I saw you and Rachel Fischer together when I was at Alvin's farm." He started walking toward her.

"Yes, I'm Martha. I wanted to get information about your sale, in case we can use anything in our shop." As if they had any room for anything else right now.

Caleb smiled. "I carted everything over to my onkel's place, where I am staying until I leave. He lives off the highway, and I figured more people would stop by there for a sale." He gestured with his free hand. "I am here cleaning. I thought I would start in the barn and then tackle the house."

Before Martha could respond, he continued. "I was thinking about my sale though, and then about your auction for little Davie. Could you sell my things there? I was considering donating all of it, and saving myself the trouble."

"Do you need the money?" Martha asked.

"Well, sure. It is a big move. I will be starting over in Kentucky."

"Then you should sell it yourself. We've had lots of donations, and I'm guessing the profits will be high. But I would love to attend your sale and see if there's anything we could resell in our shop. What day are you holding it?"

"Friday and Saturday, but come by on Thursday afternoon. We will have it all set up then." He leaned against the broom handle. "Are you looking for anything in particular?"

"Smaller items," she answered. "Glassware. That sort of thing."

"I have some of that," he answered. "My maam liked pretty things."

Martha knew Caleb had been close to his mother. He was in his early thirties and never married. She couldn't help but remember what Rachel had said about Caleb being sweet on Trudy.

"Are you selling any of your farrier tools? Or items? Or any animals?"

His face fell. "Like a saddle? Or a horse?"

Martha wrinkled her nose. Was she that obvious?

"Officer Marks already grilled me. I did not take the saddle nor Plain Beauty." He shook his head as he spoke.

Martha kept her voice low and steady. She certainly didn't want Caleb to think she was accusing him of stealing either, even if he was a chief suspect. "Do you have any idea who might have? Or might have motive to?"

Caleb shrugged. "Alvin planning to auction a horse like that would be motive for a lot of people."

"Such as?"

Caleb looped his thumbs through his suspenders. "People in the horse racing industry. There are those who believed Plain Beauty had another year of racing in her. Several thought Boss Chambers made a big mistake in selling her when he did."

"And that's what you think?"

"Ja." He pursed his lips together.

"Do you know a man named Ty Jones? Who works for a track on Long Island?"

"Worked."

Martha cocked her head. "Pardon?"

"Past tense. He took a job in New Mexico."

"Oh?"

"He stopped by here a few days ago…"

"The day of the fire."

Caleb exhaled. "Ja, it *was* the day of the fire…"

"How do you know Ty?"

"I did some work at Belmont a year ago. I met Ty then."

"Did he ask you about Alvin's farm? About Plain Beauty?"

Caleb nodded. "The topic came up… But Ty is not responsible for the fire or Plain Beauty going missing."

"Or the stolen saddle?"

Caleb's eyes narrowed.

"He stopped by Secondhand Blessings the afternoon of the fire and was interested in the saddle," Martha said. "He knew Alvin took it back to the farm."

"Well, that is interesting but circumstantial. He left the county that afternoon. He was headed for New Mexico. That is where he is now."

Martha raised her eyebrows at him. "Do you know that for sure? Do you have any evidence?"

"He left a message on my phone yesterday to say he arrived."

"Just because he said he did doesn't mean it's so. He could be anywhere." Martha's heart raced. "Or he could be in

New Mexico with Plain Beauty and the saddle. He had a hitch on his truck—I remember that. Perhaps he had a horse trailer hidden somewhere…"

"Hidden?" Caleb crossed his arms. "He was pulling a trailer when he stopped by here. A double trailer, but he only had one horse in it. His horse. An old Arabian."

Martha's heart skipped a beat. Why would Ty Jones have been without the horse trailer when he stopped by Second-hand Blessings?

As Martha backed out of Pauline's driveway, her phone rang. *Trish.* She turned the car around, pulled over to the side of the lane, and answered the call.

"How are you?" she asked after saying hello. "And how is Celeste?"

"She was better," Trish said, "but then today she spiked a fever again. We just left the doctor's office."

"What did he say?"

"That it's a mystery. That nothing is obvious. That we should do more tests. He's consulting a pediatric immunologist."

Martha took a deep breath. She had so much to do right now, but her family would always be her top priority. "I'll come out," she said. "I'll buy a ticket as soon as I get home."

"No, don't do that. Not yet… I'll let you know how she does in the next few days. And what the immunologist says."

"All right," Martha answered. "But call anytime. Give Celeste a hug from me."

"I will." Trish's voice grew heavier. "Thank you for always being there for me."

Martha swallowed a lump. Was she always there for her daughter? She'd moved a thousand miles away... "I'm praying for you both. Try to get some rest."

"I will. Talk to you soon."

After Martha ended the call, she pulled back onto the road and started toward home, her thoughts on Celeste. What did her doctor fear could be wrong?

But soon her thoughts returned to her conversation with Caleb. She wasn't ready to cross him off the list. She'd go to his uncle's on Thursday and look for more information. Ask his uncle a few questions.

She also needed to think through the night of the fire again. Had she missed something? Could Ty have parked his trailer on the other side of the woods?

But how would he have gotten Plain Beauty across the fields and through the woods without leaving any tracks? Although the day was overcast, thankfully it hadn't rained, not since a week before the night of the fire.

Martha came to the crossroads and stopped at the red light. When it turned green, she made a left-hand turn. On the other side of the highway sat Alvin's woods. She turned around in a convenience store parking lot, noticing one of Mary's signs for the auction on a telephone pole as she did. She'd seen several others around town too.

Now on the side of the highway adjacent to the woods, she pulled over, exited the car, and walked back to the far end of the trees. She took her sunglasses off and walked slowly.

Feeling foolish—who knew how many people had pulled over by the woods since Friday night—she kept walking on the narrow shoulder, her eyes on the powdery dirt at the edge of the asphalt. She didn't want to walk in the dirt and corrupt any tracks she might find.

Ahead, the trees were farther back, leaving a pull-out area off the shoulder. As Martha approached, she could make out faint tire tracks in a curve. She looked closer and finally stepped off the asphalt. There were two sets of tire tracks— could they be from a pickup pulling a trailer? It was impossible to tell.

Martha pulled out her phone and took some photos then checked them. The tire tracks barely showed. She stepped carefully over the tracks and kept her eyes on the ground. There was some sort of print. A shoe perhaps. Was that a horse's hoof in the soft dirt? She turned on the flash on her camera and zoomed in. As she snapped the photo, thunder crashed in the distance.

Then she felt a drop of rain on her arm. Then another. She stepped into the trees. Could Ty—or someone else—have gotten Plain Beauty across the fields and through the trees without leaving any tracks? The ground was either pasture or hard soil. A bolt of lightning flashed across the sky.

Martha began to count. One-alligator. Two-alligator… She got up to eight before the thunder crashed.

She felt another drop and then another. She dialed John Marks, but the call went straight to voice mail. "This is Martha. I'm in the woods on the other side of Alvin Raber's farm. There appear to be tracks here—a horse's hoof. Perhaps what could be a pickup and trailer tracks. I'll text you photos. Call me when you get a chance."

As she texted the photos, she squinted, realizing the images were of dirt. The tracks were too faint to make out. John was going to think she was ridiculous. Maybe she was.

She jumped as another bolt of lightning flashed across the sky, followed immediately by a crash of thunder. Then a torrent of rain began cascading down on top of her. She rushed toward her car, but water still ran down her face and arms by the time she reached it. Once she'd folded herself inside, she looked through the streaked window. The dirt was already spotted with rain. By the time she started the car and pulled onto the highway all traces of the tracks were gone.

CHAPTER EIGHT

Wednesday morning, Mary sat at the kitchen table with her hands wrapped around her cup of coffee, staring out the window at the hummingbird feeder. She couldn't remember the last time she actually saw a hummingbird at it, but the feeder was full of nectar. One of her sisters must have filled it.

Somebody said something.

Mary looked beyond the feeder to the field. The last crop of alfalfa had been cut the day before.

"Mary?"

She turned her head toward Martha and smiled. "Were you talking to me?"

Martha shook her head. "Who else would I be talking to?"

"Oh." Mary glanced around the kitchen. Elizabeth was nowhere to be seen.

"Are you going over to Alvin's today?"

Mary yawned, slowly covering her mouth. "I thought I would, if that's all right."

"It's fine. You should go soon. Elizabeth left a chicken casserole in the fridge for you to take."

"Doesn't she want to take it tomorrow?"

Martha shook her head. "She said to take it today. From what Trudy said yesterday, they could use something for supper tonight."

"All right."

"The sooner you go the better."

Mary glanced at her watch. It was just after nine. How long had she been sitting at the table with her coffee?

She stood. "If Alvin can use my help, I'll only stay a couple of hours. I'll be back by noon."

"All right." Martha turned to the fridge and pulled the casserole dish out. "You might ask Alvin if he saw Ty later on Friday before the fire. I'm sure he would have told John if he'd shown up at the farm—but it would be good to double-check. Also, ask if he saw a horse trailer on the other side of his woods."

Mary picked up her coffee cup. "Don't you think he would have told John if he had?"

"You'd hope so. But double-check." Martha handed Mary the casserole and took the cup in return. "Have fun. Tell Bill hello."

Mary laughed. "Is that why you're trying to push me out the door?"

"Something like that." Martha gave her a playful shove. "Remember, Alvin's expecting you to come by, but at this rate they'll have the stable rebuilt before you show up."

Martha wasn't always so easygoing when it came to Mary's comings and goings, but when it came to Bill, both of her sisters were always supportive. Mary, after her heartbreaking divorce, wasn't ready for romance again, but she couldn't convince her sisters of that. She did enjoy spending time with Bill though. There was nothing like an old childhood friend to make one feel young again.

If nothing else, Mary would be able to deliver the food and hopefully say hello to Bill. She appreciated Elizabeth suggesting that she could help with the horses, and she wanted to, but it had been a couple of years since she'd ridden last. She wasn't sure if she'd be a help to Alvin—or a hindrance. But she was excited to ride, that was for sure.

She pulled her cowboy boots out of the back of her closet and grabbed her hat from the top shelf. She'd ridden quite a bit as a girl and many times in the years since. It really was one of her favorite things to do.

The farm was like most Amish places she'd seen—neat as a pin. Except for the stable, which was nothing more than a foundation, plus a stack of partially burnt timbers. She spotted Bill first as she turned the curve in the Rabers' driveway. He was working on something out on the lawn of the house. It was almost as if he was looking for her. He grinned and waved. She'd always thought he looked like a younger Harrison Ford with his dark hair and eyes and shy smile. He wore jeans and a T-shirt, which showed off his muscles.

Bill definitely didn't look like he was in his fifties.

She parked her car, left her purse, grabbed the casserole, and climbed out. She didn't see Alvin, so she headed straight for Bill.

"Is that lunch?" he joked.

"Don't you wish. Supper. For Alvin, Trudy, and Davie. Not for you." She gave him a sassy smile.

He jutted out his lower lip. But he couldn't hold it and broke out into a grin. "Wait," he asked. "Did you cook?"

"Wrong again." She laughed. "Elizabeth made it." Looking around, she asked, "Where's Alvin?"

"He's around here somewhere. Maybe in the barn. Or the house." Bill turned toward the pasture. "Or the pasture."

In the distance, Mary made out a man standing at the fence. He was dressed Amish, but she couldn't be sure it was Alvin. "Is Trudy in the house?"

"I think so," Bill said. "I saw her hang a load of wash on the line an hour or so ago, and I haven't seen her leave."

"Thanks, Bill. See you in a bit." She turned toward the house, marching forward with the casserole held out in front of her as if it were frankincense for Baby Jesus. Certain Bill was watching her, she spun around. Sure enough, he was. He grinned and then blushed.

She held the casserole with one hand and waved, grinning back in return. "Get to work!" she called out.

"Yes, ma'am!" He saluted her, which was a little funny considering they were on an Amish farm. No one could belong to the Amish and join the military. Not only did they not take orders from a commanding officer, they didn't defend themselves. Sometimes they wouldn't even report it if a crime had been committed against them.

Bill turned back toward the framework, and Mary resumed her walk toward the house.

Mary knocked several times before she heard footsteps. Finally, the door opened, and a young barefoot Amish woman, wearing a dark purple dress and a white apron, stood in front of her. "You must be Martha and Elizabeth's sister."

"Mary." She shifted the casserole to one hand again and stuck out her hand.

"You resemble your sisters. I'm Trudy." The woman took Mary's hand. But instead of shaking it, she squeezed it.

Mary heard giggling. "That must be Davie."

"Is it safe?" came a voice from upstairs. It wasn't Davie. It was a woman's voice.

"Hold on," Trudy called over her shoulder, her face growing pink.

When she didn't explain, Mary held out the casserole. "Elizabeth made chicken casserole. For your supper. Or dinner. Or for whenever you need it."

"Danki." Trudy took the pan. "We will have it for dinner—I have been trying to feed the stable crew too."

There was an awkward moment of silence, something Mary didn't experience often, before she remembered the other reason she'd come. "Elizabeth said your father might need help with the horses. I used to ride—and would love to help."

"I know he is having a difficult time keeping up with everything. I am sure he would welcome the help… I would, but I can't take Davie out there with me."

"Of course not." Mary nodded toward the staircase. "But it sounds as if you have help."

Trudy shook her head. "She just stopped by—and can't stay."

Mary was dying to know who "she" was and why she was hiding. She smiled. "I'll go find your father."

Trudy nodded. "He will appreciate it. All of us have appreciated you and your sisters. The rides. The auction." She held up the casserole. "The food."

"You're welcome." Mary wished she could procrastinate and see who was with Davie, but she didn't have anything else to ask. "Nice to meet you. See you soon."

As soon as Trudy said goodbye, Mary turned back toward Bill. This time he was pounding nails—not looking at her. She smiled anyway at the sight of him and then waved as she passed by. He looked up and grinned, causing a nail to fall out of his mouth. He laughed as he scrambled to find it in the grass.

Mary continued on to the pasture, but as she turned onto the pathway, Alvin started out of the pasture gate, leading a brown quarter horse. She passed the barn—a huge structure—that was as neat and well cared for as the rest of the farm. She met him a few feet later.

Alvin stopped as she approached. "Are you the third Classen sister?"

"Yes. I'm Mary."

"Elizabeth mentioned you."

"I've come to help you with the horses, if you need it. I have a couple of hours this morning."

"I could definitely use the help." He nodded back toward the horse. "This is Midnight. He could use some exercise. I have trained him as a riding horse for an Englisch family—they wanted a gelding."

"Great! I'd love to ride him."

"Come on." Alvin started leading the horse again. "You can saddle him up in the barn."

Mary hurried to keep up with him. "May I ask you a few questions while we walk?"

"Go ahead." Alvin didn't sound thrilled with the idea.

"We—"

Alvin interrupted her. "Who is 'we'?"

"My sisters and I." She skipped a couple of times to keep up with him.

He slowed his pace a little. "Go ahead."

"We were wondering about Ty Jones—the man you saw at Secondhand Blessings the day of the fire."

He nodded. "I remember."

"Did you see him after that? Did he stop by here by any chance?"

Alvin wrinkled his nose but didn't respond.

"What?" Mary asked.

"I did not see him. I had other errands to run that day. But when I was at the grocery store, when I came out, the woman who parked her car across from the hitching post told me an Englischer was poking around my buggy. It sounded as if he looked like Ty. And then when I got home, Trudy said an Englischer had come to the house, asking about me. He said he was looking for a trainer and asked when I'd be back. She told him sometime in the afternoon, but he didn't return."

"And the description matched Ty's?"

Alvin sighed. "Trudy couldn't remember a lot of details. She was pretty upset about Davie that day… She said he was wearing jeans and boots. Had short brown hair. It could have been any number of Englischers."

"Or this Ty?"

"Perhaps," Alvin answered.

"Did he have any tattoos?"

"Trudy said he had a long-sleeve T-shirt on."

Mary's eyebrows shot up. "And you told Officer Marks all of this?"

Alvin chuckled. "Actually, I forgot to. But I have his number. I will give him a call."

They'd reached the barn, so Mary followed Alvin and Midnight inside. It appeared even bigger on the inside than on the outside. There were several cows in stalls and a couple of horses. At the far end was a stack of hay bales. A gray cat rubbed up against her leg as Alvin pointed to a stall. "I will put him in here, and then show you the tack room and which saddle to use. You can ride in the pasture, up the lane, on the highway, through the woods. Wherever you want. Give him a good hour ride, if you can. A little longer is fine too."

A half hour later, Mary led Midnight out of the barn. Alvin and Bill were raising the newly constructed frame on the foundation. Bill smiled as she stopped at the mounting step between the stable and the barn. Was he going to watch her climb up onto Midnight? It appeared so.

Mary took the challenge, holding on to the reins as she climbed the steps. She clutched them tightly as she swung her leg over the saddle and grabbed the horn. Midnight took a step forward. "Whoa," she said, with calmness and authority. It didn't work. The horse took a second step.

She quickly scrambled onto the saddle, holding tightly to the horn and pulling the reins. The horse stopped long enough for her to settle her rear end but then took off. Mary managed to steer him toward the pasture and away from Bill—who was laughing now.

The first half hour was harrowing. She stayed in the pasture with the horse, too afraid to go to the highway or even the lane.

But soon they found a rhythm, and Midnight seemed to have grown used to her. She gathered her courage and rode him past the barn and by the construction site, but Bill wasn't anywhere to be seen. Alvin waved at her though.

She started out toward the lane. When they reached it, Midnight took off at a trot. A warm breeze played with Mary's ponytail as the horse increased his speed. She pulled back on the reins, not wanting to go any faster.

Then a pickup pulling a horse trailer followed by a sedan started up the lane. Mary pulled Midnight's reins back and over toward the fence, wanting to give the truck and car plenty of room.

But the movement made Midnight rear. Mary, trying not to panic, spoke calmly, "You're okay. You're okay."

The horse stopped, and Mary again pulled tightly on the reins, moving the horse to the edge of the fence.

The driver of the truck, a middle-aged man, tipped his hat out the open window and grinned broadly as Midnight stomped his hoof. The driver of the next car, a middle-aged woman, gave Mary a sympathetic look.

Once the car passed by, Midnight reared again. Mary held on tightly and this time said, a little too loudly, "I'm too old for this!"

Midnight bucked, sending Mary bouncing on the saddle. She held on to the horn, but as the horse bucked again, she swung her right leg over the saddle and slid down the other side, propelling herself away from the horse. For a moment she thought she was going to stay on her feet, but then she stumbled forward and landed on her hands and knees on the lane. She glanced over her shoulder at the horse. He stood in the same spot, staring at her.

Mary stood and brushed off her hands and the knees of her jeans. As she grabbed Midnight's reins, another car came down the lane toward them, this time from the opposite direction. Mary held on tight as the horse stepped backward. "Oh no you don't," she said in her calmest and most authoritative voice. Midnight lowered his head, and she kept her eye on the car.

The driver of the pickup was now in the passenger seat of the car. He was still grinning. Again he tipped his hat out the open window.

Mary grinned back as the car passed by. She wasn't going to let on that her palms and knees stung and that she probably came close to breaking a hip.

Once the car was nearly to the highway, she began leading Midnight back toward the farm. There was no way she could get back up on him without the mounting steps. If she had more confidence—and strength—maybe she could have climbed halfway up the fence and onto the horse's back, but as it was she was just happy they were close to the barn.

When she reached the driveway and turned the corner, Bill was back at work on the frame. Someone was driving the hat man's pickup, pulling the trailer onto the driveway from where it had been parked by the corral.

It was Alvin driving, headed toward the barn.

As she reached Bill, she said, "Am I hallucinating, or did I just see an Amish man driving a truck?"

"I don't know," Bill teased. "Any chance you got bucked off and bumped your head?"

"Well, I essentially got bucked off. But I don't think I bumped my head." She ran her free hand through her ponytail. Another of the workers walked by, so she lowered her voice. "Seriously, why is Alvin driving that guy's truck?"

"It's his truck and trailer," Bill answered. "He just hires that guy to drive it."

"What?"

Bill nodded. "It's cheaper for him to own his own truck and trailer than to hire someone else's. He only drives on the property, to move it from one place to another."

Mary laughed. "I'll never stop being surprised by the Amish."

Bill smiled again. "Me neither."

As she continued leading Midnight the rest of the way to the barn, she couldn't help but wonder where Alvin's truck and trailer were the night of the fire. And if he ever made exceptions to just driving it on the farm.

CHAPTER NINE

Martha spent Wednesday afternoon and evening working on the auction items, and by the time she finally came into the house, Mary had left to run errands.

Elizabeth pointed out the three bone marrow donor kits sitting on the kitchen table. "Even though we probably won't be able to donate, we should get the kits back in the mail in the morning."

"Agreed."

"I already did mine. You should do yours now," Elizabeth said.

Martha picked up one of the kits and yawned. She hadn't been sleeping well. In the middle of the night, she'd awakened in a panic about the auction. Could she pull it off? Or she woke up worried about Celeste. Should she go to Kansas?

She put the kit back down on the table. She'd do it in the morning.

After another fitful night of sleep, Martha rose early to find that Elizabeth had placed each of the kits at their three places at the table. She chuckled and made a pot of coffee, a batch of muffins for the quilting circle, and then started making Dutch babies for breakfast before Elizabeth came into the kitchen.

Elizabeth was her usual cheery self. "Good morning," she called out. "Did you swab your cheek yet?"

Martha stifled a laugh. That wasn't something one heard every day.

"Not yet." She tried to be as upbeat as possible. "But I will. I promise."

Elizabeth pulled a mug from the cabinet. "Is Mary up yet?"

"I haven't seen her," Martha answered. It was six thirty, but Mary wasn't usually up until seven. Elizabeth was overly optimistic about their youngest sister.

When Martha put the Dutch babies in the oven, Elizabeth held up her donor kit. "Now's the perfect time to do this. It will only take a minute. I'll talk you through it."

Martha grinned and followed her big sister's instructions.

An hour later, and without a peep out of Mary, Elizabeth said, "I'll be gone most of the day. Davie has a lab appointment this morning and then a doctor's appointment this afternoon."

"We'll be fine," Martha said. "I'll probably slip out for a half hour or so in the afternoon to stop by Caleb Yoder's sale, but Mary can be in charge then."

A few minutes after Elizabeth left to pick up Trudy and Davie, Martha stepped out the back door with a basket of muffins for the quilting circle. She had just enough time to make sure her ledger and all the items were in order before Pauline and Rachel arrived.

"Wait!"

Martha turned.

Mary came rushing out of the house. "I have something I've been wanting to tell you. I didn't have a chance yesterday." She started to close the door behind her.

"Stop," Martha commanded. "Go back and do your donor kit. We need to get them in the mail."

"But I thought we were all too old."

"Well, you're probably the most likely to qualify, so I'll come talk you through it."

"All right."

Martha headed back into the house with Mary and got her test done. "I'll mail these off this afternoon."

Martha glanced at her watch. "What did you want? I have a half hour before Rachel and Pauline arrive."

"Believe me, I won't take that long." Mary linked her arm through Martha's as they walked back out the door. "Did you know Alvin Raber drives?"

"What?" She thought the Amish didn't drive.

"I witnessed it, in person, yesterday."

Martha narrowed her eyes. "Are you sure it was Alvin?"

"Positive. He was driving his truck and pulling his horse trailer."

"His?"

Mary laughed. "Yes. But believe me, I was as incredulous as you are now. Bill told me that Alvin owns the truck and trailer. It's less expensive for him to just hire a driver than to have to rent a truck and trailer too."

That made sense. "But he only drives it on his own farm, right? It's not like he drives it out on the highway."

"Right." Mary pulled her arm out from Martha's as they reached the shop. "But theoretically, he could."

"What are you getting at?"

"You said he left to make a phone call that evening. What if he put the horse in the trailer instead? And drove it to the highway or something for someone else to drive away?"

Martha shook her head. "I didn't see a pickup and trailer on the property that night." She punched in the code to unlock the front door of the shop and pulled it open.

Mary followed her in. "You said you saw tracks on the other side of the woods. Maybe Alvin took the horse there."

"I don't think he would have had time to. And he certainly wouldn't have had time to drive the trailer anywhere and then get back to the house." Martha picked up her ledger from the counter. "It doesn't make any sense."

"Well, my point is that he owns a truck and horse trailer. And he can drive it." Mary shrugged. "I thought it was information you should have."

"You're right. Thanks for telling me." Martha opened the ledger.

Mary started toward the room where the quilting supplies were stored. "I'll set up for the quilting circle."

As Martha went through the ledger, highlighting household items with pink, Mary pulled the quilting frame from the closet.

Next Martha highlighted all of the woodworking tools with yellow and the garden tools with green. She continued on through the ledger, coding each item with a color while Mary set up the chairs around the frame.

At nine, when Martha heard hooves in the parking lot, she stepped outside into the sunlight. Both Pauline and Rachel had arrived.

After Martha greeted them, she said, "I'll show you the items we have as we talk."

Carrying the ledger, she led the way into the shed first. "This is all tools—garden, farm, and woodworking." She flipped to the back of the ledger to take notes. "I need some ideas as far as what will sell the best, what should be silent auction items, what should be slated for the regular auction, and what starting bids should be."

Pauline held up a rake. "These are a dime a dozen." She nodded toward six more against the wall. "I'd put five dollars on each of them and sell them instead of auctioning them off. They're not worth your time."

Martha nodded. She was sure there were some household items that fell into the same category.

Pauline pointed toward a wheelbarrow. "Now that should be auctioned off—it's in great shape and will be a big seller."

They continued on through the shed and then into the storage unit where the furniture was stored. Rachel ran her hand over the top of one of two end tables. "These are nice. Definitely auction them off."

"There's a bedstead that matches it and a bureau."

"Consider it for a final auction piece," Pauline said. "You want to save the nicest items for last."

Martha made a note of that in the back of the ledger, although she figured she would have thought of that. They'd certainly planned to auction off Plain Beauty and her saddle last, so they needed some other big-ticket items, just in case she wasn't found in time.

"The auctioneer will come over before the auction," Rachel said. "He'll help with some of that too."

"Should I call him?" Martha asked.

Rachel nodded. "Did I give you his card?"

Martha shook her head.

"Sorry." Rachel reached into her purse. She dug out a card and handed it to Martha. It simply read, DON COBLENTZ, AUCTIONEER. And then his phone number. No website or email address.

They continued on through the items, moving into the storage room in the shop, while Martha continued to take notes. Both women were thrilled with the glassware that people had dropped off. There were five water sets—a pitcher and eight glasses—every Amish family had at least one to use at mealtime. They were big sellers in the shop. There was also some Depression-era glass. All would bring good prices.

When they'd finished in the storeroom, Rachel wiped her eyes. "I cannot tell you how grateful Alvin, Trudy, and I—and our entire family—are for what you and your sisters are doing."

"It's our pleasure, honestly." Martha patted Rachel's shoulder. "Thank you to both of you"—she smiled at Pauline—"for all of your help. I'm feeling more confident about the auction." She glanced at her watch. "We didn't talk about food…"

"I have it all covered," Rachel said. "Do not worry about a thing."

Martha knew, from other Amish events she'd attended, that if Rachel said the food was covered, it was covered. She led the way out of the storage unit. "Now we need to get you to the quilting circle."

Rachel led the way into the shop and then froze. Martha stepped beside her. All of the women had gathered, and each one was holding a quilt, either already finished or nearly so.

"Look." Mary swept her arm wide. "Everyone brought family quilts or a quilt they're making for the auction. We'll have a whole table just for quilts."

Tears filled Rachel's eyes again. But this time, as she tried to dab them away, she was unsuccessful. They streamed down her face, her gratitude evident to all.

After all of the quilting circle ladies had left, Martha slipped away to go check out Caleb Yoder's sale at his uncle's.

As she turned into the driveway, she was surprised to find other cars already parked, along with several buggies. Perhaps Caleb had decided to open the sale a day early.

It was actually a "shop" sale. The double doors were swung open, and inside were tables of items, along with tools and furniture and several people, both Amish and Englisch, milling around. On the outside was a buggy and a wagon for sale.

An ache filled Martha's heart for a moment as she stopped in the entryway to the shed. Caleb had lost both of his parents and didn't have any siblings. He was leaving the community he grew up in. Even if he found better business opportunities in Kentucky, as he'd been promised, would it be worth it?

"Martha!" Caleb waved from the back of the shed. "Come on in."

He stood beside a kitchen table. Also along the wall were chairs, three beds, and five bureaus. On the tables were dishes, serving bowls, and cooking tools. There were two other tables covered with tools. She didn't see any saddles—not that he would be foolish enough to put Plain Beauty's on display.

Martha met him in the middle of the shed. "How are you doing?"

He cocked his head. "Why do you ask?"

"This is a big change for you. The sale must make it feel awfully final."

He turned his face away. "It does," he muttered.

She couldn't help wonder what would have happened if Trudy had returned his feelings. If she had, Martha had no doubt he'd be staying in Lancaster County. "Where will you stay in Kentucky?" she asked.

"With a family friend. He works as a farrier too—the plan is that I will take over his business in a few years when he retires. He does not have any children, which is why he asked me to come, after my parents both died."

"Does he work with racehorses there?"

Caleb nodded. "With the best, including derby contenders. I believe it will be a fine experience for me, although it took me a while to decide..." He shrugged. "I can only hope it is the right decision."

Martha stepped over to the table and looked at a water set—this one a blue pitcher with eight matching glasses. "I'm interested in this for the shop. How much are you asking?"

"I was going to ask Pauline to help me with the pricing for a few items, including this one, but she hasn't shown up yet."

"How about thirty dollars?" She was sure she could sell it for forty.

"It is yours." He grinned. "And anything that does not sell."

She looked around again, not really wanting to add anything more to the auction, but the items did appear to be of good quality. "We'll sell what we can in the auction."

"Danki," he said.

She gave him the money for the water set, and as he wrapped it in newspaper and put it in a box, she looked around more.

Once she was done, she carried the box to the trunk of her car. Before she climbed in an Amish woman with gray hair under her white kapp started toward Martha, with a quilt in her arms. "Are you the woman from Secondhand Blessings?"

"Yes," Martha answered.

"I am Sally Yoder, Caleb's aunt. He told me all about little Davie being so ill—he was good friends with Trudy when they were both young. Anyway, he has been so concerned about all of them and then with the fire and all." She hugged the quilt. "I have been meaning to drop this by, for the auction."

Martha took the log cabin patterned quilt in browns and greens from her. "It's beautiful."

Sally smiled.

Martha saw her chance to ask the question she didn't ask Caleb. "Is your nephew keeping his animals?"

"Ne. He sold the cows and workhorses months ago, after his daed died. And he just sold his buggy horse."

"What about a riding horse?"

Sally shook her head. "He has not had one for the last year. He says he will buy a new one in Kentucky."

"That makes sense," Martha said. Otherwise he would have had to hire a driver with a trailer. That didn't mean that Plain Beauty couldn't be in hiding somewhere on the farm, where his aunt didn't usually go.

"Are there any other animals on your farm?"

Sally laughed. "Lots. We have a dairy farm."

"What about horses?"

"We have the usual workhorses. And a couple of buggy horses. Three dogs. Too many cats to count. Anything in particular that you are looking for?"

Martha hesitated.

"Plain Beauty?" Sally asked.

Martha nodded sheepishly.

"Caleb told me, by the questions you asked him, that he thought you suspected him of taking the horse."

Martha felt chagrined that Caleb had shared about her grilling him with his aunt. "I don't think he did," Martha said. "We're just examining all of the possibilities."

"I do not blame you for questioning him. He was one of the last people to see the horse before it disappeared. But I have to tell you that Caleb has a heart of gold." Sally sighed. "And he would never say this, not to anyone. But he has always had a soft spot for Trudy, and now for her son too. He would not do anything to jeopardize the sale to help little Davie, even though he disagreed with Alvin auctioning off the horse." Sally shook her head. "I'm sorry. I did not mean to go on and on. Caleb would not want me to defend him." She swept her arm toward the barn. "Look anywhere you would like on our farm. Plain Beauty is not on this property. Caleb did not take her."

Martha reached out and touched the woman's arm. "Thank you for sharing that. I can't tell you how much I appreciate it. Caleb is a fine young man—I'm just trying to help solve the mystery and needed to know he isn't involved. And you've helped convince me of that."

Sally stepped back. "Danki for understanding an aunt's care for her nephew. We are all praying that whoever took Plain Beauty will be caught, that the auction is a big success, and that Davie will completely recover."

Martha nodded in agreement. That was exactly what she was praying for too. She lifted the quilt in her arms. "Thank you for this. All of us appreciate it."

As she drove away from the farm, she believed Caleb was innocent. Of course, she'd be open to any evidence that might prove otherwise, but it made sense now that he wanted Alvin to get the most money possible for Plain Beauty to help Davie. Martha couldn't help but wonder, though, how big his soft spot was for Trudy. It seemed a broken heart was the reason he was moving to Kentucky.

When Martha returned to Secondhand Blessings, the parking lot was packed, but Elizabeth's car wasn't in its usual place near the house. That wasn't surprising—Martha knew her sister thought she'd be gone most of the day. But it meant Mary was on her own with a shop full of customers.

Martha grabbed the water set and the quilt from the trunk and hurried toward the barn. When she entered, she saw Mary at the cash register, ringing up items for a young woman.

"Hey." She flashed a smile at Martha. "Could you help the guy in the tool section? He's looking for something specific—I didn't catch exactly what he said."

"Sure." Mary kept a good disposition no matter how busy they got, even when she was on her own. Martha put the box on the table next to the counter.

Mary handed the customer her receipt and then said to Martha, "Oh, what do you have there?"

"A quilt for the auction from Caleb's aunt and a water set for the shop."

"I'll open up the box while you help the man in the tool section."

"I'm thinking we should sell the water set for forty dollars," Martha said. "But see what you think."

Martha tucked her purse in the cupboard underneath the counter and then headed to the back of the barn. But as soon as she arrived, her phone began ringing. *Trish*. She'd call her back as soon as she helped the customer.

He was looking for a miter saw, and Martha was able to locate the three they had in stock immediately. As he made his choice, she slipped back through the shop.

Mary was waiting on another customer. Martha held up her phone and mouthed *Trish*.

Mary nodded, and Martha hurried out the front door, wanting to talk with her daughter in private. She headed toward the house as she placed the call.

As soon as Trish picked up, she said, "Mom, can you come out? I know flying into Wichita will be too expensive, but you should be able to get something reasonable into Kansas City. I wouldn't ask if I didn't need you. Craig will pick you up."

Everything Martha had to do in the next two weeks rushed through her head.

Trish continued, not giving Martha a chance to answer. "Celeste is having more tests. And I'm exhausted. And scared."

"Of course, baby," Martha answered, her voice as soothing as a lullaby. "I'll buy a ticket right now and call you back in a few minutes."

"Thank you. You're the best."

Martha knew she had to go. Family always came first. But she had no idea how she could go to Kansas and have everything ready for the auction on time. Not to mention continue trying to get Plain Beauty back in time for the auction.

CHAPTER TEN

Elizabeth sat in the doctor's waiting room with Davie on her lap, reading him Dr. Seuss's *The 500 Hats of Bartholomew Cubbins*. Martha's kids, especially Trish, had loved that story.

Trudy sat with her head back against her chair and her eyes closed. She'd been quiet the entire day. Perhaps she was exhausted, with good cause. Not to mention emotionally spent.

Davie seemed extra tired too. He rested his head against Elizabeth's shoulder, and as Elizabeth continued reading the little boy's body grew more and more relaxed.

They'd packed a lunch and ate in a park after the lab appointment. Now, they'd waited over a half hour to see the doctor.

Soon Davie slipped into sleep. Elizabeth stopped reading, but just as she did the medical assistant called Davie's name.

When Trudy didn't respond, Elizabeth touched her arm and said, "It's Davie's turn."

Trudy sat up, yawned, and scooped Davie into her arms. "Danki," she said as she walked toward the assistant.

The appointment didn't take long. After they were back in the car, Trudy reported that the doctor said the bone marrow transplant needed to take place as soon as possible.

Elizabeth hoped Martha had mailed the kits. Even though there was a slim chance, she still wanted them to do everything they could to help Trudy and Davie.

Both were so quiet that Elizabeth thought the two had fallen asleep, but then Davie asked quietly, "Why is Caleb moving away?"

Elizabeth stared straight ahead but couldn't help but listen for the answer.

"Because he wants to live in Kentucky," Trudy said. "He has a new job there."

Davie's voice was even lower. "I will miss him."

"So will I," Trudy answered.

"Will he miss us?"

"I am certain he will." Trudy was quiet for a moment. "He said he would come over one more time and tell us goodbye."

Davie didn't speak again until Elizabeth parked the car by the Raber farmhouse. In a groggy voice, he asked, "Is Caleb here?"

"Not today," Trudy said. "It will be a few more days."

Elizabeth carried Trudy's bag to the front door while Trudy carried Davie.

"Is Grossdaddi here?" Davie asked.

Trudy shook her head. "He had business away from the farm today."

In fact, everyone seemed to be away from the farm, including the men who had been working on the stable. The framing was completed, and it appeared they were ready to start on the walls. Perhaps they were taking a late lunch or taking the day off. None of them had been there in the morning when Elizabeth picked Trudy and Davie up.

Trudy unlocked the door, and Davie pushed it open and went inside. As Elizabeth handed Trudy her bag, Davie yelled, "Aenti Faye! What are you doing here?"

"Danki," Trudy said quickly to Elizabeth. "For the ride and everything." She pushed the front door closed.

"You're welcome," Elizabeth answered as she took a step backward on the porch, and the door clicked shut.

Baffled, she walked slowly to the car. She guessed that Alvin didn't want Faye around, but Trudy did. And Davie did too. Elizabeth's heart lurched. She couldn't imagine not being able to have a relationship with one of her sisters.

As she got ready to start the car, she thought through her to-do list. Getting up to Berks County and talking with Ron Sliter was definitely at the top. Perhaps she could squeeze that in today.

She took out her cell and called Martha. After several rings her sister picked up.

Her voice sounded a little down. "Hello."

"Everything all right?"

Martha hesitated just a moment and then said, "Yes. How about on your end? Is Davie doing okay?"

"Yes, he seems to be. I just dropped them off. I was thinking I'd drive up to Berks County and try to see Ron Sliter. I'd rather show up than call ahead of time. I don't want to give him a head start in concealing anything, in case he's involved in the disappearance of Plain Beauty."

"Good idea," Martha said. "We'll be fine here."

"Has it been busy?"

"Somewhat. Mary had a rush before I arrived, but since then it's just been steady."

"Good." Elizabeth put the key in the ignition.

Martha said, "Bye—"

"—wait!" Elizabeth couldn't help but interrupt. "Did you get the kits mailed?"

"I was just going to do that..." Martha's voice trailed off.

Before Elizabeth realized it, she was saying, "You'd better hurry, or they won't go out in today's mail."

Martha sounded hurt. "I'm going right now. Don't worry."

Immediately Elizabeth regretted being so bossy. "Okay," she said. "I'll see you soon."

Lancaster County was beautiful any time of year, winter, spring, summer, and fall. But Elizabeth believed September held a special beauty all its own. She passed by farm after farm of rolling hills, pastures filled with horses and cows, fields of corn, and tidy homes and outbuildings. She played the old game from childhood—guessing which farms were Amish or not. Sometimes it was obvious—the clothes on the line or a buggy parked in the driveway would give it away. Other times, the only way to tell was whether or not there were electrical wires going to the house or other buildings.

She saw one place with solar panels on the roof of the house—and a buggy parked in the driveway. That was definitely the way of the future.

If it wasn't for the sign, she'd have no idea she'd entered Berks County. The farmland was just as fertile as Lancaster's.

Triple S Stables was southeast of Reading. A quarter mile before the turn was an old stone church with a high steeple, then an old wayside inn.

Elizabeth expected that mothers on the outskirts of Reading were happy to drive their children to take riding lessons in such an idyllic setting. It really wasn't far.

She turned onto the driveway. Ahead was a large, well-cared for red barn, red stable, a farmhouse constructed of stone, and several corrals.

As the driveway curved, a sign appeared. TRIPLE S STABLES—LESSONS, SALES, TRAINING, AND MORE.

There was a small parking area filled with SUVs in front of the stables. Elizabeth pulled into the last spot. Two adults, she was guessing they were parents, sat in their vehicles, but the rest were empty. Those parents all appeared to be along the corral watching a lesson.

Elizabeth climbed out of her car and squinted toward the corral. Several children were riding in single file around the inside perimeter, all wearing helmets. Taking lessons would have been Mary's dream as a child. Thankfully, she did have several friends who had horses, and even though she was never properly trained she did have lots of opportunities to ride.

On the other hand, Elizabeth never had an interest in riding even though she'd always admired horses. They were such majestic animals—she had great respect for them.

She doubted that wherever Plain Beauty was, she was being used for riding lessons, but still Elizabeth eyed each horse.

There were two sorrel horses, a palomino, and three quarter horses. Plain Beauty was nowhere in sight.

A young woman was leading the lesson from the center of the corral, calling out encouragement and instructions to the children. She had long dark hair under a cowboy hat and wore cherry-red boots, similar to Mary's.

Elizabeth approached the fence and asked one of the women if she knew where Ron Sliter was.

"Try inside the stable, in his office," the woman said. "That's where he was earlier."

"Thank you," Elizabeth said.

"If he's not in there, his daughter can help you." She nodded toward the young woman in the corral.

"I appreciate your help." Elizabeth started toward the stable. She stopped for a moment to let her eyes adjust and then looked to the right, where several horses were in the stalls. She stepped that way and quickly scanned the right side and then the left side of stalls. None of the horses resembled Plain Beauty.

Next, she stepped to the left. All the stalls were empty. At the far end was an open door with a sign above it that read OFFICE.

As she walked, she noted how clean the stalls were. Everything had been scooped and swept, and the stable smelled like fresh hay—and nothing else.

When she reached the open door, she said, "Knock knock."

After a moment, a deep voice said, "Come on in."

She stepped inside. Behind a small desk sat a man probably in his early sixties. His hair was silver, and he wore a goatee. A cowboy hat sat on the desk along with several files.

He looked up from writing in one of the files, fixing his steely gray gaze on Elizabeth. "How may I help you?"

"I was hoping to ask you some questions about a missing horse."

He shook his head. "You have the wrong stables. We don't have a horse missing."

"It's not a horse you own. It's one you were interested in."

"Oh?"

"Plain Beauty."

"She's not missing. An Amish man bought her."

Elizabeth kept her gaze fixed on him. "He did. Alvin Raber. But just about a week ago the horse disappeared. She either ran away during a fire or else she was stolen before it."

He put his pen down and his guard with it, for just a moment. "That's horrible."

"It is," Elizabeth agreed.

"But why would I know anything about this? My understanding is that the Amish fellow lives in Lancaster County, not anywhere near here."

"That's right. He's in Lancaster, about thirty miles from here. Alvin told me that you were interested in buying Plain Beauty."

"I was. And I regret not doing so, especially after finding out she was going to be trained to pull a buggy. I'm certain she had a year or two of racing left in her. And then, when I heard that the Amish fellow planned to auction her off, I was shocked. It seems he's willing for anyone to buy her, regardless of their background or history with horses." He pushed back in his chair. "But if you're insinuating that I had something to do with her disappearance, then"—his gaze grew even more intense—"you're mistaken."

Elizabeth exhaled. She realized her fists were clenched and relaxed her hands. "I'm not accusing you of being involved, believe me. I just wanted to ask if you had any information about the horse, like if anyone has contacted you about buying her in the last week."

"Absolutely not." He stood. "I had been planning to send someone to the auction to try to buy Plain Beauty. But now I guess I don't need to bother."

"Unless she's located."

He shook his head. "If she ran during a fire, she's traumatized. If she was stolen, she's likely been traumatized too. As much as I'd like to rescue her, I can barely keep this place afloat with the healthy horses I have." He stepped around the desk. "Now if you'll excuse me…"

Elizabeth didn't move. Instead she pulled a business card from her bag. "My name is Elizabeth Classen. Would you please call me if you hear anything?" She extended the card to him.

He took it and stepped back to his desk, opened the top drawer, and tossed the card in it. "If I hear anything, I'll let you know."

"Thank you," she said and turned toward the door.

"Ms. Classen?"

She turned back.

"I'm sorry for being so gruff. Thank you for doing what you can to find Plain Beauty. I hope you find her."

Elizabeth smiled grimly at him. "So do I, Mr. Sliter. So do I."

It was just before six when Elizabeth reached home. She hoped Mary and Martha had locked up and were getting dinner ready. She was starved.

But when she stepped into the house, they weren't in the kitchen. "Martha? Mary?" she called out.

No one answered. She put her purse on the table and walked out to the shop. It was locked. The door to the shed was open, so she headed that way.

Sure enough, as she neared, she heard her sisters' voices. Mary asked, "How long will you stay?"

"Just until Monday."

Mary said, "I can give you a ride to Harrisburg tomorrow."

"I can drive and leave my car there."

"Oh, let me take you."

"We'd better check with Elizabeth," Martha said, "and make sure she isn't taking Trudy and Davie to an appointment."

"I'm not." Elizabeth stepped into the doorway. "What's going on?"

"You're back." Martha held a rake in her hand. "I was just showing Mary which items we're going to sell and telling her the prices."

"Why?"

Martha took a deep breath and then said, "I'm going to Kansas in the morning. Trish needs me to come."

"Did she get a diagnosis for Celeste?"

Martha shook her head. "But she's having more tests, and Trish is exhausted and scared. I'll stay until Monday."

Elizabeth felt torn between wanting to tell Martha to stay longer—and wondering how they'd cope with her going at all. She managed to say, "You're doing the right thing to go. I'm happy to watch the shop tomorrow. It is definitely my turn."

"That sounds good," Martha said. "I'm going to try to get as much of this done tonight as I can, here and in the shop. And then pack."

"All right," Elizabeth said. "Any thoughts as far as dinner?"

Both of her sisters had blank stares on their faces.

Elizabeth sighed. "I'll figure something out." She turned to leave but then said to Martha, "Thank you for mailing the kits."

Martha groaned. "I forgot. We got slammed with customers, and then it just slipped my mind."

Mary chimed in, "I'll mail them tomorrow, promise."

Elizabeth hid her irritation and hurried to the house to get some supper going. Before she opened the fridge to retrieve the chicken, her better nature had surfaced, and while she cooked she prayed for Martha, Trish, and Celeste. She knew it was entirely possible that Martha might be gone longer than a few days, and as she set the table she also prayed for a critically ill Amish child, a missing horse, a successful auction, and the strength to deal with all three.

CHAPTER ELEVEN

B ack in the shop, Martha took the auctioneer's card out of her purse and gave him a call.

"Don Coblentz here," the man said in a fast and cheery voice.

Martha explained who she was and that Rachel Fischer had given her his number.

"Oh, right," he said. "I remember. The auction to raise money for the Amish boy's medical costs."

"That's right," Martha said. "Rachel said you'd come out before the auction and give me advice on organizing everything."

"I'm donating my time on that one," he said. "So I can't afford to come out ahead of time. You'll need to have everything ready."

"Pardon?"

"I'll run the actual auction, but I don't have time to advertise..."

Thankfully, Mary had already done that—not to mention they had the Amish grapevine going strong.

He continued. "...or do the setup. Someone else will have to do that. I guess I didn't make that clear to Rachel."

Martha felt defeated. "Any tips on organizing everything?"

"Arrange the items from least value to most. Have everything organized, in order, on tables with a separate form for each item—list the donor, description, beginning bid, and then leave room for the top bidder's name and phone number. Recruit someone to take payments, including debit and credit cards."

Martha jotted down notes as he talked. She would ask Elizabeth to handle the money inside the shop.

"That way I can fly right through everything on the day of the auction," Don said.

After a few more minutes of explanations, Martha thanked Don for his help. After she hung up, she exhaled sharply and then gave herself a pep talk. "You can do this," she said out loud. "It will all get done, and in time for the auction."

She spent the evening sorting through the auction items, first putting the quilt from Caleb's aunt with the others in the closet, along with the quilting frame. She would talk to Rachel about beginning bids on all of the quilts, guessing they would be marketed more to Englischers than the Amish.

Martha then put sticky notes on the items for Mary to price to sell.

She was only going to Kansas for a long weekend, but in case she needed to stay longer she wanted to finish up at least sorting the auction items so Mary and Elizabeth could continue on with the work.

Mary came out at ten and told her good night. "Elizabeth saved dinner for you. It's on a plate in the fridge."

"What did she make?"

"Chicken alfredo, French bread, and green beans."

Martha loved Elizabeth's pasta, but she was afraid it would put her to sleep. She still needed to go through the items in the storage room and then pack. "I'll be in pretty soon," she said.

It was midnight before she finished sorting all of the items. She was starving and went ahead and ate the pasta, beans, and the bread. She'd been right in waiting to eat—now she was tired from the carbs, and she still needed to pack. She could get up early. She decided that was what she would do.

But as soon as she crawled into bed, she was wide awake, her mind skipping from Celeste to Davie to the auction. And then to Trish and Trudy. Finally she got up and started packing. A couple of skirts and sweaters. A pair of capris. She'd wear jeans on the plane. She pulled out a pair of pajamas from her drawer and her robe. Once she zipped her carry-on bag, she put it at the end of her bed and changed her alarm from four to four thirty. Bless Mary for being willing to leave at five thirty to get to the airport.

The last time she looked at her clock, it was one thirty. She woke with a start and felt for her phone. Four fifteen. She might as well get up. At least she'd slept for almost three hours.

Yes, she was absolutely relieved that Mary had offered to drive her. She'd sleep in the car and then on the plane so she'd have the energy she'd need to help Trish.

Martha ended up having to wake Mary up. She stood at the door and whispered, "We need to get going." She did that several times. When Mary didn't stir, she raised her voice. "Mary, get up!" When that didn't work, Martha flipped on the light. "Mary, we need to leave in five minutes."

Mary sat up straight, opened her eyes, smiled at Martha, and then her head fell back on the pillow.

"Mary, you have to wake up. You said you'd drive me to Harrisburg. I've only had three hours of sleep…"

Mary rolled over.

Martha marched into the room and sat down on the edge of the bed. "Mary, please wake up."

Her sister groaned.

The light in the hall switched on, and footsteps fell on the hardwood floor.

"Come on." Martha put her hand on Mary's arm. "We woke Elizabeth up."

Mary opened her eyes again, and when Elizabeth stepped into the room she even sat up.

"Martha," Elizabeth said, "I'll drive you to the airport."

Mary jumped out of bed. "No, I'm taking her. I said I would."

"I really don't mind," Elizabeth said.

"Well, if you're sure." Mary climbed back in bed. "Thanks."

Ten minutes later, Elizabeth was dressed and ready to go.

Somewhere, though, Elizabeth missed all the signals that Martha needed to sleep. She kept chattering away about Plain Beauty, going on and on about meeting Ron Sliter the afternoon before. "I don't think he stole the horse. In fact, he had the same reaction Caleb Yoder did. He said it was a shame that Alvin planned to auction the horse off. Have you thought about that? About why Alvin would do that? I can see everyone's concern—absolutely anyone could buy the horse without being vetted."

"Maybe he figured only someone decent would want to buy Plain Beauty." Or maybe Alvin had changed his mind about auctioning the horse off. There was that nagging thought at the back of her mind that he'd set the whole thing up. Who had he called that night?

"Google Boss Chambers," Elizabeth said.

Martha yawned. "I thought you already did."

"I wonder if I missed something."

"I'm a little tired."

"Well, it's not like we have much time to talk about this stuff."

Martha pulled out her phone. "Why do you think I'd find anything new?"

"Google 'Boss Chambers' and 'Plain Beauty.' Find out when he bought her."

Martha followed Elizabeth's instructions, doubting that sort of information would be available. She landed on a blog about racing horses. The post was entirely about Plain Beauty. The last track that she'd raced at was Belmont on Long Island. No wonder Ty Jones knew about the horse.

"This was posted on a blog last November." So ten months ago. She read it out loud.

"Boss Chambers, of Virginia, recently purchased Plain Beauty, the mare who had been, until last year, winning marvelously at Belmont. It seems too early to put her out to pasture—or use her for riding lessons. Am waiting with bated breath to find out what Boss intends to do with her. Hopefully Plain Beauty's racing days aren't over, and Boss intends to put her on the track again."

"That's interesting. I wonder why he bought her. Is there anything about racing her again?"

"I can't find anything." Martha clicked on another post. It was from three years before about a race Plain Beauty had won at a smaller track in Pennsylvania. "Oh, wow," she said.

"What?"

"Ron Sliter was Plain Beauty's original owner."

Martha tried to sleep on the plane, but instead she kept wondering over and over why Ron Sliter hadn't told Elizabeth he'd owned Plain Beauty. And why hadn't John or someone looked into her previous owners? Why hadn't she looked into the horse's previous owners? It seemed like a no-brainer now.

She had so many questions, including where the paperwork for the horse was now. Did Alvin have it? Any chance Boss Chambers hadn't forwarded it to him? And didn't plan to?

It sounded as if the horse racing world was pretty connected. How could someone steal Plain Beauty and expect to sell her to anyone who would be willing to pay what she was worth? And then keep her a secret. None of it made sense.

During her three-hour layover in Charlotte, Martha got something to eat and tried to sleep, but all of the activity around her prevented it. Instead, she texted Trish to find out who was picking her up.

CRAIG, Trish texted back. LET HIM KNOW WHEN YOU LAND. HE'LL PICK YOU UP CURBSIDE.

That meant he was getting out of work early. He sold insurance, so it wasn't as if his schedule wasn't flexible when he needed it, but she appreciated his willingness to drive to Kansas City to pick her up.

The final flight was too short to nap. Hopefully, she could get some rest while Craig drove.

She called him when the plane landed.

"Hey, Mom!" Craig answered.

Every time she heard her oldest son's deep voice she thought of Chuck—and ached for him.

Craig asked, "How are you doing?"

"Great," she answered. And she was. Being back in Kansas had made her feel more energetic—but she still wanted that nap.

"I'm a few miles away," he said. "I'll be there by the time you're out of the airport."

When she reached the curb, she only waited a few minutes until Craig arrived in his Ford SuperCrew pickup with the king cab. Craig put it in PARK, jumped down, wrapped her in a bear hug, and said, "Welcome home, Mom!" There was that deep voice again, and the older he grew the more he looked like Chuck with his lively dark eyes and square chin.

He grabbed her bag, and then, after hugging her again, opened the passenger door for her.

As she stepped up and climbed in, a shout of "Surprise!" came from the back seat. She clutched her throat and turned around. In the back seat sat her grandsons, Kevin and Dylan. Both were howling in laughter.

The two were ten and thirteen, and full of energy and fun. She definitely wouldn't be getting a nap on the way to Hillsboro.

Martha laughed and said, "What a wonderful surprise! I'm so thrilled to see the two of you." She reached over the seat and hugged them. "I'm glad I'll get to spend some extra time with you guys." She had five grandchildren, who all lived in Hillsboro. She hoped she could see all of them as much as possible in the next four days and be able to help Trish too.

She'd been feeling as if there was never enough time in Lancaster County—and she would certainly be feeling the same way in Kansas too, even more so.

The only thing to do was to try to live as much in the moment as possible. She turned toward her grandsons.

"Dad picked us up early from school." Dylan beamed. "And brought snacks." He held up a box of crackers. "For the road trip."

"Excellent." Martha beamed back at both of her grandsons. "I've been dying to know how school is going for both of you. And all about hockey and soccer and coding and your favorite cars. Tell me everything!"

After driving through miles and miles of farmland, by the time they reached the city limits of Hillsboro, Martha knew all about Kevin's and Dylan's activities, Craig's attempt to fix the water heater, which didn't go well, and the hike their mom, Molly, had forced them to go on over Labor Day.

"It was horrible, Grandma," Dylan said. "We got lost and hiked for hours."

"One hour, buddy," Craig said, glancing in the rearview mirror. "Don't exaggerate." Then he turned toward Martha. "Want the 'grand tour' of Hillsboro?"

"Of course." The "grand tour" started with Tabor College, where she and Chuck first met. A few minutes later, Craig slowed in front of the main hall, a brick building with pillars, which always seemed a little fancy for the Mennonite founders of the college. Beyond the building were the tennis courts where she and Chuck had met in PE class, and then the library where they studied together for four years.

Classes had started a couple of weeks before, and students strolled across the front lawn. Her heart swelled at the sight of a couple walking arm in arm. She and Chuck had walked across the exact same spot exactly the same way all those years ago.

"This is where Grandma and Grandpa met," Craig said. "And where your mom and I went to school too, although we didn't fall in love as quickly as your grandparents did."

"Boy oh boy, isn't that the truth?" Martha remembered well the many girls Craig dated before he and Molly finally realized they loved each other. But Molly had been in no hurry to make a choice and settle down either. By the end of their senior year, though, they were inseparable.

"Is this where I'll go to college?" Dylan pressed his nose to the window.

"Could be," Craig replied. "Although you have a few more years to decide." He accelerated, drove through the rest of the campus and then slowed again as they passed by the house Martha and Chuck had raised their children in, a two-story craftsman style with a large front porch and a maple tree in the front yard.

Martha pointed at a stroller on the front walk. "Oh, look. A family lives there now." Nothing could warm her heart more. It had been a wonderful house in which to raise their children.

A young woman with a baby in her arms stepped onto the porch and took a handful of envelopes out of the mailbox.

Then the door slammed behind her as she stepped back inside. Martha put her hand to her throat. That had been her, years ago. The young mother had no idea how quickly the years would speed by.

Next, Craig drove by the public library. She and the children had spent countless hours there through the years, at story hours, checking out books, studying after school. It had been one of their favorite hangouts. As Craig swung around toward Trish's house, they passed the park where the boys played sports.

"There's my soccer field," Dylan squealed, pointing to the other end of the park. "I have a match there tomorrow."

"Wonderful," Martha said. "I'd love to go."

A few minutes later, Craig parked his truck along the curb in front of Trish's house. Before Martha could open her door, Elliott, who was seven, came running out of the house. For a moment Martha thought he was excited to see her, but she soon realized he was shouting, "Kevin! Dylan!"

She laughed. Of course he was excited to see his cousins. Especially since he'd probably been cooped up in the house more than usual with Celeste being ill.

By the time she opened her door, Kevin and Dylan had tumbled out of the back seat and were racing toward Elliott.

Craig offered her his free hand to help her from the car. He held her bag in the other. He was always the gentleman, just like his father.

Tears stung her eyes. How different her life would be if Chuck hadn't died. She'd still be living in Kansas, in the bosom of her family. Chuck would be enjoying their children and grandchildren, so proud of the lives they were building. Had it been the right decision to move to Lancaster, when she was missing so much of the lives of her children and grandchildren?

"You okay?" Craig asked as she stepped onto the sidewalk.

"I'm fine," she answered. "Just a little emotional is all. I hope I get to spend some time with your brother while I'm here."

He wrapped his arm around her. "I think we can persuade Kyle to honor us with his presence at least once this weekend. It's good to know you miss us."

"Every day."

He squeezed her tight and walked beside her toward the house. Elliott, satisfied with greeting his cousins, ran to Martha, wrapping his arms around her legs.

"Whoa, buddy." Craig laughed. "Be gentle with Grandma. You don't want to break her."

Martha shook her head as she hugged Elliott. "I'm far from being a fragile old lady. Hug me as hard as you'd like. I'm tough as nails."

Craig laughed again, this time throwing his head back, just like his father used to. Martha couldn't help but join him—until Trish opened the front door. She wore shorts and a T-shirt. Her light brown hair was in a messy bun on top of her head. As Trish grew older, looking into her face and delicate features became more and more like looking into a mirror for Martha—a mirror that was years out of date.

Trish looked exhausted. "There you are."

Martha opened her arms, and Trish rushed into them. "How is Celeste today? How are you?"

"I'm fine," Trish answered. "Celeste fell asleep on the couch waiting for you. Come on in." She looked over Martha's shoulder at Craig. "Hey, you. Thank you so much for picking Mom up. I have spaghetti ready. There's plenty."

"Thanks, Sis," Craig said. "But Molly went home after school and actually cooked. Our first meal of the week." He rubbed his expanding middle. "Just kidding. But I did tell her we'd be home to eat." He pointed at Elliott. "How about if we take that one with us?"

"Even though Mom just got here?"

"He'll have time with her later."

Trish called out to Elliott. "Do you want to go home with Kevin and Dylan?"

"You bet!" he shouted back.

After telling Craig, Kevin, Dylan, and Elliott goodbye, and watching Craig herd the boys into the pickup, Martha followed Trish into the house.

"I promised Celeste I'd wake her up when you got here."

The house was a classic ranch style with a kitchen and dining area separated by an eating bar. The family room was on the other side. Trish worked from home, doing medical transcription work. It meant she could be home with the kids, but Martha also knew she did a lot of her work early in the morning or late at night.

It was a blessing that Trish was home as much as she was because Jared worked in Wichita in the IT department for the state bank commissioner. His commute was an hour each way.

Celeste was curled up on the couch with her legs tucked up to her chest. Her blond hair was pulled back in pigtails, and her eyelids fluttered a little as she slept.

Trish knelt beside her. "Sweetie, Grandma's here."

The little girl didn't stir. Trish put an arm on her shoulder. "Celeste."

Her eyes fluttered and then closed again. Trish put her hand on Celeste's forehead. "She's warm."

Martha leaned over and took a turn. "She's burning up." She guessed her fever was a hundred and three or four. "Call your doctor," Martha said to Trish. "But I'm guessing we should take her to the ER." The community hospital was on the edge of town, just a few miles away.

Celeste opened her eyes again and smiled at her grandmother. "Hi," she managed to say, but then her eyes drifted closed again.

Trish dialed the doctor's office. After she explained what was going on, she asked, "Should I call 911?"

Martha knew they could get her to the hospital sooner than waiting for an ambulance. The nurse must have known that too because Trish said, "Okay. We'll take her."

Martha bent down and scooped Celeste into her arms. "Grab your keys," she said to Trish. "Let's go."

CHAPTER TWELVE

Trish sat in the back seat with Celeste and called Jared as Martha drove to the hospital.

"Meet us there," Trish said to him then ended the call. "Jared left Wichita nearly an hour ago and will be here soon," she told Martha.

Martha pulled the car to the ER entrance, and Trish quickly rushed Celeste through the double doors while Martha parked the car. A couple of minutes later, when she walked through the double doors, Celeste and Trish were already in a room.

"Mrs. Watts," the nurse said. "Follow me."

As Martha hustled after her, the attendant at the front desk introduced herself. "I'm Tessa Johnson. Now Coleman. I went to school with Kyle."

"Oh, Tessa," Martha said. "How nice to see you. When did you get married?" When Martha left Hillsboro a year ago, Tessa was still a single woman.

"In June." She beamed. "I married Brad Coleman. He was a year ahead of me. We couldn't stand each other in high school." She shrugged. "But things change."

"They certainly do."

Tessa pointed toward the last room. "They're in there." She motioned for Martha to go on in. A nurse was just taking

Celeste's temperature with a forehead thermometer. She removed it and read, "It's 103.6."

"I would have tried to get her fever down at home," Trish said, "except that she's been so ill, so I thought I better bring her in right away. She's been having tests done at the children's hospital in Kansas City."

"What for?"

"The specialist believes she has an autoimmune disease," Trish answered. "We're waiting to get the results back for some blood tests and imaging."

"All right," the nurse said. "In the meantime, we'll get her fever down and get her hydrated. I'll be right back, and the doctor will be in soon."

As they waited, Trish sat beside Celeste on the bed and held her hand, but she looked at Martha, who sat in the chair. "Do you think we should have taken her to Kansas City?"

"No." Martha patted her daughter's arm. That was much too far to drive with a sick child. "Let's see what the doctor says."

The nurse came back and started an IV. "This will bring her fever down."

Celeste whimpered and raised her head as the nurse inserted the IV, but then put her head back on the pillow. The nurse took a cloth and ran it under cold water and rubbed it across Celeste's arms and neck.

Jared slipped into the room with the doctor. He said hello to Martha, gave Trish a peck on the lips, and then moved to the head of the bed and bent down and kissed Celeste's forehead.

"Daddy," she said, grasping Jared's hand.

"Daddy's here, Celeste. I'm glad Mommy and Grandma brought you up here. You're gonna be okay."

Celeste pointed to the IV in her arm.

"That's going to help you feel better in a hurry," Jared said.

Martha's eyes filled with tears. She was so thankful Celeste was well cared for by both of her parents.

Four hours later, after blood had been drawn and analyzed, it was determined that there wasn't anything more pressing than what Celeste was already being tested for. The ER doctor had consulted with the doctor in Kansas, and neither thought she was in danger. "But I'd like to keep her overnight," the doctor said. "For observation and to make sure she's hydrated."

Once the doctor left, Jared turned his attention to Celeste while Martha motioned to Trish to step out of the room with her. Once they were in the hall, Martha said, "I didn't want to talk about this in front of Celeste, but I'd love to spend the night up here with her tonight. That way you and Jared could get some rest."

"I don't want you to do that." Trish's eyes were full of concern. "You must be exhausted from your flight."

"I'm not exhausted, and I would really like to spend the time with Celeste."

"All right. I'll ask her."

"I'll go get a cup of coffee," Martha said, "so Celeste doesn't feel any pressure." Celeste hadn't seen her grandma much in the last year, and she'd understand if Celeste didn't want her to stay. But she hoped she would.

During the night, from her spot in the recliner, Martha stared at her granddaughter, who was illuminated by the nightlight over her bed.

The night nurse came in, and Martha said hello to her.

"I was hoping you'd be asleep," the nurse said.

"I've dozed some," Martha replied.

The nurse took Celeste's temperature. "Much better—it's 100.4 now."

That was better. Martha breathed a grateful prayer.

After the nurse left, Celeste stirred and opened her eyes.

"Hey, sweetie," Martha said. "Grandma's right here."

The little girl smiled and went back to sleep.

Martha continued to stare at her, as she would a newborn, and then she began to pray, asking the Lord to reveal what exactly was wrong with Celeste, what the proper treatment was, strength for all of them, healing for little Davie.

When the sun started to peek into the room, Martha headed down to the bathroom to wash her face and brush her teeth, but what she really needed was a shower. When she returned to the room, the nurse was taking Celeste's temperature again. "It's down to 99.9."

Celeste smiled at Martha and said, "I'm hungry."

"Oh good." Martha sat down beside her. "They'll bring you a tray soon."

"I want to go home."

"I know, sweetie." Martha brushed Celeste's hair away from her eyes. "We'll need to see what the doctor says."

Thankfully, the doctor made his rounds early, and when Trish came to the hospital at eight, the doctor said Celeste could go home. "Make sure she gets plenty to drink, and if her fever climbs again, give her ibuprofen. And, of course, keep your Monday appointment with the pediatrician in Kansas City."

Trish nodded. "We will."

On the way home, Craig called. Martha put it on SPEAKER.

"Hey, Mom," he said. "Jared just picked Elliott up and said you're on your way home. Want to go to Dylan's soccer game?"

"What!" Trish called out. "Are you trying to steal her away from me?" She laughed.

"That's exactly what I'm doing," Craig answered. "It's my turn." The two were only eighteen months apart. Now they argued in fun, thankfully.

"I'm fine with it." Trish gave Martha a smile.

"Sure," Martha said. "Where and when?"

"Ten."

"I'll see you there," Martha said. She could walk.

After a quick shower, Martha grabbed a mug from the cupboard.

"Do you want that to go?" Trish asked.

"Sure."

Trish took a travel mug from another cupboard. It used to be that Martha knew where everything was in Trish's kitchen, but she'd moved things around some. It was another indication that life was always changing.

"You can take my car," Trish said. "Jared and Elliott are on their way home."

"Can I take Elliott with me?"

"Sure." Trish grinned. "He'd love that." She stepped away from the sink and wrapped her arms around Martha. "Thanks for coming. I've missed you so much."

Martha swallowed hard, fighting back her tears.

Craig invited Kyle, his wife, Laura, and their little boy to the soccer game too. As Martha and Elliott walked to where the spectators were gathered, Kyle came jogging toward her with Mick, who was two, in his arms.

As she hugged her youngest child, holding his child, she choked back tears again. She loved her sisters dearly, and all of their friends in Lancaster and her childhood home, but the people she loved most in all the world lived in Hillsboro, Kansas.

Kevin and Elliott played with Mick, and Kyle, Laura, Craig, and Molly all chatted on the sidelines with Martha while Dylan and his team warmed up.

Her sons and daughters-in-law asked her about Secondhand Blessings and her sisters. Martha updated them on all the latest news and then described the upcoming auction. "It's to raise money for a little boy named Davie," she said. "He's just been diagnosed with leukemia."

"Oh goodness." Molly ran her hand through her hair. "Don't the Amish have insurance?"

"Most don't," Martha said. "They do have a mutual fund, where everyone pitches in to cover medical expenses. But sometimes the fund is low or the expenses are too much, and then everyone pitches in to raise the money."

"Fascinating," Craig said. "Any new mysteries you, Aunt Elizabeth, and Aunt Mary are attempting to solve?" He elbowed her.

Martha chuckled. All three of her kids found it remarkable that she and her sisters had become amateur sleuths, that mysteries practically kept falling into their laps. "Actually, there is. A missing—most likely stolen—racehorse."

All of them listened with interest as she explained what she knew about Plain Beauty. "We have some leads but no clear suspect," she concluded. "And the auction is just a week from today."

"Goodness." Molly stood by Craig but didn't seem to find the idea of another mystery as amusing. "That sounds horrible. That poor horse."

Martha agreed. "Hopefully whoever has her is taking good care of her."

Molly was a gentle soul with a heart of compassion. The perfect balance for Craig. It wasn't that he couldn't be compassionate—but he definitely saw the amusing side of life first.

Once the game started, they all focused on Dylan. First he played offense, but after a couple of goals and three assists the coach moved him back to defense, where he stopped several goals.

"He's good," Martha said.

"Isn't he?" Craig beamed.

"He's definitely improving," Molly said. Martha appreciated her modesty. "And he's learning to pass to his teammates. So we're happy with that."

Craig chuckled again.

"It's a good thing Dylan has such a conscientious mother to balance you out." Martha elbowed her son. He'd never been known for his intuition or foresight.

"I know, I know," he said. "That used to be your job—Molly learned it well."

Martha put her arm around her daughter-in-law and gave her a hug. And then hugged Craig too. The upside of his personality was that he knew and loved everyone in town, was a big support to the community through both the Chamber of Commerce and the boosters at the high school and the college, and ran a fair and profitable business.

Martha searched for Kyle as she let go of Craig. He'd found a quiet spot and was showing Mick how to kick a soccer ball. All three of her children were so different. Craig was outgoing and gregarious. Trish was conscientious and kind. Kyle was thoughtful and quiet. She was truly blessed by all of her children and grandchildren.

After Dylan's team won the soccer match seven to two, Molly said, "How about if everyone comes to our house for dinner? Craig can barbecue."

Craig's face lit up in a faux shocked expression, but then he nodded his head in agreement.

"I don't know if Trish will want to bring Celeste," Molly said. "But maybe she and Jared could take turns, and each one could drop by long enough to eat."

"That's a wonderful idea," Martha said. "What can I bring?"

Without missing a beat, Craig said, "Your baked beans."

"No," Molly chimed in as she shook her head at Craig. She turned toward Martha. "I have your recipe—I'll make them. I don't want you to do a thing."

Martha spent the afternoon doing laundry, cleaning the kitchen, changing the sheets in Celeste's bedroom, and making casseroles to put in the freezer for Trish. In the evening she drove Trish's car over to Craig and Molly's with Elliott, while Trish and Jared both stayed home with Celeste. They said that was what they needed. Some peace and quiet.

Sunday morning she took Elliott to the Mennonite church she and Chuck had raised their children in. She couldn't help but yawn a few times during the service. She'd gotten a better sleep than she had in the last few nights, but sleeping in the guest room she heard Trish get up several times with Celeste. After the second time, Martha got up too and told Trish to go back to bed.

As the pastor started a closing prayer, Martha bowed her head and prayed for her granddaughter again and then the rest of her family too. She finished by praying for her sisters, who seemed far away in Lancaster County.

After the service ended, she chatted with friends, women she'd relied on as she raised her kids, women whose husbands had been Chuck's best friends. Again, she ached for him.

And she realized how much she missed her old friends too. Yes, she had friends in Lancaster, even some she'd known her entire life, but she had so many shared experiences with the women from her church. They'd taken care of her babies in the nursery, traded childcare, prayed each other through the teenage years, and celebrated marriages and grand-babies together.

As Jan Gingrich approached her, Martha broke out in a grin and opened her arms for a hug. The woman had always been shy, but she was also warm and caring. They'd first met as freshmen at the college. Janet was from Hillsboro and stayed in town to teach the third grade after graduation. She hadn't married until she was in her thirties and never had children.

"How are you?" Martha asked. "Ready to retire?"

"I did, in the spring," Jan answered. "I took the summer off, and now I'm looking for somewhere to volunteer."

They caught up on each other's lives, then Jan asked about Martha's children. She gave her a quick rundown and told her about Celeste.

As they chatted, Martha walked with Jan into the church fellowship hall. Thankfully, there was a potluck that day, which gave Martha more time with friends. She felt such joy fellow-shipping with everyone and only wished that Trish, Jared, and Celeste had been able to come too.

Several people in the congregation approached Martha to ask about Celeste and said they were praying for her. Martha was overwhelmed with gratitude.

As she drove Elliott home he asked, "Grandma, why did you move to Pennsylvania?"

"Well…" Martha tried to choose her words carefully. "My sisters live there, and it seemed like a good idea to go back to where I grew up and live with them for a while."

"I wish you'd move back here. I miss you when you're not here."

"I miss you too," Martha replied. "But thankfully, we can talk all the time."

He sighed and then said dramatically, "It's not the same."

"I know, sweetie." Martha stayed silent the rest of the way to Trish's because she was afraid if she spoke, she'd cry.

Both Craig and Kyle stopped by later in the day to tell her goodbye. Again, she choked back her tears.

That night, she slept fitfully again, although she didn't hear Trish up with Celeste. The next morning, Martha rose early.

Celeste had her appointment in Kansas City, so Trish would drop Martha off at the airport on the way. There was a tearful goodbye from a still pajama-clad Elliott, then Martha told Jared goodbye after he'd carried Celeste out to the car.

"Thank you so much for coming," he said. "I won't say it, because you've heard it too much already...but I hope you know how much we all miss you."

Martha knew she couldn't ask for a better son-in-law. He loved Trish and was a good father to his kids. He leaned in the back seat and kissed Celeste and then kissed Trish. "Call me as soon as you can."

"I will," Trish answered as she hugged him.

Martha settled into the front seat. She wouldn't know how the appointment went until she landed in Harrisburg. Thankfully, she'd gotten a direct flight home.

As Trish backed out of the driveway she said, "Did you see everything you wanted to see while you were—" She paused. "Back?" It was obvious she almost said *home*.

"Actually," Martha answered, "there's one more place I'd like to go, on the way out of town."

"Where's that?"

"The cemetery."

Five minutes later, Martha stood in front of Chuck's tombstone. CHARLES WALLACE WATTS. There was a cross and then BLESSED ARE THE PURE IN HEART, FOR THEY SHALL SEE GOD inscribed in the stone.

She ached as she read the words over again. Only God knew the number of their days, and He'd known all along that Chuck's were fewer than hers. She was grateful for the time she had with him, but she missed him. She ached for him. She longed for him.

She turned back toward the car. Trish stood with the passenger door open, a look of concern in her eyes. Martha tried to smile at her, but she couldn't.

Coming back to Kansas had been what she needed to do, no question about it. But she did have a question racing around in her heart. Should she have ever left?

CHAPTER THIRTEEN

Mary parked in the cell phone waiting area and sipped the iced mocha she'd picked up at the coffee place a couple of miles from the Harrisburg airport. She'd bought one for Martha too—she figured her sister could use the caffeine and sugar after her long weekend.

The weekend back at Secondhand Blessings without Martha had been pretty long too. What with running the shop and getting ready for the auction, Mary had hardly had a moment to sit down—until she crawled into her car to come pick Martha up.

Elizabeth had volunteered to do it, but Mary had insisted. Elizabeth had been doing so much driving for Trudy and Davie that Mary was happy to drive to Harrisburg.

Martha's flight was late—twenty minutes or so. Hopefully it would arrive soon. Elizabeth needed to pick up Trudy and Davie, which meant Mary needed to get back to watch the shop.

Her phone dinged with a text from Martha. MEET ME AT ARRIVALS. Mary put her drink in the cup holder, slipped the car into DRIVE, and headed for the passenger pickup at the terminal. She spotted Martha right away. She wore a pair of black capris and a cobalt blue top. She held her cell phone up to her ear with one hand and the extended handle of her carry-on bag with the other.

Mary pulled up to the curb, hit the Down button on the passenger window, and called out, "Here I am!"

Martha fluttered her fingers and then said into her phone, "Trish, Mary is here. I'll call you once I'm back in Lancaster."

Mary popped the trunk. Martha plopped her bag into it and then climbed into the passenger seat. "Thanks for picking me up," she said.

"No problem," Mary said. "It gives me a chance to finally sit down."

"Oh dear."

Mary laughed. "It hasn't been that bad. Just busy." She nodded toward the far mocha. "That one's for you."

"Aww, thank you," Martha answered. "Don't mind if I do..." She picked it up and took a sip.

"How's Celeste?" Mary asked.

"They saw the pediatric immunologist today, the one in Kansas City, and just got the diagnosis." Martha's voice choked a little as she said, "They had to diagnose it by a process of elimination, but they've determined that it's juvenile arthritis."

That didn't sound too bad to Mary. It could have been worse—it wasn't like she had cancer or anything. "Is it a bad case?"

"I'm not sure what a bad case is." Martha took another sip of her mocha. "She ended up in the ER on Friday night with a high fever."

Alarmed, Mary asked, "Why didn't you let us know?"

Martha wrinkled her nose. "I would have if she hadn't been released the next morning."

"She spent the night?"

Martha nodded. "I stayed with her so Trish could get some sleep. Celeste has been in so much pain that Trish hasn't been sleeping much."

"Wow, here I was complaining about our busy weekend." Mary was aware, once again, that she'd rushed ahead about her own life instead of asking about Martha's first. "Sounds like your weekend was worse than ours."

"Oh, it wasn't bad. In fact it was wonderful. I was so happy to get to spend that time at the hospital with Celeste. And I had lots of time with Elliott and the other grandkids too. And with Trish and Jared. And Craig and Molly. And Kyle and Laura." She sighed. "It was a great weekend, except for Celeste being ill. I'm so glad I was able to go." Martha took another sip of the mocha. "Thank you for making it possible for me to spend that time with my family."

Family. The tone in Martha's voice alarmed Mary. Out of the three sisters, Mary believed Martha had given up the most to live in Bird-in-Hand.

Martha had loved her life in Hillsboro. She had so many good memories there of her marriage to Chuck, of her friendships, of her children. She had five grandchildren she adored.

Honestly, Mary had been shocked when Martha said she was going to move back to Bird-in-Hand. The decision to leave Indiana had been easy for Mary. Brian had left her for another woman. Her kids were grown and doing well.

She didn't have too much to tether her to her old life.

But that wasn't the case for Martha, not at all.

"We were so busy all summer that I didn't realize how much I missed the kids and grandkids," Martha said. "But that was crystal clear this weekend."

Mary stared straight ahead as she turned onto the interstate. Martha had every reason to return to Kansas to live—but Mary couldn't bear to think of her sister doing so. As much as Martha's perfectionism grated on Mary, life in Lancaster County wouldn't be nearly as fulfilling without her.

When they arrived back at the house, Mary told Martha to get settled while she relieved Elizabeth in the shop. "She's going to pick up Trudy and Davie for a late appointment."

"All right." Martha opened the passenger door. "But I'll be right out to get to work on the auction."

"About that…" Mary wasn't sure what to say.

"Yes?"

"Well, I did work on it some but didn't get as much done as I hoped to." Mary climbed out of the car and slammed the door. "I'll explain things to you when you come out." Honestly, she didn't get that much done at all. Martha's directions had been confusing, and she was afraid anything she did do wouldn't be up to Martha's standards. At least she could relieve Elizabeth now, so she could go help Trudy and Davie.

But when Mary arrived in the shop, Elizabeth didn't seem to be in a hurry to leave. She waited on a customer chatting away about the production at the Sight & Sound Theatre in Lancaster. "What a joy," the woman said. "I came all the way from Illinois, and it was well worth it. Not to mention seeing all of the Amish farms and businesses. We have Amish settlements back home, mind you, but they're not like here…"

"Do you need to go?" Mary mouthed.

Elizabeth shook her head. The woman didn't notice as she continued on. Elizabeth placed her purchase—a tile trivet with a rooster on it—in a bag.

Mary decided to pretend like she was a customer and picked up a pillowcase set from a shelf and approached the counter.

The woman laughed. "I've really been taking up your time. Sorry."

"No problem," Elizabeth said.

"It's just that all of this is so exciting, and I'm traveling alone."

Mary felt a pang of regret for trying to hurry the woman along.

"I'm going to go look around Bird-in-Hand more," the woman said.

"Make sure and stop by the bakery," Mary said to her. "They have the best sticky buns."

"Thank you." The woman grinned. "I will."

Mary wondered if she was a recent widow. Or perhaps her husband had left her. Who could know the stories other people carried?

When the woman left, Mary placed the pillowcases on the counter.

"Smooth move," Elizabeth said.

"I thought so." Mary laughed. "So why aren't you in a hurry to get out of here? I thought I was late."

"I told you a half hour early because I *knew* you'd be late." Elizabeth wrinkled her nose. "But as it turns out, I'm not going. Trudy called and said they didn't need a ride, that someone she knew was headed that way."

"Oh? Do they have many Englisch friends?"

Elizabeth shrugged as an expression of sadness passed over her face. But then she smiled. "I needed more time here anyway. It's not a big deal."

"But you enjoy spending time with them, don't you?"

"I do..." Her expression turned sad again. "I prayed for Trudy when she was a teenager. I was so glad when she married and then had Davie. I prayed for her when her husband died." She sighed. "I want the best for her and Davie, I really do. But I can't deny that I enjoy taking them to appointments and spending time with them."

"Well, they're only getting a ride today, right?" Mary asked. "You'll be their driver again in no time."

Elizabeth shrugged. "We'll see."

Mary took a step toward the storage room. "Martha will be out in a few minutes, but before she gets here, tell me. Do you think we can pull off this auction? We only have five days, no horse, no saddle. And what seems like a million random items. It's so much harder than I thought it would be..."

Elizabeth laughed.

"It makes me think of when I worked at the art gallery in Indianapolis," Mary said. "We'd have these fund-raisers to try to make payroll. We'd sell tickets to cocktail hours with artists. Beg artists to paint giveaway copies of their work. Auction off birthday parties in the gallery."

"So what happened?"

Mary shrugged. "We didn't make payroll two months in a row, and I lost my job."

"That's it? How does it relate to our auction?"

Mary laughed. "The uncertainty is my point."

"You lost your job—things didn't work out."

"Actually they did." Mary ran her hand through her hair. "I got the job as a barista after that, and the gallery ended up signing a super prolific painter who turned out to sell a ton of paintings. Several times they hired me to run their coffee bar for special events."

Elizabeth threw her hands up. "Well, we only have one chance with this auction. We have to get it right the first time. And we're running out of time to find the horse and saddle, not to mention"—she pointed toward the storeroom—"get all of this stuff organized."

Mary smiled and said, "We will." She knew how much she, her stories, and her lack of organization exasperated her sisters. But they could stand to relax a little.

As she turned to go to the storage room to do what she'd told Martha she'd do over the weekend, the phone rang.

Elizabeth picked it up. "Secondhand Blessings. How may I help you?"

After a short pause, Elizabeth said, "Rachel, slow down. I didn't catch all of that."

The next thing Elizabeth said was, "I'll be right over."

CHAPTER FOURTEEN

Ten minutes later, Elizabeth turned down the Fischers' lane. As she drove, she breathed a prayer of thanks that Trudy and Davie had gotten a ride to the doctor's appointment with someone else. The Lord knew she'd need to give Rachel and Alvin a ride to the hospital, where Davie had just been admitted.

As Elizabeth approached the house, Rachel came out the back door, her bonnet on over her white kapp, her cape over her shoulders, her purse in one hand, and a cloth bag in the other. She walked straight to the car, but then Phoebe yelled, "Maam!" from the front porch.

"Hannah," Rachel called out, "help your sister."

A moment later, Hannah appeared on the back porch, drying her hands on her apron.

"Phoebe is out front." Rachel opened the car door. "See what she needs."

Hannah headed down the steps, waving as she did. "I will see to Phoebe. Tell Trudy we are praying for Davie."

Rachel waved back and settled into the front seat with a sigh. "Goodness," she said. "I feel pulled in ten different directions today."

"I can only imagine." Elizabeth backed the car around.

"I am just so glad Silas was near the phone shed and answered the phone when Trudy called."

Elizabeth turned onto the lane. "Did you reach Alvin?"

Rachel shook her head. "I left a message, but I doubt he will get it before we arrive."

"What exactly did Trudy say?" Elizabeth asked.

"Just that Davie's numbers were low, and he needed to be hospitalized. She'd left a message for her daed too and then called me. She asked that both of us come to the hospital. Poor thing."

Elizabeth nodded. Trudy was strong, but this was all so much for her to handle. Of course she needed her father and her aunt to help her through a time like this.

Five minutes later, Elizabeth came to a stop in Alvin's driveway, adjacent to Bill, who stood next to a sheet of plywood on two sawhorses.

Rachel lowered her window. "Is Alvin around?"

Bill nodded toward the stable. Between the framework, Elizabeth could see Alvin working with another man. Rachel waved to him and told Elizabeth to honk.

That got his attention, and he started toward them. Rachel told him Davie was in the hospital.

"I will go wash my hands and change." Alvin looked down at his sawdust-covered beard and blue shirt.

As Elizabeth backed the car up and parked it in her usual spot, Alvin ran into the house. Rachel climbed out of the car and followed him inside to get a change of clothes for Trudy and other items she'd need to spend the night.

Bill hurried over to see what was wrong. Once Elizabeth explained through the open window, he said he'd be praying.

Then he leaned down a little more and said, "Any chance Mary is coming by to ride one of the horses?"

"Not today," Elizabeth answered. "We're trying to get ready for the auction."

Bill took his hat off and ran his hand through his hair. "Anything I can do to help?"

"Actually," Elizabeth said, "there is. Not today, but Friday the tents and tables will be delivered. We'll need help putting out the auction items. On Saturday too."

"I'll come by as soon as work is over," Bill said. "I'll see you then. Tell Mary hello and that the horses over here need attention." He winked.

Elizabeth smiled at him. He was such a good man, and she truly hoped Mary would see that, in time. When she was ready. "I'll do that," she said.

In no time, Alvin hurried out of the house, wearing a white shirt and a clean pair of pants. The sawdust was also gone from his beard. He climbed into the back seat on the passenger side. "Danki, Elizabeth, for giving us a ride. You have been a good neighbor to us."

Then he stared out the window, not saying another word. A couple of minutes later, Rachel appeared with the cloth bag hung over her arm. Once she'd buckled her seat belt, Elizabeth backed the car up and turned down the driveway to the lane and then onto the highway.

Alvin's presence made Elizabeth self-conscious. She wanted to ask him about Plain Beauty and what he thought of Boss Chambers and Ron Sliter, but she knew now wasn't the time. Besides, how could she ask him questions without giving away that she and Martha were still unclear as far as what his role could have been in Plain Beauty's disappearance?

Rachel commented a couple of times on crops in the fields along the way or a cow or a horse. Elizabeth guessed all of them were on the lookout for Plain Beauty. No doubt the thief wouldn't be foolish enough to pasture her in plain sight, but just in case, Elizabeth looked for the horse everywhere she drove too. Of course, if Alvin had anything to do with the horse's disappearance, it wouldn't be in the area. For that matter, if either Boss Chambers or Ron Sliter was involved, the horse wouldn't be in Pennsylvania or West Virginia either. Plain Beauty would be far, far away. She sighed. What were the chances they'd figure out who took the horse in the next five days?

She slowed as they entered Lancaster, first past the large Federal-style homes and then the row houses. By the time they reached downtown, the late afternoon traffic was thick, and it took quite a while to get to the hospital. "Did Trudy say if they were in the emergency department? Or on the floor?" Elizabeth asked once they were a block away

"On the floor," Rachel said. "Pediatrics is what she said."

"I'll drop the two of you off at the front door and then park," Elizabeth said. "I can wait in the lobby."

"Oh, no." Rachel patted Elizabeth's arm. "You are family. Come on up to the room."

When Elizabeth found Davie's room, the door was closed. She decided to wait outside, not wanting to interrupt if the doctor

was consulting with the family. She sat in a chair in the hall and checked her phone.

She had a text from Martha asking how Davie was. She texted back that she didn't have any new information but that she'd let Martha know as soon as she did.

Elizabeth watched the staff at the nurses' station scurrying around, and a housekeeper pushing a cart down the hall.

Finally, Davie's door opened, and Rachel came out. "There you are." She had her bonnet in her hand, along with her cape. Her white kapp on her head certainly stood out.

"How's Davie?" Elizabeth asked.

"He is getting a transfusion, and they need to monitor him." She sat down in the chair next to Elizabeth. "It is actually a good thing you didn't come in. They're only allowing immediate family and, of course, no children. They're worried he could get sick."

"Of course." Elizabeth didn't need to see Davie.

"Alvin is holding Davie right now, giving Trudy a break. I'm not sure how long he'll want to stay."

"I'm in no hurry," Elizabeth said.

Rachel smiled. "I know you are pulled in as many directions as I am. You have been such a help to Trudy. I am shocked you could drop her off here and then come get us. When I called the shop, I expected for Mary or Martha to answer, not you."

"Oh, I didn't take Trudy and Davie to the appointment today. She called and said she was getting a ride with someone else."

"Really?" Rachel spread her cape over her legs, which was a good idea. It was chilly in the hospital from the air conditioning, and Elizabeth wished she'd brought a sweater.

After a long pause, Rachel asked, "Do you know who she got the ride from?"

"No," Elizabeth answered. "She didn't say, and I didn't ask."

When Rachel didn't respond, Elizabeth began talking about the auction. There was no reason to waste the time they had together. "Tell me about the food vendors."

"We have a crew of men barbecuing bratwursts and chicken, along with corn on the cob. A crew of women will make mashed potatoes and slaw. We will have one booth for slices of pie and another for donuts covered with vanilla crème."

"Yum." Elizabeth's mouth was watering.

Rachel smiled and continued. "One for Martha's baked goods. Mary should make a sign, promoting what she sells through your shop. And one for lemonade and coffee and bottled water. All of the food will be donated. The bishop and his wife are going to purchase paper plates, plastic forks, and cups tomorrow. Oh, and because the auctioneer is donating his services too, we will pass out his cards—I am sure he will get enough future business to make it all worth it."

"Wow," Elizabeth said. "It seems you've thought of everything."

"I hope so. I have ten barbecues that will arrive Saturday morning. A couple of troughs—" She smiled. "Clean ones, for water bottles. I have asked everyone to bring lawn chairs, and even though we will have tents, we have asked for extra canopies for shade for our older and younger folks."

"Perfect," Elizabeth said. "We've ordered portable toilets. They'll be delivered Saturday morning and picked up on Monday."

Rachel laughed. "Sorry you will have to have them around that long."

"No worries," Elizabeth answered. They'd thought about having them picked up on Sunday but were afraid that might offend their Amish neighbors, who didn't do any work on the Sabbath and didn't believe in making others work either. None of them ate at restaurants or shopped on Sundays.

Rachel sat a little straighter in her chair. "Hannah will help me organize the food vendors on Saturday morning and then make sure everyone has what they need during the auction. We have also sent out notices to every district in the county and in Chester and Berks County too."

"Wow." Elizabeth fought back the anxiety that threatened her. "I hope we have enough parking at the shop."

"I thought of that," Rachel said. "We will open up our pasture adjacent to your property. And I have recruited five young men, organized by Adam, to manage all of that."

Rachel's oldest son was the perfect choice to be in charge of the parking crew. "Danki." Elizabeth laughed at her own use of the Pennsylvania Dutch word. "I didn't do that on purpose."

"It is music to my ears." Rachel smiled. "Do not worry about how many people attend the auction—these things always turn out. God leads exactly the right people and just the right amount. We just need to do our tasks and see how He works out the details."

Elizabeth nodded, grateful for the reminder that the Lord was in charge. Out of the corner of her eye she noticed a woman wearing jeans and a T-shirt stepping out of the elevator. A woman who looked familiar.

"I think I know who might have given Trudy and Davie a ride to the doctor," Elizabeth said in a quiet voice, "and then to the hospital."

"Who?" Rachel asked.

"Faye."

"Faye!" As Rachel turned toward the elevator, the young woman froze. And then, like a flash, darted toward the stairwell door. In a split second, she was gone.

CHAPTER FIFTEEN

Tuesday morning Martha rose before dawn, showered and dressed, and started a pot of coffee. She'd finally gotten a good night's sleep, but it hadn't calmed her. She felt as unsettled as ever.

She sat down at the table and opened her Bible. Butterscotch rubbed against her leg, and Martha reached down and petted him. "Hungry?"

The cat raised his head.

Martha sighed and went to get food to feed the cat and the dogs too. Then she returned to the table.

Thankfully, Elizabeth wasn't up yet. She needed some time to regroup.

As the coffee began to drip, Martha opened her Bible to Second Timothy, chapter one. She'd finished First Timothy on Monday before leaving Kansas. She read the first several verses and then reread verse seven. *"For God hath not given us the spirit of fear; but of power, and of love, and of a sound mind."*

She didn't feel of sound mind. She felt divided between Kansas and Bird-in-Hand. And, yes, she had a spirit of fear. For Celeste's health. For Trish's strength. For the upcoming auction. For Davie and Trudy.

But God had given her a spirit of power and love. And sound mind. She bowed her head and prayed that He would reduce her fear and increase her love and power. And show her His plan for her—should she stay in Bird-in-Hand or return to Kansas?

"I need a sound mind," she whispered. "I can't help anyone if I'm wallowing in fear."

The coffee had stopped dripping, and she stood to pour herself a cup and get started on her to-do list. As she settled back down at the table, she wrote *baking* on the top of her list. And then *call Boss Chambers*. She needed to pick up where she'd left off last Friday as far as finding Plain Beauty. And then *call Pauline* and *forms for auction items*. As she took a sip of coffee, her phoned dinged with a text from Trish. It was 5:45. Why was she up so early?

Anxiety filled Martha as she read her daughter's words. I FIGURED YOU WERE UP. GUESS WHO CALLED ME YESTERDAY?

WHO? Martha texted back.

JAN GINGRICH.

Martha smiled. WHAT ABOUT?

SHE WANTED TO KNOW HOW CELESTE WAS DOING, AND IF SHE COULD BRING DINNER TONIGHT.

THAT'S GREAT. Martha felt so grateful to her friend. HOW IS CELESTE?

SHE SLEPT BETTER—ONLY UP TWICE. HOPEFULLY NEW MEDS ARE HELPING. WILL CALL LATER WITH DETAILS.

Martha sent a smiley face, slipped her phone back into her pocket, and reached for her cookbook just as Elizabeth came into the kitchen. Martha had been in bed before her older sister returned the night before, and she didn't expect her up so early.

"How is Davie doing?" Martha asked.

"Not well," Elizabeth answered. "At least he wasn't last night. Trudy says he needs the bone marrow transplant as soon as possible."

"Is she a match?" Martha cradled her mug of coffee in her hands.

Elizabeth shook her head. "So far they haven't found one."

"What about Amanda?"

"She's not."

"Rachel? Any of her cousins?"

"Not that I know of," Elizabeth answered. "At least not by late last night when I gave Alvin and Rachel rides home. Hopefully they'll identify a stranger soon." She sighed. "I wish I could be a match, but I know I'm too old. I'd do anything I could to help Trudy and Davie."

Martha put her arm around Elizabeth. "I know you would. You've been such a good friend to them. They really appreciate it."

"There's one more person who I hope has gotten tested."

"Oh?"

"Trudy's oldest sister, Faye."

Martha let go of Elizabeth and took a step backward. She'd been under the impression that Faye had only been with Trudy that one day, when Elizabeth had met her. "She's still around?"

"Apparently," Elizabeth said. "Alvin seems upset with her, but I believe Trudy wants her to be close. In fact, it seems Faye gave Trudy and Davie a ride to the doctor and then the hospital yesterday. But I don't think Alvin knows that."

"What about Rachel?"

"She knows." Elizabeth poured herself a cup of coffee. "It makes me so sad. Trudy's had so many losses. I can see why she'd want her sister around."

"I can too." Martha met Elizabeth's gaze. "I know I'm thankful for mine."

"Ditto," Elizabeth said.

No matter how much Martha missed Kansas, her kids, and grandkids, she was thankful for her sisters. She couldn't imagine her life without them.

She took a deep breath. God had given her a spirit of love and power and sound mind. She prayed she'd truly be able to live by that.

While the blueberry muffins baked, Martha sat down at the computer and looked up the phone number for Boss Chambers's stable. She jotted it down on her to-do list and then began mixing up dough for the lemon scones. At eight on the dot, she called the number for Boss Chambers, but the call went straight to voice mail. Martha gave her name and cell number and then said she was looking for information on Plain Beauty. "Please give me a call as soon as you can," she said. "The funding for a little boy's healthcare is on the line."

She continued baking until Mary came into the kitchen a half hour later, yawning and stretching her arms. "Good morning," she said. "I overslept. I'm just going to get a cup of coffee to take in the shower with me." She laughed.

Martha could never understand how Mary could be so *not* a morning person but happy as soon as she rose, nevertheless.

After she took the scones from the oven, Martha packaged up the baked goods, placed them in her basket, and headed out to the shop. It had rained on the farm the afternoon before, but not for long. Thankfully, it had already dried.

When she reached the shop, she saw that Elizabeth was already there, straightening things up before she gave Rachel and Alvin a ride back to the hospital.

Martha had an hour until Secondhand Blessings opened— she'd do what she could to finish organizing the auction items.

Just after ten, Elizabeth left on her errand. By then Mary was in the shop, and Martha kept working on the auction items, placing price stickers on the "for sale" items, making notes about the silent auction items and about the beginning bids on the regular auction items, all information she would transfer to the forms she still needed to create.

By early afternoon Elizabeth had returned, and the three sisters gathered around the counter in the shop during a momentary lull in business.

"How is Davie?" Martha asked.

"The same," Elizabeth answered.

"And Trudy?"

"Exhausted." Elizabeth sighed. "I took her home to rest, and Rachel is going to spend the night with Davie."

"What about Alvin?"

"He didn't go up today. He stayed to work on the stable. He hopes to have it done in the next few days."

"Any word about a bone marrow donor?" Martha asked.

Elizabeth shook her head. "But Trudy told me on the way home that Faye has been tested."

"That's good, right?"

"I hope so. Although, I wonder what Alvin's response will be if she's a match."

Martha's jaw dropped. Finally she managed to say, "Surely he'd be fine with it, right?"

"I hope so."

Two college age women came into the shop and began looking at the vintage clothes. A few minutes later, John Marks walked through the open front door.

"Hello," he said to Martha and then to Elizabeth, followed by a smile. He took out his notebook. "I wanted to check in about Plain Beauty."

Martha's heart raced. "Have you found her?"

He shook his head. "I did talk with the manager of the Belmont track about Ty Jones. He gave me a cell number for him, but it's no longer in use. He said Jones was headed to the Albuquerque Downs Racetrack in New Mexico, but when I called out there, the manager said Jones had had problems with his truck on the way down and was delayed. Last he heard, Jones was in Denver."

Martha groaned. "Plain Beauty could be anywhere."

"It's a pretty tight industry. I'm hoping someone will talk soon," John said.

"I left a message for Boss Chambers, the man who sold Plain Beauty to Alvin," Martha said.

"Good," John said.

"And I found out that Ron Sliter, who has a horse farm near Reading, was Plain Beauty's original owner," Elizabeth said. "He didn't mention that when I visited him, which I find odd."

"How about Alvin's phone call?" Martha asked. "Right before the stable burned down."

"I asked him about that." John held his pen in midair. "He said he'd called Caleb, asking him to stop by one more time before he left for Kentucky."

"Why?"

John hesitated before answering. "I told him I wouldn't share that information—it has nothing to do with the case."

"Could you confirm that Alvin was telling the truth?" Martha asked, cringing that she was practically accusing an Amish man of lying.

"I confirmed it with Caleb," John said. "There's no discrepancy between the two accounts."

"Oh." That hadn't been exactly what Martha was expecting. And it didn't mean for sure that Alvin wasn't involved in the disappearance of Plain Beauty. Although it seemed less likely that he was.

"How about the fire chief's report?" Martha asked. "What caused the fire?"

"A knocked-over lantern," John said. "In the stall next to Plain Beauty's. There were four stalls down at the end that were unoccupied, thankfully. Or Alvin would have most likely lost some horses."

"Have you determined whether Plain Beauty was stolen or not?"

"Stolen or released out that far door. Otherwise she would have burned."

"I doubt Alvin left the lantern burning," Martha said. "It certainly wasn't burning when I was in the stable that evening."

John nodded. "That's what both Alvin and Rachel said too."

He consulted his notes again and then said, "Thank you for the updates. I want you to know we haven't forgotten this case."

Martha smiled at him. It was obvious he hadn't.

"I know the auction is coming up," John added, "and the horse is an integral part of it."

"At this point," Elizabeth said, "we're just praying she's okay. It would be great to have her as the big item at the auction…but her safety is our biggest concern."

"I understand," John said. "I hope to be at the auction and contribute to Davie's medical bills."

"Thank you," Elizabeth said. "We'll look forward to seeing you then."

After John left, Martha stepped into the storage room and called Boss Chambers again. This time someone answered— but it wasn't Boss Chambers. "This is his assistant." The voice was masculine and a little harsh.

"May I speak with Mr. Chambers?"

"No," the man said. "He's not available."

"Could I leave a message?"

"If you'd like."

Martha again said she was looking for information on Plain Beauty and rattled off her phone number.

The man grunted.

"Did you write that down?"

"Yeah," the man said.

"And my phone number?"

"Give it to me again," the man said.

After she did, she thanked him and hung up, feeling unsettled. She'd be surprised if the man gave Chambers her message at all. Hopefully he would listen to the voice mail she left earlier.

Martha returned to the counter where Elizabeth and Mary were still chatting. "Do either of you mind if I go track down Boss Chambers?" she asked.

Elizabeth's eyebrows shot up. "Doesn't he live in West Virginia?"

Martha nodded. "It's two hours away. I can go there and be back by dinnertime."

"Want me to go with you?" Mary asked.

"No, that's okay. Would you work on the auction items while Elizabeth minds the shop?" Martha updated Mary on what she'd done. "I'll work on it more tonight."

A few minutes later, Martha was on the road. Soon her thoughts had turned away from Boss Chambers and to Celeste.

Trish hadn't called her back yet. Martha wasn't sure if that was a good thing or not. She hoped it was. She decided to believe it was, instead of choosing fear. At least until she could send a text. Or call.

Martha headed west on Highway 30, rehearsing what she would ask Boss Chambers when she arrived. The weather was muggy, and clouds built on the horizon. She hoped they wouldn't get rain, or if they did that the ground around Secondhand Blessings would quickly dry out. It would be difficult to set the auction up in mud. Sure, the Amish held mud sales in the fall and spring, sales that were inevitably held in muddy fields. But she didn't want that for the auction.

She passed through Gettysburg and realized it had been years since she'd visited the battlefield. That would be a good day trip when her family visited from Kansas. Both the adults and children would enjoy it, at least she hoped so. The kids might be a little young yet. Maybe in a few years.

As she left Gettysburg, the sky opened up in a torrent of rain, but it didn't last long. When it stopped, she lowered her window and breathed in the fresh scent of the rain, mixed with the fields of alfalfa and corn. The rain hadn't soaked the ground. Hopefully, if it rained back home it wasn't much either.

She continued on, crossing the border into Maryland and then soon after into West Virginia. Boss Chambers's horse farm and stable were near the town of Hedgesville. She followed the directions on her phone's GPS and soon found the farm amid rolling green hills and woods. She turned down the driveway, slowing as she neared a barn. There were corrals but no horses in them. There were no children either. Unlike Ron Sliter, it seemed Boss Chambers didn't offer riding lessons. On the hill ahead was a house made of bricks with a stately front porch.

Martha wasn't sure whether to drive up to the house or get out at the barn and was still trying to decide when a young man sauntered out of the barn. She waved and lowered the window.

"Excuse me," she called out. "I'm looking for Boss Chambers."

"Is he expecting you?" It wasn't the same man as on the phone—at least this man's voice was much softer and kinder.

"Maybe," she answered. "I left a voice mail and then left a message with an assistant, who didn't give me his name. He sounded a little—" She hesitated.

The young man laughed. "That would be R.J. He's a trainer here and likes to answer the phone when Granddad isn't around."

"Granddad?"

The young man extended his hand. "I'm Lucas Chambers."

Martha introduced herself as she shook his hand.

He took his phone out of his back pocket. "Granddad is up at the house. I'll give him a call." A second later, he held the phone up. "That's funny. It went straight to voice mail. I'll go up and ask him."

"Before you go..." Martha fished the photo of Plain Beauty from her purse. "Any chance you recognize this horse?"

"Sure. That's Plain Beauty."

Martha's heart raced. "When was the last time you saw her?"

"When Granddad sold her to that Amish guy. He came down and got her." The young man pivoted toward the house. "Stay here. I'll go get Granddad."

Martha was tempted to go inside the barn but figured she shouldn't. Instead she walked over to the field and leaned against the white fence. She couldn't see a horse in sight. Perhaps they were in the barn.

She checked the time on her phone. Finally, after she'd been waiting for about fifteen minutes, the young man drove toward her in a pickup with an older man wearing a cowboy hat in the passenger seat. The older man lowered his window. His face was leathery and solemn, and his eyes were a watery but piercing green.

Martha approached the truck and introduced herself.

"I figured," the man said.

She tried to smile, but the scowl on his face stopped her.

In a low voice, he barked, "What do you want?"

Martha took a step backward. He didn't seem to be a nice man, not at all.

As he leaned his arm against the open window frame, Martha noticed that it shook a little. Perhaps he was ill. She took a deep breath and said, "I'm looking for information about Plain Beauty. She disappeared—"

"I know all about that," he said. "I've had at least five messages about that horse—four from that Amish man—"

Martha spoke up. "Alvin Raber."

He glared. "And one from a policeman."

"John Marks?"

"Could be." Boss shook his head, as if in disgust. "I have to say you're the first person to actually find your way down here."

"Do you have any information on the horse's disappearance?"

"Of course I don't," he said. "Although I don't know what to do with her paperwork. Send it on to the Amish man, I guess. I can't believe he lost Plain Beauty. She's a fine specimen of a horse. I never should have sold her to him."

"I'm hoping you don't mind me asking where you were on the night of September sixth."

"Of course I mind." He scowled again. "You're accusing me of horse thievery."

"He can't drive anymore," Lucas said. "He doesn't get around much. He can barely ride down here."

"All right," Martha said, looking behind her to the field. "Where are your other horses?"

He gestured widely. "Do you see any horses?"

"No." Martha's face grew warm. "I don't. That's why I asked."

"I'm selling them all," he said. "I only have one left in the barn."

Martha stepped closer to the truck. "May I ask why?"

"No." Boss stared her down with another glare. "But believe me, it would be ludicrous for me to steal Plain Beauty. What would I do with her? I couldn't resell her. Or race her. And I certainly can't ride her." He turned toward his grandson. "Boy, take me back up to the house."

Lucas leaned toward Martha and mouthed, "Sorry."

Martha nodded. She appreciated his help.

As Lucas turned the pickup around, Martha kept watching Boss. He kept his arm on the window frame and stared straight ahead.

Once the pickup headed back to the house and she could only see the back of his hat, she realized she had one more question. Why did he still have an assistant when he was selling all of his horses?

CHAPTER SIXTEEN

Mary rose at six thirty on Wednesday morning. She was determined to get over to Alvin's and ride before another busy day began. The horses needed exercise, and she loved to care for them.

She headed to the bathroom for a quick shower. She always used to grow restless in September. When her kids were home, the month meant summer was over, school had started, and she had to figure out what to do with her time. Sometimes she had a job—that she would quit. Other times, she'd taken the summer off to spend it with the kids and would be looking for a new job.

She'd never been the kind of person who stuck with one job for long.

But here she was in Lancaster County, working with her sisters, running Secondhand Blessings. How long would she find it fulfilling?

Of course both Martha and Elizabeth were already up and drinking coffee when Mary staggered into the kitchen. Martha was talking about her trip to Boss Chambers's horse farm the day before. She'd already given them every detail the night before, but now she and Elizabeth were deconstructing the visit again, picking apart everything Boss said, trying to figure out if there was anything he might have meant between the lines.

"I'd love to know about R.J.," Elizabeth said. "Is there a photo of him on the website? Maybe we can get a last name and get more information on him."

"Great idea!" Martha said. "I'll do that right now."

Mary grabbed a mug and began pouring herself a cup of coffee. "I'm going over to Alvin's to give the horses some exercise this morning."

"When?" Elizabeth sounded as if she had a frog in her throat.

Mary held up her full cup. "As soon as I finish this."

"For how long?"

"A couple of hours. I'll be back before we open."

"I haven't heard from Rachel, so I don't know if she needs a ride…" Elizabeth's voice trailed off.

"I'll have my phone. Call if you need me back sooner."

Elizabeth turned toward Martha at the desk. "Did you have plans for this morning?"

"Pauline's coming over. We're going to work on the auction…"

"I won't be gone long." Mary reached into the cabinet for a travel mug. "In fact, I'll take my coffee with me and drink it on the way, to save time."

She finished the coffee as she sat in Alvin's driveway, not sure what to do. No one was working on the stable yet. What if they'd decided to take the day off?

As she tried to decide what to do, Alvin came out the front door, snapping his suspenders. He squinted in the morning light, and Mary waved.

She climbed out of her car. "I came to ride. Is that all right?"

"Ja..."

She zipped her sweatshirt against the chill of the morning and retrieved her hat from the back seat.

"I already fed the horses," Alvin said. "But I have not brushed any of them down. Come into the barn with me. You can ride Midnight again."

"Oh, how about another one?" Mary suggested. "He did his best to knock me on my backside—and succeeded."

Alvin laughed. "That's right. Well, he is my gentlest horse."

"Really?"

He nodded.

"All right. I guess I'll give it another go."

Alvin worked quickly, brushing two horses in the time it took Mary to brush one.

Just as she finished Midnight, Bill's voice boomed through the barn. "Anyone home?"

"Back here," Alvin called back.

Mary led Midnight out of the stall just as Bill started toward her.

"There you are," he said. "I saw your car and thought maybe you were already out riding."

Mary smiled. "Headed that way. What are you up to today?"

"Working on the stable. I drove over to the other side of the county to give a bid on a kitchen remodel—that's why I'm late." He smiled back. "If I had known you were going to be here, I would have waited until tomorrow to give the bid though."

"Business first," Mary said. "That's always been my motto."

He laughed. They both knew that was far from the truth. As she gazed into Bill's eyes, for the moment she hoped she'd stick with the family business and stay in Pennsylvania.

Midnight didn't buck Mary off, although he did try to scrape her off along the pasture fence. She managed to redirect him and mostly enjoyed the rest of her ride. At nine thirty she headed back to the barn.

Alvin, who had been helping Bill on the stable, followed Mary. She had Midnight back in his stall by the time Alvin caught up with her.

"How was the ride?" he asked.

"Better."

"You handled him well when he brushed against the fence. I appreciate you coming over to ride—I know you are busy too."

"I'm happy to help," Mary responded, surprised at Alvin's expression of gratitude.

"I wanted to let you know that I had a phone call about Ty Jones, the young man interested in the saddle."

Mary nodded. "I remember."

"It was from a trainer at Belmont. He heard about Plain Beauty going missing and that Ty had been around, wanting to buy the saddle." Alvin held up his hand and took the glove off. "He gave me Ty's cell phone number." The numbers were written on Alvin's palm.

"Great," Mary said. She pulled her phone from her back pocket. "I'll just take a photo of the number." She started to click and then froze. "Is it all right if I take a photo of your hand?"

Alvin threw his head back and laughed. "Ja, that is fine. Just do not get my face."

"I won't." Mary snapped the photo. Although she did get a wisp of his long white beard. "I'll give Ty a call and see what he knows," she said. "Do you mind if I make the call here?"

He shook his head. "Do you mind going to your car? I ask Bill to go to his truck when he needs to make calls."

That was fair. She agreed and strode out of the barn toward her car. As she walked, she was surprised to see someone riding a horse down the lane toward the farm. The horse appeared familiar, perhaps one of Alvin's. The rider was an Englisch woman, maybe in her late twenties. She wore a cowboy hat, with her hair in braids, and she rode with confidence and control. Mary had never seen her before, but obviously other Englischers were helping Alvin out too.

Mary climbed into her car, looked at the photo again, memorized the number, and then called it immediately, before she forgot it.

A man answered.

Mary froze. What was she supposed to say? Did you take Plain Beauty's training saddle? Did you take the horse too? Why hadn't she planned out what to ask before she called?

"Hello?" he said again. His voice sounded worried.

"This is Mary Baxter," she said. "From Secondhand Blessings in Bird-in-Hand, Pennsylvania. I think you stopped by a couple of weeks ago."

"I remember," he said. "I bought a horseshoe there."

"That's right."

"Hey," he said. "I heard about Plain Beauty, the Amish guy's horse. Has she been found?"

"Not yet," Mary said. "In fact she's the reason I called. I was wondering if you might have any idea where she could be."

He hesitated and then finally answered. "Of course not. A buddy of mine told me she was gone."

"Have you heard anything about her during your travels? Any chance anyone said anything?"

"Like who?"

"Well, you're traveling with a horse, right? Don't you stop at stables along the way? Places where people would be talking about a missing horse?"

He laughed. "Not those kinds of places. I'm stopping at mom-and-pop joints along the way. Not any sort of place Plain Beauty would be."

Mary was growing in confidence. "Could you tell me why you were pulling a horse trailer when you stopped and saw Caleb Yoder but not when you stopped by Secondhand Blessings?"

"As a matter of fact, I can. The trailer was in a shop getting a flat tire fixed."

"Where was your horse?"

"In a pasture behind the tire shop."

That didn't sound very likely. "What's the name of the shop? Where is it located?"

He laughed. "You're ruthless, aren't you?"

When Mary didn't reply, he said, "I can't remember the name. But it's on the main highway, not far from your place. It has a pasture behind it where I left my horse while the tire on my trailer was repaired. There's a diner up the road a short ways from it. That's where I found out about the auction."

The shop sounded unlikely to Mary—she had no memory of it. But she'd drive by, just to be sure.

"Why didn't you answer your phone when the police officer from here called?"

Ty chuckled. "I broke my phone in Nebraska and had to get a new one."

"Fair enough," Mary said. "And why are you taking so long to get to New Mexico?"

"I'm here now," Ty said. "It took so long because my truck broke down in Colorado. But I think you all already know that. My boss here said someone called…"

Mary's face grew warm. "You should probably expect another call from the officer investigating the abduction of Plain Beauty."

"I will," he said. "And I'll gladly speak with him. Tell him to call any time."

"Thank you," Mary said, ready to end the call. "You've been helpful."

"I haven't given you any new information," he said.

"Have a good day," she answered.

"You too."

As she started to hang up she could hear him mutter, "That was weird."

Based on her intuition, she really didn't think Ty had anything to do with the disappearance of Plain Beauty or the saddle. Then again, her intuition wasn't always right. It certainly hadn't been with the demise of her marriage. It had taken her far too long to figure out Brian was cheating on her.

She climbed back out of the car and headed over to the stable to give Alvin an update. After she did, the young woman on the horse rode by again.

Mary nodded toward the woman and then said to Alvin, "I see you've recruited more Englisch help."

"You could say that," he said.

"Who is she?"

"Faye," Alvin answered. "My oldest daughter."

Mary almost called Elizabeth from Alvin's driveway to tell her Faye was on the farm, but she decided that would be rude. What if Alvin could read her lips? She'd assumed the pickup that wasn't Bill's was another carpenter's, but maybe it belonged to Faye.

On the way back to Secondhand Blessings, Mary slowed as she approached the tire shop. She'd been sure Ty was lying, but there it was. She'd driven by the shop a thousand times, although she couldn't remember the name and had never noticed a pasture and certainly no horses behind it.

The shop was called Top Tire and was one of those non-franchise tire businesses.

She pulled into the parking lot and didn't see a pasture behind the shop until she drove to the far side. Sure enough, there was a pasture with a gate from the parking lot. There were currently four horses in it.

Mary pulled in front of the shop. There was a horse trailer inside one of the bays, getting a new tire on the back. It was likely Ty had gotten a flat tire, put on a spare, and then had the original tire repaired and reinstalled.

The diner was just down the street, maybe a quarter mile.

It seemed Ty Jones wasn't lying after all.

CHAPTER SEVENTEEN

With five minutes left before opening, Elizabeth left a message for Rachel to ask how Davie was doing. "Call me back when you get a chance," she said.

Just before it was time to turn the sign to OPEN, Elizabeth's phone rang. Expecting Rachel, she answered quickly with a cheery, "Hello!"

"Hello." It was a man's voice.

Elizabeth looked at her screen. RON SLITER. Putting the phone back up to her ear, she said, "Oh, hello, Ron. How can I help you?"

"I need some more information," he said. "About the auction. I didn't ask why the Amish man—"

"Alvin Raber."

"That's right. Why was Alvin planning on auctioning Plain Beauty off?"

"His grandson is ill," Elizabeth answered. "Davie is his name. He's four, and has leukemia."

"I'm so sorry to hear that. And they don't have insurance, right?"

"That's correct." Elizabeth turned the sign and opened the front door. Thankfully, no vehicles were in the parking lot. "They have their church mutual fund, but Davie needs a bone marrow transplant, and the church doesn't have enough money to cover that and his treatment. Plus, he's in the hospital right now."

"I see."

After a long pause, Elizabeth asked, "Is there anything else I can help you with?"

"Would you let me know if the horse shows up? If Alvin ends up auctioning her off?"

"Of course," Elizabeth said.

"You can text me at this number. I know you're busy getting ready for the auction."

"I'll do that," Elizabeth said.

"And thank you for doing this—the auction, helping to make sure the boy gets the medical care he needs."

"My family has known this little boy's family for years and years," Elizabeth said. "It's our privilege to help." Then, instead of saying goodbye she asked, "Do you mind if I ask you a question?"

"Not at all."

"Why didn't you tell me you were Plain Beauty's original owner?"

She could hear him sigh.

"I'm sorry," she said. "I don't mean to pry."

"No," he said. "It's fine. I was the horse's first owner. She was born on my farm. I knew right away she was a beauty, and there was nothing plain about her—thus the name. I thought I had a winner for sure, and so did a lot of other people. But then my youngest daughter, who was in her teens, was in a horrible accident. She got bucked by a horse she was training and broke her neck. I ended up selling Plain Beauty to pay for her care."

"Oh, I'm so sorry," Elizabeth said. "How is your daughter now?"

"She passed away. She survived the injury but then got pneumonia…"

"Oh, I'm really sorry." Elizabeth's heart ached for the man.

"That was four years ago, but you know…" His voice trailed off.

Elizabeth whispered, "You never get over that sort of thing."

"That's right," Ron said. "Thank you for your kind words."

After Elizabeth told Ron goodbye, she slipped her phone into her apron pocket, touched that Ron seemed so concerned about Davie. But he'd lost a child—of course he would be. He seemed understanding now about why Alvin would auction off the horse. Knowing more of a story certainly could change a point of view.

She supposed she should have told him about Alvin's situation when she first met him, but it hadn't entered her head that he would be so opposed to Plain Beauty being auctioned off. She was definitely a well-loved horse.

Mary arrived at ten thirty, popped her head into the shop to say she was back, and then headed to the house to change her clothes. When she returned, she told Elizabeth she'd spoken with Ty Jones.

"He sounded really nice," she said. "I doubt he took Plain Beauty or the saddle."

Elizabeth nodded toward the door. "Why don't you go out and help Martha and Pauline? They're going through items in the shed and then the container. I'll holler if I need help in here."

Right before lunch, Martha and Pauline came into the shop chattering away as if they'd known each other all their lives. Pauline's white apron was dusty, there was a smudge of dirt across her cheek, and she held a rag in her hand. Martha wore her work jeans and had the sleeves of her blouse rolled up to her elbows. As she brushed her hands together she said, "We've been cleaning some of the auction items. I didn't realize how dirty some of them were."

Pauline stepped into the gift shop area and twirled the carousel of postcards. "Do you sell many of these?" she asked.

Elizabeth stepped to her side. "Quite a few. We also sell lots of pot holders. And the soap sells well too."

Pauline turned toward the handmade goods. "Where do you get these?"

"Rachel Fischer makes the pot holders—her girls help her," Elizabeth explained. "The soap comes from an Amish woman on the other side of the county, a friend of Rachel's."

Pauline kept looking at the items.

"Do you want to go get something to eat?" Martha asked. "Pauline is going to dust the items in the storage room, but I can watch the shop."

"All right," Elizabeth said. "I won't be long."

When she entered the kitchen, she made herself a turkey sandwich and sat down at the desk to eat it. She logged on to the computer and began googling horse trainers in Pennsylvania. She copied and pasted the names and phone numbers into a document as she took bites of her sandwich.

Her plan was to start calling the trainers and see if any of them knew anything about Plain Beauty. She moved on to West Virginia trainers next, and then Maryland and Virginia.

Once she had the list complete, she printed it out and took her plate to the sink. She'd add other eastern states if none of the trainers on the list panned out. Before she left the kitchen, she pulled her cell phone from her pocket and called Rachel's number again. Of course no one answered. "Hi, Rachel. It's me, Elizabeth," she said. "I was just wondering how Davie is doing. Call when you get a chance. Oh, and let me know if the quilting circle tomorrow will work for you. If it doesn't, we'll totally understand."

She didn't want to bother the Fischers unnecessarily, but she couldn't help wondering how Davie was doing. She longed for an update. If she didn't hear anything by late afternoon, she'd call Trudy at the hospital.

After she returned to the shop, Martha and Pauline went to the house to get some lunch. Elizabeth started calling trainers. Of course, she mostly just reached voice mails. She did reach the third trainer on the list.

"I have no idea what you're talking about," he said gruffly. "Please don't call here again."

Elizabeth sighed as she hung up. Mary came in the shop just before two, saying, "I'm starving."

"Go get some lunch," Elizabeth said.

As soon as Mary left, Elizabeth's phone rang. She didn't recognize the phone number and expected it to be one of the horse trainers. It wasn't. It was Trudy.

"Davie is getting discharged this afternoon. Could you come get us?"

"Of course," Elizabeth answered. "How soon should I be there?"

"As soon as you can. Our ride fell through."

Elizabeth said she'd be on her way as soon as possible and then called Mary, asking if she could return to the shop.

"I'm just making a sandwich," she said. "I'll be right there."

An hour later, Elizabeth stepped into Davie's hospital room. He was on the bed, dressed and ready to go. Trudy cuddled next to him. It took Elizabeth a moment to realize they were both asleep. She stepped closer to the bed but neither stirred.

"I'm here," Elizabeth said. When Trudy still didn't budge, Elizabeth touched her arm.

Her eyes fluttered. "Oh, hallo."

Elizabeth stepped to the chair and picked up Trudy's bag. "Is there anything you need to do to discharge Davie?"

Trudy shook her head as she reached for the call button. "Just buzz the nurse."

After she pressed it, she rubbed Davie's arm and said, "It's time to go home."

"Grossdaddi?"

"Ja, we'll see Grossdaddi."

Davie smiled.

A couple of minutes later, a nurse appeared with a wheelchair. "Where's your sister?" she asked Trudy.

"At the meeting."

"Great!" The nurse lifted Davie from the bed and placed him in the wheelchair. "That sounds really promising."

Trudy climbed off the bed. "I hope so."

Elizabeth wondered what they were talking about but didn't ask—at least not until they reached the car.

As Elizabeth backed out of the parking place, she asked, "What meeting was the nurse talking about?"

"An informational meeting to become a donor."

Elizabeth smiled. "Your sister is a match?"

"Maybe." Trudy yawned. "They want her to get all of the information about the procedure and the recovery before she gets tested further. And the side effects. If she agrees, she'll sign a consent form."

"Wonderful." Elizabeth glanced in the rearview mirror as she drove out of the parking lot.

Trudy shrugged. "We'll see, if she actually agrees to do it."

"Why wouldn't she?"

"It's complicated."

Elizabeth assumed the problem was between Alvin and Faye, but Trudy hadn't said that. She'd mind her own business.

When they reached the Raber farm, Alvin and Bill were working on the roof of the stable.

"I wish he wouldn't do that." Trudy pointed to her father.

"I help," Davie chirped in English even though he usually spoke Pennsylvania Dutch.

Trudy glanced toward her son and smiled. "Ach, not for a few years."

That was a wonderful thought to think of a healthy Davie helping Alvin in a few years.

Elizabeth parked the car, turned off the engine, and grabbed Trudy's bag. Davie reached for her from his car seat.

"Oh, that's so sweet," she said.

"Do you mind getting him?" Trudy asked. "I need to go talk to Daed for a minute."

"Sure." Elizabeth hurried around to the other side of the car, the bag slung over her shoulder. She unbuckled Davie and then awkwardly slipped the straps from his shoulders. He squirmed.

She placed her hands under his arms and pulled him out, grateful she didn't bump his head on the frame of the door. She stood by the car with him in her arms, enjoying the moment until Alvin waved at Davie and Davie started talking in Pennsylvania Dutch. Elizabeth recognized grossdaddi several times.

Trudy reached her father, and they spoke for a couple of moments then started toward the house. Elizabeth headed up the front steps and sat down with Davie on the porch.

As Trudy and Alvin grew closer, Elizabeth could make out Trudy saying, "What if she is a match but she does not want to do it?"

"She will do it," Alvin said. "I will talk with the bishop and have him speak with her."

Trudy shook her head. "That will only make it worse."

"Why would she not do it?"

"She feels isolated and as if you do not love her."

"Love? I am her father. Of course I love her. She is the one who left—but I know Faye. She will not hold anything I have done over Davie's needs."

"Well, maybe you could let her know you love her. That you still care for her even though she left."

"Why could you not be the match? Or Amanda? It does not make sense."

"That is how genetics work. It is up to Gott." Trudy turned toward the porch, and Elizabeth ducked her head.

Alvin brightened as he saw his grandson and took the steps two at a time. "Davie!"

The little boy squirmed off Elizabeth's lap. "Grossdaddi!"

Alvin scooped him up and held him tight then turned to Elizabeth. "We have not seen your police officer friend for a few days. Has he given you an update?"

Elizabeth shook her head. "I know he's been working on it. I imagine you'll hear from him soon."

After she told Trudy, Davie, and Alvin goodbye, she climbed back in her car. It wasn't like John not to give updates. She sent him a text, just to check in, and then backed out of the driveway.

When Elizabeth arrived home, she checked her phone. There was no return text from John.

Mary was still watching the shop, but spread across the counter was a piece of poster board and a collection of markers. She, with her artistic talents, really was the best one to make the signs.

Several customers were milling around but none were ready to check out.

"Where's Martha?" Elizabeth asked as she grabbed her apron.

"She went to see if she can track down some footage."

"What?"

"Video footage. From businesses along the highway from September sixth. She's hoping to see a horse trailer."

"Great idea," Elizabeth said. "Maybe Ty Jones isn't as innocent as he sounds."

Mary gave her a sassy smile. "Or Caleb Yoder. Or Ron Sliter."

Elizabeth laughed. "I deserved that. Let's hope something cracks this case soon. We have two days to get Plain Beauty back."

CHAPTER EIGHTEEN

Martha parked on the highway side of Alvin's woods and then crossed the road. There was a gas station and convenience store, a tire shop—the one where Mary said Ty Jones had the flat tire on his trailer repaired, and then about a quarter mile down the road a café, where Ty had breakfast that morning and heard about the auction at Secondhand Blessings from the waitress. Had he been honest about the waitress telling him about the auction? Or had he heard about it from another source? She'd stop by the café too.

But she'd start at the convenience store. Several people were gassing up their cars, and there was a line inside at the register with people buying snacks and drinks. Martha glanced around, hoping to find someone who might be a manager, but the only staff person on the premises was behind the counter. She stepped into line.

After several minutes she reached the counter. The man behind it appeared haggard and overwhelmed. "Is the manager here?" she asked.

"I'm the manager," he answered. "My clerk called in sick today."

"Oh, that's too bad." Martha smiled kindly. "I'm hoping you can help me."

"Are you buying?"

She quickly grabbed a bag of chips. "I'll take these. And your help, if possible. Do you have a security camera out front?"

He rang up the chips. "Yep."

She handed him a five-dollar bill. "I was wondering if I could look at the footage from Friday, September sixth."

He laughed.

Martha kept her voice calm. "Is that a yes?"

"Depends on whether I still got it or not." He handed her change. "I have a clerk coming in soon. Come back in a half hour, and I'll see what I can find."

"Thank you." She tucked the chips into her bag and stepped out of the store.

Next was the tire store. There were several men working, rolling tires here and there and raising cars on hydraulic lifts.

She headed inside. There was a woman at the counter and a couple of customers waiting in chairs.

"How may I help you?" the woman asked.

"I'm looking for security footage from Friday, September sixth."

The woman looked behind her at a man sitting in a glass-enclosed office. Then she turned back toward Martha. "I have no idea if we'd have that or not. Hold on."

She picked up the phone on the counter and pushed a button. "I have a lady wanting to know about security camera footage. Could I send her your way?"

Martha watched the man in the office. He nodded as he spoke.

"Go on back," the woman said.

Martha thanked her and headed to the glass office. The man stood and opened the door for her. As she entered, he positioned himself with his back to the window.

"We don't have any security footage," he said. "But I don't want anyone to know that. Right now we just have cameras that aren't hooked up to anything."

"All right," Martha said. "How about the pasture behind the shop? Do you let people who are hauling a horse trailer and need a tire changed put their horses back there?"

"Yep," he said. "It doesn't happen very often, but it does happen."

"Do you remember a young man with tattoos on his arms with a horse trailer? Maybe with New York plates."

"Yeah, a two-horse trailer. With a flat tire on the back right side. The horse was a paint, brown and white."

"Thank you," Martha said. "That's very helpful."

"May I ask what this is about?"

"Alvin Raber has a horse missing. I'm helping the family figure out what happened to it."

"Oh, Plain Beauty."

Surprised, Martha asked, "You've heard of her?"

"A police officer stopped by last week to see if I'd seen or heard anything about the horse. That's a pity. I sold Alvin a set of tires for his trailer a few months ago. Great guy."

Martha nodded in agreement. "He is."

"I heard there's an auction coming up to raise money for his grandson, for medical bills."

"That's right," Martha said. "At Secondhand Blessings, the shop my sisters and I run. It's this Saturday, starting at noon." Saying the day and time made her anxiety rise.

"I'll be there." The man put his index finger to his lips. "Now mum's the word about our laxity in the security department."

"Of course," she said.

When she reached the café, she wondered how she'd possibly find the right waitress. But there were only two on duty in a nearly empty dining hall. After describing Ty Jones, the younger waitress said, "I remember him."

"Can you recall if he knew about the horse Plain Beauty being in Lancaster County?"

Her face reddened a little. "I don't think he did. He seemed surprised to find out that she'd ended up in Bird-in-Hand. Alvin had told me earlier that morning that he planned to auction the horse—he comes in fairly often for a cup of coffee and to talk with other farmers in the area."

"What was Ty's reaction when you told him about the auction?"

"Well, at first he was confused. He couldn't understand why someone would auction off a horse like that. I guess she was really something."

Martha nodded. "Did you know her saddle was for sale too?"

"Yes. Alvin told me he planned to auction it off too." She rubbed the back of her neck. "I told Ty there wasn't a date for the auction yet, but he said he was going over to Secondhand Blessings anyway. I think he hoped you'd sell him the saddle or give him Alvin's address at least. Did you?"

"No," Martha responded. But Alvin might have. It was hard to know. "Thank you for your help." She pulled out her business card and handed it to the girl. "If you think of anything else, will you let me know?"

"Of course."

Martha walked back down the highway, past the tire shop. The leaves on the trees at the far end of the pasture behind the shop were turning orange and gold. As Martha walked along at a brisk pace, she called Trish.

"Hey, Mom. Can I call you back in a few?"

"Of course. Just tell me how Celeste is."

"Not so good... We're trying to get her meds figured out. I'll call soon. Love you."

Martha's heart raced as she slipped her phone back into her bag. She was certain she needed to move back to Kansas. It was ridiculous for her to be so far away from her children and grandchildren.

She kept walking along and soon reached the convenience store. When she stepped inside, the line wasn't as long—and there was a woman at the counter.

The manager had a clipboard in his hands and was counting boxes of crackers.

Martha approached him. "I came back."

He gave her a blank stare.

"To see about the security footage from September sixth."

"Oh, that's right." He wrote down a number on the top piece of paper on the clipboard. "The footage is back in the office."

She followed him to the office, to a desktop computer in the corner of the room. The desk was cluttered with papers and coffee cups.

"The system can save footage up to sixty days, but sometimes, if nothing has happened, the owner deletes it sooner." He opened up the computer. "Let's see what we have."

He clicked on an application Martha didn't recognize and then on the September date.

"What time of day?" he asked.

"Between six and seven thirty that evening." She didn't want to underestimate when the trailer might have passed by the convenience store.

"Okay." He moved the mouse around. "It will show the video between those two times. You can speed the video up, freeze a frame, and zoom in." He showed her how to do each. "You have to pay attention if you want to catch anything. Watching this can be pretty mesmerizing, like being trapped in a snowstorm."

"You're all right with me staying back here and going through it by myself?"

"Is there a reason I shouldn't be?"

Martha laughed. "No. And I appreciate your trust."

The manager left the room, and Martha began going through the footage. It *was* mesmerizing—but mostly boring. The black-and-white film showed cars pulling into the gas station and people approaching the convenience store.

She had to concentrate on watching the traffic on the highway. She froze the frame of a pickup truck. Then zoomed in to read the license plate. She could tell it was a Pennsylvania plate but that was all.

She kept going through the footage, reaching the six thirty marker. Soon after, at 6:37, a pickup pulling a horse trailer entered the screen. She froze the footage but couldn't make out the license plate.

She kept going through the footage. A different pickup and horse trailer appeared. The time was 6:45. She froze the frame and zoomed in. It was a white license plate with blue trim. She couldn't read the state but it was possible that it was a West Virginia design.

She took a photo of the screen with her phone and then looked through the rest of the footage. At 7:23 the same pickup and trailer appeared again, but this time they were traveling much faster than they had been before and going the opposite direction.

Martha texted John and asked if she could meet him at the East Lampeter Township Police Station.

Next, she asked the manager the best way for a police officer to look at the footage.

"From East Lampeter?"

"That's right," she said.

"I'll email it to them—we do it fairly frequently. Did you write down the time they need to look at?"

"Yes." She glanced down at her phone. "6:37 and 7:23."

"Sounds like a stakeout."

Martha just smiled.

"With a horse trailer as the getaway..." His head shot up. "Wait a minute, is this about that missing horse?"

"Yes, it is." Martha didn't see any reason her mission should be a secret. She'd already asked about the horse at the café and tire store.

"Nice guy. He gasses up his truck here. You know, someone else drives it, but he always pays." The manager pointed to one of the empty cups on the desk. "Gets a coffee. That sort of thing. I don't know much about horses, but he always has beauties in his trailer."

"Yes," Martha said. "He's a respected trainer."

"Wow." The manager drummed his fingers on the desk. "You know a police officer stopped by here a while ago, asking to see footage for some particular night. I can't remember when—but the owner said he'd already erased it."

"That's odd."

The manager shrugged. "It was probably for a different night anyway."

Martha extended her hand. "I appreciate your help."

"You're welcome. I really hope you can find that horse."

Fifteen minutes later, Martha arrived at the police station. John met her in the lobby. After greeting her, he asked where the video was from.

"The convenience store across the street from Alvin's woods."

John shook his head. "I asked about that, but the owner told me he'd already erased it."

Martha grimaced. "The manager said the owner had said that about some date, but he wasn't sure it was the same one I was looking for."

"I wonder if someone paid him off." He shook his head. "But if that's the case, you'd think he would've deleted the footage."

"Hopefully he was just confused." Martha took out her phone. "The manager sent you the footage, but I also took pictures with my phone."

John took a look. "It's pretty blurry."

"Yes," Martha said, "but I'm pretty sure that's a West Virginia license plate."

He chuckled. "I'm not so sure, but I take it you're thinking Boss Chambers."

"Perhaps. Ty Jones has a two-horse trailer. At least that's what the guy at the tire shop said. This is definitely bigger."

"Elizabeth said you went down to the Chambers place. Did you see any trailers?"

She shook her head.

"How about trucks?"

"One—it wasn't this big. But he has a huge place, although he said he's selling off his horses. Anyway, I'm sure he has more trucks around."

"I'll see if I can enlarge it and get a license plate number." He nodded down the hall. "You can look too."

John led the way into an office with several rolling chairs. He pulled two up to a desk with a computer. It took him a few minutes to locate the email and open the document and the footage.

Martha told him the first time frame, and he scrolled ahead to that.

Once he had the image, he froze it and then enlarged it, zooming in on the license plate. But it was still too blurry to make out the state or any of the numbers or letters.

"Let's try the other frame."

"7:23."

He did the same thing to the next image, but it wasn't clear enough to see the license plate either.

"But don't you think the design looks like West Virginia?" Martha asked.

"It could be, but there are so many other states that have a relatively plain design like that—it's hard to tell." John crossed his arms. "I can't tell the make and model of the pickup and trailer, but I'll look into that further."

He paused for a moment. "But let's say Boss Chambers did take Plain Beauty. What would he do with her?"

"Well, I thought maybe just keep her." Martha rolled back in her chair a little. "Like he regretted selling Plain Beauty and wanted her back. But when I visited, he said he was getting rid of all of his horses. And he seems to be in poor health."

"So if he didn't plan to keep her, what would he do?"

"Sell her again," Martha said.

John stood. "But to whom? Wouldn't anyone in the business be leery of buying her?"

Martha's voice sounded high, even to herself. "There might be some unsuspecting buyer."

"That's true," John said. "But we don't know it's Boss Chambers. We have no evidence that it is."

Martha agreed. It could still be Alvin, for that matter.

When Martha returned to the house, Mary and Elizabeth had already closed up the shop and were in the kitchen fixing a Caesar salad with chicken for dinner. Martha filled them in on what she'd seen on the security footage. "It appeared to be a West Virginia plate, but John said not to jump to conclusions."

"How about the make and model of the pickup and trailer?" Elizabeth asked.

"John is going to look into that." Martha washed her hands as she spoke.

Elizabeth's phone rang, and she stepped toward the table to answer it. Martha couldn't help but overhear her side of the conversation. "Thank you for calling me back." There was a pause, and then Elizabeth said, "That's a good tip. We'll look into that."

As she hung up, Martha asked, "Who was that?"

"A trainer in Delaware that I called. No one has contacted her about Plain Beauty, and she hasn't heard anything about her, but she said that there are online chat groups where trainers trade a lot of information about horses. Sometimes someone will post about a recent acquisition, that sort of thing. She said it's mostly bragging, but it won't hurt to look."

"Great," Martha said. "I'll get started tonight after dinner."

CHAPTER NINETEEN

The next morning Martha crawled out of bed to look for more horse trainer chat rooms. She started a pot of coffee, showered, dressed, and then fed the dogs and the cat. Next she hurried outside, collected the eggs from the hens and fed the chickens and the goats, who kept butting up against her leg. They made her think of her grandchildren and that Trish hadn't called her back. She glanced at her phone. Five forty. It was too early to call or text.

Back in the house, Martha poured herself a cup of coffee, mixed up a double batch of muffins and slid them into the oven, then sat down at the computer to resume what she'd started the night before until it was time to take the muffins out. Once she had them cooling, she returned to the computer. After a half hour of finding sites, bookmarking them, and scrolling through the messages since September 6, she came across a post from two days ago.

JUST LOOKED AT A BEAUTY OF A HORSE. MARE. QUARTER HORSE. BLACK AS MIDNIGHT. HAVEN'T DECIDED WHETHER TO PURCHASE HER OR NOT. I'LL KEEP YOU POSTED. The online handle was @horseship. Perhaps the trainer planned to breed Plain Beauty. Martha didn't know much about the horse business, but at five, Plain Beauty had years of breeding ahead of her.

She couldn't find out any more information about the person who posted—not a location or phone number or business. She bookmarked the page and jotted down the information. She'd check back later to see if the person posted again. Then she kept on scrolling as both Elizabeth and Mary finally came down the stairs. While the other two made breakfast, Martha asked, "What would a person do with a retired racing horse?"

"I actually asked Alvin that soon after Plain Beauty went missing." Elizabeth put a lid on the oatmeal. "He said retired racing horses might race at smaller tracks. Or be bred. Or trained to work as a ranch horse, cutting cows and that sort of thing. Or sent to the slaughterhouse—but that wouldn't happen to Plain Beauty. She's worth too much and has years of value left in her."

Martha took a sip of her cold coffee and decided to do some research on horse tracks, or "downs," as they were called. There were six in Pennsylvania, two in West Virginia, and three in Maryland. Of course, Plain Beauty could be anywhere in the US by now. There were five tracks in New Mexico, including Albuquerque Downs, where Ty was. She'd call the track in a couple of hours and ask if there was a horse there that looked like Plain Beauty.

Next she researched horse breeders, just in Pennsylvania and West Virginia. There were at least one hundred fifty listed. She sighed. That would be a lot of places to contact.

"What's the matter?" Elizabeth asked.

"I was thinking about contacting horse breeders in Pennsylvania and West Virginia—you know, and other nearby states—but there are so many. I feel like Plain Beauty is a needle in a haystack."

Elizabeth poured herself a cup of coffee. "That's how I felt about the trainers."

"How many called you back?"

"Three out of twenty-five. And I have scores more to call."

Martha logged off the computer and said, "Maybe this isn't the best use of our time."

She created a template to keep track of all the auction items. She would need to work quickly to get the forms made and printed off. She opened the auction ledger that she'd left on the desk the night before and filled out the form for the first item, then printed it. Thankfully, she'd recently changed the ink in the printer.

After breakfast Martha gathered the muffins she'd wrapped, and they all headed to the shop to get ready for the day, including setting up for the quilting circle, which, according to Elizabeth, Rachel planned to lead. Martha wished they'd gone ahead and canceled it—she didn't want any more pressure on Rachel.

As she walked to the shop, Martha fell behind, breathing in the sweet scent of the hay that Silas had cut the day before. Again her thoughts fell to Trish. She didn't want to be the imposing mother, but she was beginning to worry.

Normally by this time, Trish would have dropped the kids off at school before going home to work. Martha stopped, looping her arm through the handle of the muffin basket as Elizabeth and Mary continued on to the shop. Martha texted Trish. CAN YOU TALK?

Not right now, she texted back. Will call asap.

Martha had been praying all week about moving back to Kansas. If she lived there, she wouldn't be wondering how Celeste was doing. She'd know. And she could help Trish.

In fact, her pull to move back to Kansas was more to help Trish than to think she could make a difference in Celeste's health. Because if Trish wasn't so tired and spent, she'd have more energy to care for Celeste.

Martha had to get through the auction, and then she'd talk with Elizabeth and Mary about what she needed to do next. She'd feel as if she were letting her sisters down, but hopefully they'd understand.

Martha stood in the entryway to the shop for a moment to let her eyes adjust to the dimmer light. Elizabeth was already processing some new items from the day before that needed to be shelved, and Mary was sorting through the vintage clothes rack.

Mary grinned at Martha. "I'm going to come up with a really cool fall outfit to display."

Martha smiled back, thinking of twenty more important tasks, but maybe Mary needed to do something creative before buckling down to work.

Martha arranged the muffins in the display case and then concentrated on getting ready for the quilting circle. First she pulled the frame out of the closet, which was now also stuffed with auction items, like every other nook and cranny in the shop. Once she had the frame with the quilt set up, she placed the folding chairs around it.

She checked her phone, hoping she'd find a text from Trish. She didn't. It was five minutes until ten. Time to open up and welcome the quilting circle women.

Mary had put together three vintage outfits. An eggplant-colored flapper dress, a gold '70s pantsuit, and a brown calico prairie skirt with a white peasant blouse. "Nice work," Martha said as she walked by the rack.

Mary grinned. "We're getting a reputation for our vintage clothes."

"Thanks to you," Martha said as she headed to the storage room to call the track in Albuquerque. After calling the main number, she was transferred to the HR department. She explained that she was inquiring about Ty Jones, not expecting to get any answers to her questions.

However, apparently the woman wasn't worried about confidentiality. "He started yesterday," she said.

"Any chance he brought horses with him?"

"Yes," the woman said. "One horse. A paint."

"Thank you," Martha said. "You've been quite helpful." She hung up. Unless Ty had managed to completely hide Plain Beauty or sell her, it seemed he was innocent.

She headed out to the shop and unlocked the front door.

Anne and Betty were coming toward the shop carrying more quilts. "We want to auction these off," Anne said. "And some of the other women are bringing more too."

"Oh, that's wonderful!" Martha exclaimed. "Thank you."

"Where is Rachel?" Betty asked.

"We're expecting her any minute." Martha shot Elizabeth a look.

Elizabeth nodded. "Come get a cup of coffee and a muffin."

Thankfully, Rachel, along with Phoebe, arrived a few minutes later, walking in with Marietta and Leora. Sure enough, several of the other women brought more quilts.

"We are all very grateful," Rachel said. "This is far more than we expected."

Marietta and Leora nodded in agreement.

"We'll have a table with just quilts on it," Martha said.

"I'll make a sign," Mary added.

Martha wasn't sure if the quilts should be placed in the silent auction or the general one. She'd ask Pauline.

The women chatted as they helped themselves to muffins and cups of coffee.

Finally, Elizabeth gestured toward the quilt in the frame. "Let's get going. If we finish this, we'll have another one to auction off."

The women sat in their chairs, with Phoebe in her usual place next to Rachel. With the nine-patch quilt spread out in front of them, they threaded their needles and began quilting. The conversation turned to Davie, of course.

"He is home," Rachel said. "As of yesterday."

"How about a bone marrow donor?" Anne asked. "Has one been found?"

"There is a possibility," Rachel reported. "This person has gone to a meeting and now has further tests to go through."

Martha knew she was talking about Faye and admired Rachel for being discreet.

Phoebe looked at her mother and smiled but didn't say anything. Rachel patted her hand in affirmation.

"How is Trudy doing?" Leora asked. "I have not called—I know she has so much to do. But I have been wondering how she is."

"Tired," Rachel said. "But staying strong." She smiled at her sister.

The conversation turned to the auction. Martha gave an update about the items that had been donated and the plans for Saturday. "We'll have the main auction, silent auction, and sales items. Plus great food. Hopefully everyone can come."

One after another, the women all said they planned to attend and bring family and friends with them.

Rachel smiled and thanked them.

Secretly Martha feared no one would come, and they wouldn't make any money—or everyone would, and they wouldn't have enough room for parking or enough food to feed everyone.

But Rachel caught her eye and smiled calmly. Martha remembered what her friend had said about trusting the Lord to bring just the right number of people. Martha returned Rachel's smile.

"Any news on Plain Beauty?" Marietta asked.

Rachel glanced at Martha again.

"No," Martha said. "The police are still working on it."

"Any leads?" Betty asked.

Martha wasn't sure what to say. Finally she said, "There have been some, but so far none have panned out."

The conversation shifted to Betty's buggy horse, who was getting old. "I'll have to buy another one soon."

Marietta suggested she see Alvin, and others offered advice on what kind of horse to look for.

A few minutes later, a young woman dressed in jeans and a sweatshirt came into the shop. Martha didn't recognize her, but by how quickly Rachel stood, it seemed she did. Marietta and Leora leaned toward the woman, as if expecting her to say something.

So did Mary and Elizabeth.

Confused, Martha studied the young woman. She had long, loose blond hair, piercing blue eyes, and a petite build.

"Aenti Rachel—"

Rachel stepped toward her. "What do you need, Faye?"

Faye. She was Trudy's sister. Alvin's oldest daughter.

"I need to speak with you," Faye answered.

Rachel turned toward her sisters. "Marietta and Leora too?"

Faye shook her head. "No, just you."

While Faye and Rachel spoke outside the shop, the quilting circle women chatted quietly except for Marietta and Leora, who both had their heads bowed, as if they were praying.

Martha glanced toward Elizabeth. Her head was bowed too. Martha followed suit, asking the Lord to give Rachel wisdom and to help Faye make her decision in line with the Lord's will. She prayed that if any animosity between Faye and Alvin was in the way, the Lord would heal that too.

Anne laughed at something Betty said, and the mood of the group lightened a little.

Martha lifted her head and asked Phoebe if she was working on a quilting project at home.

She beamed and nodded. "For Davie."

Marietta asked what she was making.

"A nine-patch," she said, "in his favorite color—blue."

"That sounds lovely," Elizabeth said. "What fabrics are you using?"

"Scraps from Daed's and the boys' shirts." Phoebe beamed. "All colors of blue. Sky blue. Midnight blue. Plain blue. Baby blue."

"The quilt will match Davie's eyes," Elizabeth said.

"Ja." Phoebe smiled again. "You are right." Then she ducked her head and concentrated on her quilting again.

Rachel returned a moment later, without Faye. She cleared her throat and said, "Would any of you Englisch ladies with a car be willing to give Faye a ride to the clinic in Lancaster?"

Phoebe's head shot up. "What about her truck?"

Rachel sighed. "She does not want to drive…"

"I'd be happy to," Martha said.

"Ach." Rachel's voice was low and kind. "You have so much to do in the next couple of days…"

"It won't take long." Martha stood and started toward the door. "I just need to grab my keys. I'll tell Faye I'll take her." Martha turned toward Elizabeth, realizing she should have checked with her, but her sister nodded in agreement.

"Danki," Rachel said.

Martha told the women goodbye and pushed through the door. Faye leaned against a silver pickup.

Martha approached her. "I'm Martha Watts," she said. "Elizabeth's sister. I think you've met her."

Faye nodded.

"And Mary is our youngest sister. She saw you at your father's yesterday."

Faye nodded again.

"I can give you a ride to the clinic," Martha said. "I just have to get my keys and purse."

A few minutes later they were on the highway, going through Bird-in-Hand to Lancaster.

"I need to get my blood drawn," Faye said. "Thank you for driving me. I'm a little squeamish and didn't want to drive home."

"I'm glad you asked." Martha had a million questions for the young woman but didn't want to intrude. Her first one was answered, maybe. At least it sounded as if Faye was going through with the testing to donate to Davie.

"Where do you live?" Martha asked.

"Outside of Harrisburg. I work at a farm supply store. But they're giving me a couple of weeks off."

"Where have you been staying?"

"I was staying at a friend's. But now I'm staying in Daed's dawdy haus. Since yesterday."

Martha was surprised to hear that, considering that Alvin seemed opposed to having Faye around, but maybe that was why she was in the dawdy haus and not the main house.

Faye didn't say any more. Martha searched for a nonintrusive topic. Finally she said, "I sure like your aunts. It's been so fun to have Rachel lead our quilting circle and to have Marietta and Leora in it too."

"Ja, they're all really great. Daed really won the lottery when it came to sisters."

Martha almost laughed at Faye's response. She definitely spoke like an Englischer.

"I wasn't so lucky," Faye said.

Martha concentrated on keeping her voice casual. "Oh?"

"Well, Trudy is cool, but Amanda has never forgiven me for leaving." She turned her head toward the passenger window and gazed out at a market as they passed by. "She's miffed that I've come back home and angry with Daed for letting me stay."

"That's too bad." Martha stared straight ahead.

Faye didn't say anything for another long moment but then said, "She even talked to the bishop about me not being allowed to donate my marrow to Davie, saying that God has to have someone else in mind."

Martha had a hard time understanding that. "Oh dear."

"It broke Trudy's heart." She slouched in her seat. "She's never been angry with me the way Amanda has…"

Martha slowed for a stoplight. "What about your father?"

"He was really disappointed in me," Faye said, "but not so much angry. Maybe more embarrassed than anything. I told him last night to stop caring what other people think, although I know it's hard."

"What does he think about you donating bone marrow?"

"He's okay with it." Faye sat up a little taller. "He wants Davie to get well. The little guy is his only grandchild."

"Were you having second thoughts about donating because of what Amanda was saying?"

Faye shook her head. "Of course not. I'd do whatever I could for Davie. And for Trudy." She ran her hand through her long hair. "I don't relish doing this—the meeting frightened me. Now the thought of that painful procedure has me queasy." She shuddered. "Those big needles in the back of my pelvic bones. Having to stay in the hospital most of the day, maybe even overnight."

Martha didn't usually get queasy, but listening to Faye made her empathetic. Perhaps the issue for her hadn't been the way she'd been treated when she left the Amish, but her fear of needles.

Faye continued. "Possible side effects are hip pain, fatigue, nausea." She sighed. "But if I really am a match, I'll do it. No doubt about it."

CHAPTER TWENTY

Faye directed Martha through downtown Lancaster to the clinic for her blood test. "The actual bone marrow transplant would take place at the hospital, but they sent me to this clinic for the blood test."

As Martha parked her car in the lot, Faye asked, "Would you come in with me?"

"Of course." Martha admired the young woman for doing what she feared. That was true courage.

Unfortunately, the clinic was busy, and they had to wait. Martha tried not to think of all the work that needed to be done back at Secondhand Blessings to get ready for the auction.

Finally, a lab technician called Faye back.

"Come with me," she begged Martha.

"I'd be glad to." Martha walked beside Faye down the hall, wondering if Faye would have left the Amish if her mother hadn't passed away. She also wondered why Alvin hadn't remarried. Most Amish widows and widowers remarried within a year or two after losing their spouses.

The technician led Faye, who'd taken a piece of paper out of her purse, to a chair. Faye handed the document to the phlebotomist, who then stepped to her computer.

After a few minutes, she asked, "Which arm?"

"My left," Faye answered.

Martha stepped closer to Faye as the phlebotomist put a tourniquet around her upper arm.

"Don't look at the needle, look at me." Martha reached for Faye's free hand.

Faye followed her instructions but still winced when the needle went in.

The technician filled up three tubes and then finally took the tourniquet off. "How are you feeling?" she asked Faye.

"All right," Faye said. But she didn't look all right. She looked up at the phlebotomist. "Will my fear of needles and all things medical disqualify me from donating to Davie?"

The technician smiled at her. "I'm not an expert on all of this, but I've never heard of anyone being disqualified because they're squeamish. You'll do fine."

The technician left with the vials, and Faye started to stand.

"Oh no you don't," Martha said. "Sit here for another couple of minutes."

Faye did, but when she started to get up she still swayed. Martha linked her arm through Faye's and forced her to sit down again. The next time she stood, she seemed all right.

"We should get you something to eat," Martha said. It was nearly one o'clock. Past lunchtime.

"Ja, that sounds like a good idea. I forgot to eat breakfast."

"Oh dear." As much as Martha needed to get back to the shop, she needed to take care of Faye first.

The technician said there was a coffee shop around the corner that served soup and sandwiches.

Martha held on to Faye's arm as they walked out of the clinic and then down the street. Once they entered the café,

Martha led Faye to a table and seated her. Then she went up to the counter to order soup and sandwiches for both of them.

Once they had their food, Martha led them in a prayer.

"Thank you for everything," Faye said after Martha had finished praying.

"Oh, I haven't done much."

"No, you did. I hate doctors and clinics and needles. You got me through that. I really appreciate it."

"I'd be happy to stay with you through the bone marrow donation too, if that works out." Martha realized as soon as she said it that she might not be around. What if she'd returned to Kansas by then? But she wasn't going to correct herself. Not now.

"I'd like that." Faye took a small bite of her turkey sandwich. "Most Englischers ask me why I never joined the Amish."

Martha smiled as she dipped her spoon into her squash soup. "I didn't want to pry."

Faye appeared awfully pale. "I can tell you're a Lancaster County Englischer. Up in Harrisburg everyone wants to know what my accent is. Then why I left. If I'll join the Amish, in time, after all."

Martha couldn't help herself. "Will you?"

Faye shook her head. "I left six years ago, when I was twenty-two. I thought it through before I left. I miss my family and friends, but I needed to leave. That doesn't mean I think everyone should. In fact, I begged Trudy to stay."

Martha wiped her mouth with her napkin. "You did?"

Faye nodded. "She wanted to leave because she was fed up with Daed. I told her that wasn't enough of a reason."

"Why did you leave?"

"Because I longed for more freedom." She glanced down at her sandwich that only had a half bite missing. "To have more opportunities to work with horses. To support myself." She met Martha's gaze. "To drive. Ja, that sounds so shallow, but I really like my independence."

"Did Trudy take your advice right away?"

"Well, not completely. She still entertained the idea, even though she'd joined the church. If she'd left, she would have been shunned, which, technically, I'm not." Faye took a sip of water. "It wasn't until Sam started courting her that she decided to stay, for sure." She sighed. "Which is one of the reasons Amanda was—is—furious with me. She said that she'd lost our maam, and then me, and she couldn't bear to lose Trudy too. I think when Sam died, Amanda thought Trudy might still leave and take Davie with her, of course."

Martha could only imagine how hard the thought of that would have been for Amanda. And she surmised Amanda was having a hard time starting a family of her own because young married Amish women didn't choose not to have children. Which would only add another layer of stress for her, feeling as if her only nephew might be taken away.

"Even though I would have loved for both of them to come live with me after Sam died, I never encouraged it," Faye said. "And I'm so glad I didn't."

"Why is that?"

"They wouldn't have all the support and care they have now. Here, they have Daed. Aenti Rachel, Aenti Marietta, and Aenti Leora. Everyone in our district. You and your sisters. In Harrisburg they'd only have me."

Martha leaned over the table, toward Faye. "Who do you have?"

Faye's eyes immediately filled with tears. Instead of answering, she ducked her head and stared at her soup. "I'm still not feeling well," she said.

Martha assured her that was fine, and they left the café with their arms linked again.

Once they left the Lancaster city limits, Martha headed toward Bird-in-Hand, while Faye sat with her head back against the seat rest and her eyes closed.

About a mile from the shop, Faye said, "Could you take me to Daed's house? I'm still feeling light-headed. I don't think I should drive."

"Of course." Martha turned right at the next intersection.

"I'm not sure how I'll get my truck, but I'll figure something out."

Again Martha started going through everything she needed to do, but then she chided herself. What was more important than taking care of Faye? Than taking care of the person who could be the answer to Davie's healing? "Give me the key, and Elizabeth and I can bring it over in the morning."

"Thank you," Faye said. "God has really used you to care for me. I know you're doing it for Davie, but I appreciate it."

Martha wasn't sure what to say. She had just thought the exact same thing. But now she was convicted by those thoughts. "I hope I'd be helping you regardless," she said. "Now that I know you, I'll help you any way I can." If she did go back to Kansas, she'd need to wait until after Faye's donor procedure.

"Thank you." Faye put her head back against the seat and closed her eyes again.

"Do you mind if I ask you a couple of questions?" Martha asked. "About your life in Harrisburg."

"Go ahead."

"Do you date Englischers?"

"Sometimes. I just broke up with a guy who works construction. He wasn't right for me."

Martha asked her second question. "Do you go to a church in Harrisburg?"

"Ja," she answered. "That's where I met the construction guy. I've been going there since I left. It's nondenominational. The people are really nice." She shrugged. "It's not like the Amish church, but I'm thankful for it."

"How is it not like the Amish church?"

Faye, her eyes still closed, chuckled a little. "They don't gossip as much, at least not to me. But then, I don't think they'd take care of me if I was sick or pay for my medical costs or stuff like that either."

Martha agreed. "It's amazing how the Amish community cares for their people."

Faye sighed. "That's what I miss the most. Knowing that I'd always be cared for."

"I'll pray you'll find that in your new life," Martha said as she turned down the lane toward Alvin's farm.

Once Martha parked her car, she helped Faye get out. The ring of hammers filled the air, but Martha couldn't see anyone on the house side of the stable. Alvin and his crew must be working on the field side.

Martha walked closely beside Faye up the stairs to the house and knocked on the front door. Trudy soon answered it, holding Davie in her arms. Before even saying hello to Faye or Martha, she turned so she was blocking Davie and said to her sister, "Are you ill?"

"Just queasy—not contagious," Faye answered.

Trudy chuckled and shook her head. "Poor Faye." She glanced at Martha. "She has been like this since we were little. It is so funny, she can care for a wounded animal or person, but if it is her, she is a mess."

Faye rolled her eyes. "I'm going to go straight out to the dawdy haus and rest."

Trudy took Faye's arm and said to Martha, "Danki for your help. We all appreciate it."

"You're welcome. Elizabeth and I will shuttle Faye's truck over in the morning."

Trudy chuckled again and then nudged her sister. "You really have it bad this time, ja?"

Faye nodded and pointed toward the dawdy haus out the back door.

Martha pulled the front door shut and headed back down the steps.

Alvin popped up from the other side of the roof and walked to the peak of the stable and waved. So did Bill. Martha didn't think Alvin should be up on the roof, but she doubted he would listen to her.

"Any new leads on Plain Beauty?" Alvin shouted down.

"No," Martha replied. The "lead" from the day before wasn't enough to base any hope on.

"Guess we'll have to have the auction without her."

Martha reluctantly agreed. Thankfully, they hadn't advertised the horse as part of the auction.

"How's everything else shaping up?"

"Good." Martha shaded her eyes against the afternoon sun. "We'll start setting everything up by tomorrow afternoon and finish by Saturday noon, when the 'doors'"—she made air quotes—"open."

"Wunderbar!" Alvin called out. "I will be over Saturday morning. I am going to run one of the barbecues."

"Oh." Martha took a step closer to the stable. "I was hoping you'd greet people."

"Oh, I will do that too. Caleb Yoder is going to help me barbecue."

"Caleb? I thought he'd left for Kentucky."

Alvin shook his head. "He is staying a little longer than he thought he would."

"I see," Martha said, even though she didn't. She thought it odd that Pauline hadn't mentioned anything.

Then, as she was leaving the Raber farm, she passed Caleb driving his buggy toward her. She waved, and he waved back. Was he visiting Alvin? Or Trudy and Davie?

It was after three by the time Martha returned to Secondhand Blessings. The shop was packed with tourists. Elizabeth was ringing up a sale at the counter, with three other people waiting in line, and Mary was helping a customer at the vintage clothes rack.

"How can I help?" Martha asked Elizabeth as she tucked her purse into the shelf underneath the counter.

"We're doing okay with the shop, but Caleb Yoder dropped off some things for the auction."

"Oh? I just passed him on his way to the Raber farm."

"Interesting," Elizabeth said. "The boxes are back by the storage room. Go ahead and work on those."

"Okay." Martha grabbed a ledger. Even though she'd expected Caleb to drop off his extra items, she felt overwhelmed by them. At least there were only three boxes. He must have sold most of his things.

When she was done she retrieved her clipboard. She'd already drawn a map of the property, and now she walked along and paced out where the food tents and eating area would be, where the auction would take place, where the holding area would be, where the corral would be set up for Plain Beauty in case she was found in time, where the silent auction and sales tables would be located, and where the portable toilets would be dropped off. Several times she had to erase something when she realized it wouldn't work logistically. By the time she finished, it was five o'clock, and Elizabeth was turning the sign to CLOSED.

"When will everything be delivered?" Elizabeth asked.

"Tomorrow afternoon," Martha answered.

Mary came out of the shop. "I'll mow the yard, finish up the weeding, and water all the plants."

"Bless you." Martha was filled with appreciation. Those were all tasks Mary did with little effort, but if Martha was to do them—except the watering—it would take her twice as long.

"And then I'll work on the posters," Mary said. "But I may need to finish those up tomorrow evening."

"No worries." Martha smiled at her sister. "We'll get it all done in time."

Mary took a step backward. "Are you feeling all right?"

"What do you mean?"

"You seem…more relaxed than usual. We still have a missing horse, a huge auction to put together, a sick boy here in Lancaster, and a sick girl in Kansas. And yet you're saying 'we'll get it all done.'"

Martha laughed. "I'm trying really hard to trust the Lord with this one."

Mary smiled. "Well, it's great. It makes working on this much more enjoyable."

Convicted about her past behavior, Martha guessed being more relaxed did make it more enjoyable for Mary. And probably for Elizabeth too. She headed back into the shop to help Elizabeth close up for the day.

An hour later, after feeding the goats, chickens, dogs, and cat, the sisters sat down to eat a chef salad Elizabeth had tossed together.

The conversation soon fell to the auction. "Will we have the tents on the premises for two nights?" Elizabeth asked.

Martha nodded. "The rental company is only charging us for one though—that's how the delivery worked out. It's to our advantage."

"Aren't you worried about vandals?" Mary asked.

"Oh, I forgot to tell you." Martha put her fork down and reached for her glass of iced tea. "Pauline is hiring two young

Amish men who'll be on site tomorrow night, with lanterns and a couple of dogs."

"Oh, perfect," Mary said.

"The weather is the other thing that's going to be perfect," Martha said. "Seventy degrees and not a cloud in the sky."

Elizabeth beamed. "That should bode well for the turnout, the auction sales, and the food sales."

Martha and Mary both agreed.

After supper, Mary pulled out the poster board and her art supplies. "I think I'll work on the sign for the quilts next."

Martha did the dishes and then sat down at the computer to produce more of the auction item forms. When she took a break to stretch her back, Mary was still working on the quilt sign.

It was gorgeous with lots of colors and shapes. Martha stepped closer. The illustration was of the log cabin quilt the circle was working on.

"Oh, I forgot to ask," Martha said. "Did the quilt get finished today?"

"It did." Mary filled in a block with a purple marker. "Marietta and Leora stayed until it was done, until just before you got back."

"So we'll auction it too?"

"That's right," Mary said. The sign read SILENT QUILT AUCTION INSIDE SHOP. "Rachel thought putting them as part of the silent auction will work best—and they'll stay cleaner in the shop. We'll need to have an attendant in the shop the whole time though, so people will focus on the quilts and not try to buy any of our items, but the quilting circle ladies all said they'd take turns and worked out a schedule."

"Perfect." Martha hoped people who attended the auction who'd never shopped at Secondhand Blessings would return to the shop in the weeks after the auction.

Sometime after nine, Martha realized how tired she was. With a yawn, she checked her phone, hoping to have a text from Trish. But there was nothing.

As she debated whether to call or not, her phone began to buzz. TRISH.

She answered it and headed out to the patio where a cool breeze was blowing. "Hi, sweetie," she said. "I'm so glad you called. How is Celeste? How are you?"

"Celeste came home from school today in a lot of pain..." Trish's voice trailed off. "Just a sec." In the background she asked Jared to check on Elliott. Then she said, "I'm back."

"Listen," Martha said. "I just need to finish up this auction, but then I'm going to talk to Elizabeth and Mary about moving back to Kansas. I shouldn't be here when you and Celeste need me."

"Oh, Mom, that's so sweet of you, and I appreciate it." She paused.

"But?" Martha couldn't believe her daughter didn't want her to move back.

"But I can't get the image of you at Dad's grave out of my mind. You looked so sad."

"I was..."

"And that's why I think it's better if you stay in Lancaster. You have your own life there. If you came back to Kansas, you'd have reminders all over the place. Yes, come visit more often, but don't uproot the life you just planted."

Martha leaned against the patio post. "Are you sure? I want to help you."

"Which I truly appreciate, but something really cool has happened this week."

"Oh?" Martha stood up straight.

"Jan came over and helped me with laundry and getting dinner ready two afternoons this week," Trish said. "And today when Celeste wasn't feeling well, Jan was working at the school and called me. She brought Celeste to the house and stayed with her while I finished up my work for the day."

"Wow." Martha's heart filled with gratitude for her friend.

"I know, isn't it great? That much help is making a big difference."

"I bet it is, and for Jan too." Martha's heart swelled at the thought of sharing her grandchildren with her friend.

"So, thank you, Mom. But I want you to enjoy your time back in Bird-in-Hand. Who knows what the future holds, but right now it makes me happy to think of you in Grandma and Grandpa's old house with your sisters."

After they chatted a little while longer, Martha told Trish goodbye and hung up. Full of relief, she headed back into the house. Yes, there was a part of her that did want to return to Kansas—but there was another part of her content to stay in Lancaster County.

The poster boards and markers were still on the table, but Mary was nowhere in sight. She probably planned to work on the signs in the morning.

Martha yawned again and was tempted to go to bed, but instead she sat back down at the computer to check the horse chatrooms. She went to the bookmarked sites and scrolled through. She didn't see anything new posted. Then she went to the last one she'd bookmarked, the one where the breeder had posted about hoping to buy the black mare.

There was a new post by @horseship, the first one on the thread. He'd posted two minutes before. GREAT NEWS! I'M BUYING THIS BEAUTY, AT LEAST I HOPE SO. THE OWNER IS BRINGING HER TO SAIL AWAY FARMS TOMORROW! ETA, 10 A.M. HERE'S THE ONE PHOTO I HAVE. I'LL POST MORE PICS ASAP.

The photo under his comment wasn't very good quality, and Martha couldn't tell if it was Plain Beauty for sure. She logged on to the site on her phone and took a screenshot of the post. Then she googled Sail Away Farms, and found one just south of Taneytown, Maryland. It was only an hour and a half away.

Martha leaned back in the desk chair. She needed to set up for the auction tomorrow. Did she have time to run a reconnaissance mission in search of Plain Beauty too?

CHAPTER TWENTY-ONE

Martha rose at 5 a.m., showered, dressed, fed the animals, petted the dogs, rubbed the cat's neck, and made the coffee. Then she mixed up a breakfast casserole and a double batch of pumpkin muffins and popped both in the oven. It was six fifteen. Where was Elizabeth?

She returned to the computer and checked the chat thread. There were a few congratulations but nothing more from @horseship.

Finally, she heard Elizabeth in the shower. She entered the kitchen at the same time Martha pulled out the casserole and muffins.

"The breakfast casserole smells good," Elizabeth said, heading for the coffee. "What's the special occasion?"

"We have a busy day. I thought a good breakfast was in order." Martha turned toward her sister. "Plus I need to talk with you about something."

"What is it?"

"I may have a lead on Plain Beauty." She explained what she'd found on the chat thread. "I'll talk with Alvin about it when we shuttle Faye's pickup over."

Elizabeth rubbed her hands together. "Oh, I hope the horse is Plain Beauty. Wouldn't it be great to get this solved before the auction?"

"It would be." Martha couldn't think of anything better.

"I think we should let John know."

"Yes." Martha had thought of that last night when she tossed and turned before falling asleep. "I'll send him a screenshot of the chat thread and a photo of the horse. And you call him."

Martha listened as Elizabeth spoke to John. Finally, she said, "That sounds like an excellent idea." She hung up and said, "John is going to call the sheriff in Carroll County, Maryland. He'll call back and let me know what he finds out."

A couple of minutes later, Elizabeth's phone rang. Finally, she said, "I see. Thank you for trying." Then, after a pause, "We'll let you know what we find out."

She ended the call and said, "The local sheriff doesn't think there's enough reason to send anyone out. They're short-staffed. And John can't get away today either. He said if you go to be careful. Call 911 immediately if it's Plain Beauty—or if you have any problems. In that case, a deputy will get over as soon as possible."

"Sounds like a good plan." Martha smiled, but inside she didn't feel as sure. Would it be a good idea to go down? What were the chances the horse was Plain Beauty?

An hour later they left Mary in charge and headed over to Alvin's farm with Martha driving Faye's pickup and Elizabeth driving her car. When they arrived, Alvin and Bill were installing windows in the stables.

As they climbed out of the vehicles, Elizabeth said, "Look at that. They've nearly completed the stable. What quick work."

Martha nodded in agreement and pulled her phone from her purse. "I'm going to go show the chat thread and photo to Alvin."

It took her a minute to get his attention as he pounded away on a window frame. Finally, she raised her voice. "Alvin!"

He turned toward her.

She held up her phone. "I need to show you something."

He slipped the hammer into his tool belt and stepped toward her. Bill paused for a moment but then kept hammering away.

Over the racket, Martha explained what she'd found online. "Read this," she said, handing him the phone.

When he finished, he said, "Sounds like a long shot."

"I agree," Martha said. "Now look at this." She took the phone back, clicked on the photo of the horse, and then handed it back to him.

He studied it for a few moments. Finally he said, "I cannot be certain, but I changed my mind. I think it would be worth looking into."

"I know you don't have the bill of sale on Plain Beauty, but do you have any documentation?"

"I do," Alvin answered. "A canceled check."

"Any chance you could go with me to see what's going on down at Sail Away Farms?"

Alvin tugged on his beard. "Right now?"

Martha nodded. "We'd need to take the trailer, just in case."

"Can you drive my truck?"

Martha cringed. She'd just driven Faye's pickup, but it wasn't towing a trailer. "I can try," she said.

"Great. I will go talk with Bill, hitch the trailer, and then get the canceled check." He pointed toward the house. "Go get a cup of coffee—the girls are all inside. I will be in as soon as I am done."

Martha followed his instructions, and once she was on the porch and reached the door, she knocked. And then knocked again.

"Coming!" someone finally yelled.

A moment later, Trudy opened the front door. Her eyes were rimmed with red.

"Oh dear," Martha said. "Have I come at a bad time?"

"No." Trudy gestured for her to enter the house. "It's actually a good time."

Martha stepped into the house. At the table sat Elizabeth and Faye, with Davie on her lap. Amanda stood behind Faye, with her hands on her shoulders. Everyone except for Davie had been crying.

Martha sat down at the end of the table, next to Elizabeth.

"I have been having a come-to-my senses moment," Amanda said. "Your sister has been giving us all wise counsel."

"Oh, I just gave a few ideas. The three of you are the ones doing all of the work."

Trudy stepped toward the counter. "Martha, would you like a cup of coffee?"

"Please." Martha kept her eyes on Elizabeth.

While Trudy poured the coffee, Amanda said, "I have been convicted of my anger toward Faye. I believed she was selfish, and that was why she left. But I can see by her willingness to help Davie that she is not as selfish as I have been portraying her." She patted Faye's shoulder. "Will you forgive me?"

"Of course," Faye said. "Honestly, the way you and others treated me when I left is exactly what I expected. I knew Trudy wouldn't, and I figured Daed wouldn't be horrible to me... But to have you apologize for the way you treated me is really a gift."

Amanda brushed a tear away. "I am truly sorry. And I am truly grateful that you are willing to help Davie. I am praying you will be a match for Davie."

Faye bounced Davie on her leg. "We all are." She turned her head up toward her sister. "I hope you realize that even though I never joined the church, I truly love him too."

As Amanda nodded, Alvin came through the front door.

"Faye!" he called out. "Can you go to Maryland with Martha and me?"

"What?"

"I need someone to drive my truck and trailer."

Faye stood and slipped Davie into Amanda's arms. "Ja, I can do that. Right now?"

Alvin nodded. He held up the documents. "We are going after Plain Beauty."

As everyone talked at once, Elizabeth told Martha she would call Ron Sliter and see if anyone had contacted him about buying Plain Beauty.

"Good idea," Martha said. "Call me and let me know what he says."

Davie begged to go with Faye and Alvin in the "twuck and twaila," but his grandfather told him he needed to stay home this time. "We'll have an adventure soon."

Martha told Elizabeth, Trudy, Amanda, and Davie good-bye, and then followed Alvin and Faye out the front door, relieved that she wouldn't have to drive.

The pickup and trailer were by the barn, hitched, pointing the right direction, and ready to go. Martha climbed in the back seat of the king cab. They all waved at Bill as they passed by the stable.

Martha found the website for the farm on her phone and clicked on directions.

Faye braked too hard before she turned onto the lane. "Sorry," she said.

"No need to be," Alvin answered. "I just had the brakes redone. They are touchy."

Martha couldn't help but think of her own father and how patient he'd always been with her.

Alvin directed Faye to turn left on Highway 30 just as Caleb Yoder slowed to turn down the lane to the Raber farm.

Martha watched him turn and said, "So is Caleb doing work at your place?"

Faye shot her father a look.

Alvin cleared his throat and said, "I think he is going to spend some time with Davie this morning." Before Martha could ask for more information, Alvin said to Faye, "Head toward York."

Martha smiled. Perhaps Caleb had delayed leaving to see if he had a reason to stay.

Traffic was thick, and several times they were delayed behind buggies. Alvin laughed the fourth time it happened and said, "I will not complain."

They continued on, through Gettysburg. This part of the route was the same as when Martha drove to Boss Chambers's farm.

Elizabeth called just after they passed through the town and said she'd gotten through to Ron Sliter. "He said someone 'anonymously' contacted him about a special horse he'd be interested in, but Ron told him he had no interest in anything from an anonymous source."

"When was that?" Martha asked.

"Tuesday."

That would have been the day before @horseship posted in the chat room.

"Thank you," Martha said.

"You're welcome," Elizabeth answered. "Let me know what you find out."

She kept checking the clock. What if the seller of the horse got there early and left before they arrived? If that happened, they'd have to ask the owner of the farm if he'd just bought a horse—and hope he'd be honest.

Several times Faye pressed on the brakes too hard. Each time, Alvin said, "That is all right. You are doing fine."

After a while they turned onto Route 134, south toward Maryland. It was beautiful country with green pastures, strips of woods, and stately homes, barns, and stables.

Faye slowed down as they entered the Taneytown city limits. It was a sweet, old-fashioned town with a population of around seven thousand filled with red-brick buildings. South of town, they turned down a lane. Martha checked her phone. It was 9:10.

Stopped at a gate, leaving the farm, was a truck pulling a horse trailer. With West Virginia plates. A young man was walking toward the gate, most likely to open it. Inside the cab of the pickup was another person, but he ducked his head and turned his cowboy hat down.

"Pull up right to the gate," Alvin said as he grabbed a pair of binoculars out of the glove box. "Turn the truck and trailer across the lane. Make sure he cannot open the gate."

Faye accelerated, following her father's instructions, and slammed on the brakes, stopping the truck within inches of the gate.

The man jumped back and began cursing. The man in the cab ducked his head even more.

"Move your truck!" the man at the gate yelled.

Faye shifted into PARK and leaned back against the driver's seat, as if she could get away from the man.

In the distance, probably a quarter of a mile away, was a barn and corral. There were banners flying by the corral in the shape of sails. Martha could make out a black horse and a person.

Alvin whistled. "I am almost certain that is Plain Beauty."

"I'll call 911," Martha said, punching in the numbers.

"I would try to alert the man at the corral, but I need to stay here to stop Boss Chambers."

"Are you sure it's him?" Martha asked as the phone rang.

"Positive. It is the truck and trailer he used to deliver Plain Beauty. And that man at the gate is his assistant, R.J."

CHAPTER TWENTY-TWO

Holding her phone to her ear, Martha prayed R.J. wasn't a violent man.

The dispatcher answered. "911, what is your emergency?"

"I'm at Sail Away Farms, outside of Taneytown, 10211 Sail Lane. There's a horse thief trying to get away. Officer John Marks from Bird-in-Hand contacted the local sheriff this morning about—"

The dispatcher cut her off. "Is everyone safe?"

"I think so," Martha said. "We have the thieves pinned in, with the gate between us."

"Don't confront anyone," the dispatcher said.

Martha nearly laughed. They were practically face to face with both Boss Chambers and his assistant.

"We'll stay in the truck," she said. "With the doors locked." At least that was her plan. She hoped it was Alvin's too. "How long until someone arrives?"

"A deputy is three miles away. Sit tight but stay on the call."

"I will," Martha answered.

"Daed, I can run down there and alert the man with Plain Beauty while you stay here."

"No," Alvin said. "That is too dangerous. You would have to run by that man. He might grab you and hold you hostage."

"Daed!" Faye said. "You sound as if you've been watching detective shows."

"I have not. I just know these things happen."

R.J. climbed the gate and came around to Alvin's window. He yelled for Alvin to lower it, and when he wouldn't the man began pounding on it.

Faye started honking the horn.

"What's going on?" the 911 dispatcher asked.

"One of the thieves is banging on the window."

R.J. kept yelling but then abruptly stopped and climbed back over the gate.

"He is going to get something from his truck to break the window." Alvin turned to Faye. "Go ahead and sneak down the other side of the truck and trailer. I'd rather have you risk that than stay in the truck with him going crazy. I will keep up with the honking."

As R.J. opened a toolbox in the bed of the truck, Faye jumped down from the cab and Alvin kept pressing on the horn.

She scurried over the gate and began running, as if she were a racehorse.

"She has always been fast," Alvin said. "She always won all the foot races when she was a girl."

Just as she passed Boss Chambers's door, he opened it and began yelling.

"What's going on?" the dispatcher asked.

Martha gave her an update as R.J. realized what Faye was doing.

R.J. ran back to the cab and jumped in. As he backed the truck and trailer up, Martha feared he intended to run Faye down, but then he shifted forward and plowed through the fence into the pasture.

"He is going cross-country." Alvin shook his head. "That is ridiculous."

The truck bounced along the pasture as R.J. cut a tight corner and drove through another fence, going down into a ditch. But he came back out, onto the road, just as a siren wailed in the distance.

Martha and Alvin jumped down from the cab as the sheriff's car, with two officers inside, came to a stop and blocked R.J. and Boss Chambers from going any farther up the road.

R.J. jumped down from the cab, yelling, "We can explain everything. We were just escaping from those crazy people."

Martha wondered if she, the fifty-five-year old grand-mother, and Alvin, the Amish man in his sixties, should hold up their hands.

The sheriff, an older, tall, thin man, climbed out and then a younger, shorter deputy joined him. "Everyone remain calm," the sheriff said in a slow, quiet voice. "We had a call about a stolen horse."

"That's right," R.J. said. "These two are trying to steal a horse we just delivered." He nodded toward the barn. "They've got another woman with them. She's already on the farm."

Martha crossed her arms. My, the man was a fast talker.

"I have documentation that I paid for the horse," Alvin said, "four weeks ago. The man in the cab, Boss Chambers, never sent me the bill of sale as he promised he would. The horse in question disappeared from my farm in Lancaster County on September sixth. I fear Boss Chambers stole her back, along with her saddle, and then resold her today."

"All right," the sheriff said. He turned toward Boss. "Out of the pickup."

Boss took his time but managed to climb down, leaning on a cane.

"Close the door," the deputy added.

He complied and took a step away from the truck. He kept his head down and certainly didn't act with bravado as he had just a few days before on his farm in West Virginia.

The sound of a motor made them all turn. A man was driving a pickup toward them, with Faye in the cab. He jumped down, opened up the gate, and yelled, "R.J.! What's going on? Why did you drive through my fences?"

R.J. waved his hands at him. "It's all right, Sean. We've got this under control. Just a misunderstanding is all."

Faye jumped out of the other side of the pickup and called out to the driver, "It's more than a misunderstanding. Like I already said, you bought a stolen horse."

The man looked like he might cry. "But he gave me the registration papers. And a bill of sale. And now my fences need to be repaired."

"Well, he stole the horse from my daed. And he had no right to sell it."

As Sean, followed by Faye, walked toward the group, the sheriff and deputy exchanged glances. Then the sheriff shrugged and said, "Anyone got a gun on them?"

Everyone said no.

"All right," the sheriff said, "everyone pull out any documentation you have and bring it over to the hood of the cruiser."

Sean pulled a couple of pieces of paper from the front pocket of his shirt while Alvin opened the front door of his pickup and pulled out his canceled check. R.J. took a check out of the pocket of his work shirt and held it up.

As they all gathered around the hood of the cruiser, Alvin turned to Sean. "Any chance Boss sold you a training saddle?"

Sean nodded.

"That was stolen from my tack room on the evening of September sixth too."

R.J. laughed. "Any proof it was in your possession that day?"

"Actually, there is." Martha held up her phone. "I have a photo of it, taken that afternoon."

"You can't prove it was in Alvin's possession. There's no way he's in the picture."

"Actually—" Martha scrolled through her photos. "Alvin's hands are in the photo…"

R.J. snorted.

"And his beard."

She held her phone up for the sheriff to see.

"That very well could be Alvin." The officer pointed to Sean. "Is this the saddle you just bought?"

Sean stepped closer and took a look. "Yep." He sneered at R.J. "You dirty trickster." Both the sheriff and the deputy stepped between the two men and held Sean back as he demanded, "Give me back my check."

CHAPTER TWENTY-THREE

It turned out the sheriff had spoken with John that morning and remembered the background of the story, but he had each person tell their side of the story anyway. Alvin went first and told the story Martha already knew.

When it was R.J.'s turn he deferred to Boss.

He grunted and pointed at Alvin, saying, "I have no idea what this man is talking about."

"Then why did you deposit my check?" Alvin held up his canceled check. "This check was cashed on September seventh, the day after I purchased the horse."

When Boss didn't answer, Alvin took a step toward him. "Why did you do it?"

"You didn't deserve that horse."

"Then why did you sell her to me?"

"That's just it, I regretted selling her immediately."

Martha stepped forward. "And you thought if you stole her back, the nonresistant Amish man wouldn't go after you? Wouldn't press charges?"

"Wait," R.J. said. "You told me the Amish guy's check bounced, but he wouldn't return the horse. And the saddle. That's why we—"

"Be quiet!" Boss yelled.

Everyone stood stunned for a moment.

Finally, Alvin turned to R.J. "Did you set the fire on purpose, or was it an accident?"

"Fire?" Boss barked.

R.J. hung his head. "Accident. It was darker than I expected, so I lit the lantern to get a better view of the horses, to make sure I had Plain Beauty. But as I was leading her out, she reared, and I bumped the lantern. I panicked and fled."

Boss shook his head in disgust.

"I was relieved to hear you got all of the other horses out," R.J. added.

When no one had anything more to say, the sheriff asked for all the evidence, then asked Boss and R.J. if they would willingly come to the station for questioning.

"I will," R.J. said.

"Only with my lawyer," Boss retorted.

"You can call him from the station," the sheriff said.

"What about the horse?" Alvin asked.

"You're the last legal owner," the sheriff said. "You can take her—but don't sell her or anything."

Alvin's face fell. "I was hoping to auction her off tomorrow."

"Nope." The sheriff shook his head. "Assure me you won't."

Alvin frowned. "All right." He turned to Sean. "Sorry for all of this trouble."

The man nodded. "So am I, but I'm glad you showed up today and not a week from now. She's a beauty. The sooner you claimed her the better." Then he turned toward the sheriff. "What about my fence?"

"I'll write it into the report as destruction of property. Call your insurance and have them request the report." The officer rubbed the back of his head. "But in the meantime, I'd get it repaired. Before you lose your livestock."

Sean nodded. "Thankfully, they're in the south pasture right now…"

R.J. walked ahead of Boss, and the old man struggled as he made his way to the cruiser. Martha stepped to his side and took his arm.

"I'm a foolish old man," he said to her. "First I regretted selling Plain Beauty. Then I regretted stealing her." He sighed.

As they neared the cruiser, R.J. was talking with the younger officer. "I don't know why I believed him about needing to steal the horse back. He hasn't been himself. He said he sent the bill of sale before he cashed the check. And he's doing fine financially, but he's been worried about money. He believed he should have sold the horse for more, that he could get more for her."

The officer opened the back door. "How about his health? He seems rather frail."

"Oh, he didn't mention that? He has a brain tumor." R.J. sighed. "I thought he was okay, mentally. I believed what he said about the Amish guy. But apparently I was mistaken."

Martha inhaled, sharply. Finally, the theft of Plain Beauty was beginning to make sense.

Once the deputy moved Boss Chambers's truck and trailer to the side of the lane, and joined the sheriff in the front of the patrol car, Faye, Alvin, and Martha climbed into their pickup and followed Sean up the lane to the barn.

He parked in front of the corral. They all climbed out and walked up to the fence. Plain Beauty raised her head and pranced her feet. She'd been on quite a journey, but it appeared as if she'd been well cared for. Plus, she'd been at a familiar place.

"How long have you had Sail Away Farms?" Alvin asked Sean.

"I inherited it from my uncle a couple of months ago," he answered. "My parents were missionaries in Argentina, out in the country, and I grew up working on a nearby horse farm. I'd work here, with my uncle, when we were on furlough and then during the summers through college and vet school. I was working on a farm in upstate New York when my uncle died unexpectedly. I'm going to try and do my best to continue what he started."

"I think you will," Alvin said.

Sean took off his hat. "May I ask a question?"

"Of course," Alvin answered.

"Who tipped all of you off?"

Alvin nodded toward Martha. "She is the one who figured it out."

Martha shrugged. "I saw your post in the trainer chat room on Wednesday night about wanting to buy a 'beauty' and then your post from last night. I thought it was worth the risk of coming down, to see for ourselves."

Sean rubbed the back of his neck. "I'm so thankful I posted—and that you saw it. I hate to think I would have been in possession of a stolen horse."

As they all watched Plain Beauty, Sean asked about the auction. Alvin began talking, and Martha was afraid he might never stop. He told him about Davie and the need for the bone marrow transplant and their hope that Faye would be a match, and how they were raising money for Davie's medical care with the auction.

"Obviously you won't be selling this horse at the auction, but will you be selling any other ones?"

Alvin turned toward Martha. "That is brilliant." Grinning, he turned back to Sean. "As a matter of fact, now that you mention it, I have one I plan to sell. Another quarter horse, for sure."

"Daed? What are you talking about?"

"Caleb Yoder's horse," he said. "I bought it—I just have not brought it to the farm yet."

"Maybe Caleb will buy it back," Faye said. "Once he decides to stay."

Martha smiled. It seemed everyone was hoping Caleb would stay in Bird-in-Hand.

"He'll need a horse for his courting buggy." Faye grinned.

Martha's mouth dropped open.

Alvin shook his head. "He just comes over to play with Davie."

"Daed," Faye said. "Don't be obtuse."

Sean cleared his throat. "Could we talk about the auction?"

Faye laughed. "Sorry."

"What other items are being auctioned? Any tack items? Farm equipment?"

"Definitely," Martha said. "Other saddles, besides Plain Beauty's. Harnesses. Halters. Stirrups. Really, everything you can imagine, including a couple of troughs that are in good shape." She pulled a business card out of her purse. "Here's the address. It starts at noon tomorrow." Just the thought made her heart race. She really needed to get home.

"We should probably load Plain Beauty and get going," she said to Alvin.

He ignored her and said to Sean, "We will all be at the auction. So that is another benefit. You will get to see all of us again."

Martha laughed. "If we don't get back to Bird-in-Hand and actually set up for the auction, none of us will be at the auction, because there won't be one."

"All right, all right." Alvin chuckled. "I get the message." He extended his hand to Sean. "I am sorry for the reason, but it has been a pleasure to meet you. I hope we will see you tomorrow."

"I think you will," Sean answered. He turned toward Martha and shook her hand. And then did the same with Faye. "You are a brave lady," he said. "Will you be at the auction too?"

Faye smiled and nodded.

On the way home, Faye drove much more slowly with Plain Beauty in the trailer. Martha finally stopped checking the time on her phone and put her head back. Breathing deeply, she said a prayer that everything would work out. They retraced their route through Gettysburg and York and then on toward Lancaster.

"Could you drop me off at the shop?" Martha asked Faye. "Since I don't have a vehicle at your farm."

"Of course," Faye answered.

A few miles from the shop, Martha's phone buzzed. It was the rental company. As she answered it, she expected her contact to tell her that the drop-off was complete.

Instead, he said, "We have a complication."

"What?" Her heart began to race again.

"We're running late because the truck broke down about an hour ago. I thought it would be an easy fix, but the mechanic we sent out said it needs a new transmission. So…" The man hesitated.

"Yes?"

"Let me check the paperwork again." She could hear the rustling of papers. "Here it is. We'll deliver your order tomorrow morning."

"Tomorrow morning?"

"That's right. By seven."

"There's no chance you can get it to us tonight?"

"Sorry," the man said. "We have two weddings this evening. Those take priority. We'll give you a discount for the inconvenience."

"All right," Martha said. There was nothing to do but be gracious—and pray some more.

CHAPTER TWENTY-FOUR

It turned out her prayers were quickly answered. As soon as Alvin found out what the situation was, he said, "We will have plenty of help tomorrow morning. Make out a plan tonight on the best way to set everything up once the tables and tents arrive. I will bring the crew."

A few minutes later, Faye pulled the truck and trailer straight through the parking lot of Secondhand Blessings. "We'll see you in the morning."

Alvin lowered his window as Martha climbed out of the back seat. "Danki for everything you have done for us. I will see you in the morning too."

"Thank you," Martha said. "See you tomorrow."

As she hurried into Secondhand Blessings, she hoped Pauline had stuck around. She could really use her help to get everything organized.

Elizabeth stood at the counter, ringing up a sale.

Martha waved and asked, "Is Pauline here?"

Elizabeth pointed toward the storeroom. As Martha hurried by, she said, "The tent and tables delivery is delayed until tomorrow morning. I'm hoping Pauline can help me come up with an extra efficient rollout plan."

Elizabeth's mouth dropped open, but she quickly closed it and turned her attention back to the customer, with a smile on her face.

Pauline and Mary were in the storeroom.

"No delivery truck, so far," Mary said. "They must be running late."

Martha explained the situation, and Mary and Pauline reacted with shock.

"Alvin is going to recruit a crew to help in the morning, so we need to come up with a comprehensive plan."

"Let's do it," Mary said.

"I propose we go into the house and sit at the table," Martha said. "We can map everything out, make sure we have a sign for everything, and come up with a time line—as long as they deliver the items by seven o'clock as promised."

"What if they don't?" Mary asked.

"There is no reason to think like that now," Pauline replied. "We need to trust the Lord that they will."

Elizabeth agreed to run the shop while the others worked in the house. Martha grabbed the ledger of auction items and her planning notebook.

Once they'd settled around the table with cups of coffee and sandwiches, Martha said, "First, we need to go over who is in charge of what." She flipped to her list. "Mary, you are in charge of making sure every last sign is done by the time you go to bed tonight, no matter how simple it is. Artistic is good, but functional is essential."

"Got it." Mary nodded in agreement.

"I'll be in charge of directing where the tents and tables go," Martha said. "And then I'll put the signs on each table."

She turned toward Pauline. "Then I'll have you direct our crew as far as placing the right items on the corresponding tables."

"Will do," Pauline responded.

"Mary, can you help make sure all of the items end up on the correct tables?" Martha opened up the ledger. "We'll arrange the items and documents so they'll all be easy to access during the actual auction." Thankfully, Pauline had already indicated that she would oversee that job too.

The three went through every detail of the auction they could think of, writing down notes and making adjustments to the map that Martha had already started.

"We'll put Elizabeth in charge of the food tents and directing our vendors to the right spot when it comes time to set up." Martha checked her list again and tapped her pencil on the table. "We'll need someone to buy ice in the morning and fill all of the cold boxes we have."

"I'll call Bill and ask him to do that," Mary said. "And tell him not to come by tonight."

"That'll work." Martha continued to scan her notes to see if she'd forgotten anything.

Mary drifted off and returned with her stack of poster board, markers, and a list of signs that still needed to be made.

Finally, just before five o'clock, Martha and Pauline finished with the planning. Pauline said she would be back by quarter to seven the next morning.

"Will the crew Alvin recruits expect to be fed?" Martha asked.

Pauline shook her head. "They will eat breakfast before they come, but it would be good to have coffee and muffins, that sort of thing."

Martha agreed. She'd do more baking before bed. She thanked Pauline profusely.

"Ja," the woman answered. "Gott is good with His planning, is He not?"

"Absolutely." Martha was grateful for Pauline's confidence that the Lord had His hand in their planning.

That evening Martha baked multiple batches of muffins while Elizabeth helped Mary with the signs. The last ones weren't quite as fancy as the first ones, but they were all attractive. Between taking batches of muffins from the oven, Martha finished up the auction item documents.

Finally, all three sisters cleaned up the kitchen—both the baking items and the poster supplies—and then fell into bed.

As Martha said her prayers, she thanked the Lord that Trish had the help she needed, that Celeste was getting the medical care she needed, and that Plain Beauty had been found. "Dear Lord," she whispered out loud, "now please help us pull off this auction." That would feel like a miracle indeed. "And heal Davie of his cancer."

The next morning Alvin arrived at six thirty with Faye, who had driven the pickup and horse trailer over. They brought a large propane barbecue and several coolers.

"I will be selling ribs," Alvin said.

"They're quite famous," Faye added.

"Do not brag," Alvin admonished.

Faye laughed. "How about infamous, then?"

Alvin grinned and said, "I had a phone call from the police station in Maryland. They got as much of a confession out of

Boss Chambers as possible. R.J. was able to fill in the holes. I am convinced Boss's mental capabilities have been affected by his tumor. I decided not to press charges."

"Really? Don't you think R.J. should have figured out that what Boss was asking him to do was criminal?"

Alvin shrugged. "It is not our way to press charges against others."

Martha inhaled sharply, but then let her breath out slowly, realizing it was Alvin's decision, not hers. "You're right," she said. "This is entirely your decision." And she shouldn't be surprised. She knew Amish people rarely pressed charges or sued.

Alvin smiled kindly at her. "I do not expect you to completely understand, but I have to follow my own convictions. It is what I believe the Lord wants me to do."

Martha nodded. "I do understand that. And I don't think Boss Chambers is a threat to anyone else—or R.J. either. I'm guessing justice has already been served."

"Ja," Alvin said. "If there is one thing I have learned in life, it is that the Lord's justice is often different than our own."

Martha agreed. The Lord's ways were not people's ways—in all sorts of areas of life. She nodded to the horse trailer. "Did you bring one to sell?"

He nodded. "Midnight—the family I was training him for decided they didn't want him after all."

As Alvin led the horse from the trailer and toward the corral, Mary caught sight of the horse and came running over. "I wish I could buy—"

"No!" Martha said.

Mary laughed. "I was just dreaming. I promise."

The delivery truck arrived just as the Amish crew did. It took a couple of hours to unload all the tents and tables and get them placed correctly.

Task after task was completed, and once everything was set up, Martha invited everyone into the house for a coffee break with muffins while Pauline gave directions to set up the auction items.

Martha headed outside with the signs and placed them on the tables, and soon the crew was distributing all the goods, under Pauline's direction.

The food crew, including Rachel and her girls, arrived by ten, and Elizabeth directed everyone to their booths. Soon the barbecues were fired up, coolers were filled with salads and beverages, and desserts were unpacked.

By eleven thirty, the parking crew, headed up by Rachel's oldest son, Adam, had arrived, both to direct the cars to the Fischers' field to park and to unhitch horses from the buggies and lead them into the Fischers' pasture.

At noon, right on time, the event opened with the sale items and the silent auction. As Martha scurried around, making sure everything was in order, she said hello to Caleb, who was helping Alvin finish up his ribs.

Later she saw Trudy walking around the grounds with Caleb. "Who's with Davie?" Martha asked.

"Amanda," Trudy answered. "She said she wasn't interested in coming to the auction and would rather stay with him. I'll only stay an hour and then go to be with him."

By midafternoon Martha spotted Sean from Sail Away Farms walking with Faye over to the corral. He definitely seemed interested in Midnight.

Martha hurried into the shop to check on Elizabeth and the quilt sale. Marietta and Leora were in the shop, looking at the quilt table. There were multiple bids on all of the quilts.

Martha turned toward the register, where Elizabeth sat with John. They were deep in conversation. Martha simply smiled and slipped back out of the shop.

It was nearly three o'clock, close to the time for the auction to start. As Martha neared the main auction tent, Pauline waved at her. The auctioneer had arrived and was finishing up looking over the tables and forms. "It looks like everything is in order and ready to start. You have done a fine job," he said.

Martha turned toward Pauline and expressed her thanks. "I couldn't have done this without you."

Pauline beamed. "I am so grateful you asked for my help. It has been a joy to work with you."

As the auctioneer opened the bidding on the very first item, Martha saw Faye running toward the tent. Alvin must have seen her too, because he intercepted her before she reached the crowd. She said something to him and hugged him. Then she took off toward the parking area, and Alvin came back into the tent.

Martha hurried to him. "Alvin, is everything all right?"

Alvin looked at her and broke out in a grin from ear to ear. "Everything is better than all right. Faye just received a call from the clinic, and she is an exact match for Davie. The procedure will take place very soon."

"Oh, Alvin," Martha said. "What could be better news than that?"

"Faye is on her way to the house to tell Trudy," Alvin said. "We will now pray for Gott's will to be done through the transplant."

Martha's heart was bursting with gratitude as her gaze swept the tent, looking for her sisters. Her family, her home, her community, her village—she knew God's will for her life was wrapped up in this time, in this place, and she couldn't be more content to be right in the center of it all.

A NOTE FROM THE AUTHOR

Dear Reader,

The first time I visited Lancaster County was with my husband and oldest son, who was just a baby at the time. It was in late summer, the same time of year that *Plain Beauty* is set. That was back in 1987, and I absolutely fell in love with "Amish Country." I have been back countless times since. The loveliness of the landscape never escapes me. Pristine farms of emerald green fields, immaculate houses, and massive barns. Splashes of color from the laundry drying on the wash lines and the flowers blooming in pots on the porches. Cows, mules, and all kinds of horses, from draft horses to miniature ones. Chickens and turkeys. Prancing standardbred horses pulling buggies and workhorses hitched to wagons.

It truly is a magical place.

As I wrote *Plain Beauty,* I thought of the beautiful Lancaster County landscapes, but mostly I thought of the people. I have friends and acquaintances in Amish communities from Lancaster County, Pennsylvania, to Nappanee, Indiana. The interactions between the Amish and their Englisch neighbors truly fascinate me, which made writing *Plain Beauty* a joy.

As Elizabeth, Martha, and Mary help their Amish friend Rachel Fischer and her extended family, both groups of people grow in faith and love. That's truly what it's all about and holds far more beauty than even the idyllic landscapes.

Leslie Gould

ABOUT THE AUTHOR

Leslie Gould is the #1 bestselling and Christy Award-winning author of over thirty novels. Besides writing, she also teaches part time at Warner Pacific University. Leslie and her husband, Peter, enjoy traveling, research trips, and hiking. They live in Portland, Oregon, and are the revolving-door parents of four grown children and two cats.

MORE TO THE STORY

It's well known that the Amish often buy retired racehorses and train them to pull their buggies, as I wrote about in *Plain Beauty*. But what isn't common knowledge is that the Amish also sell their horses to work in other places too. On a recent trip to Charleston, South Carolina, the horse that pulled the tour wagon I rode in came from an Amish farm in Lancaster County. And when I was in New York City a few years ago, the driver of a carriage in Central Park said his horse had come from an Amish farm too. The Amish are known for their love of horses and skills in training them. Just as it's a pleasure to witness the retired racehorses pulling buggies in Lancaster County, it's also a thrill to see Amish workhorses in communities far away from Plain settlements.

FRESH FROM MARTHA'S KITCHEN

Apple-and-Caramel Muffins

Muffin Ingredients:

2 cups all-purpose flour

¾ cup sugar

2 teaspoons baking powder

2½ teaspoons ground cinnamon

½ teaspoon salt

1 large egg

1 cup milk

¼ cup butter, melted

2 teaspoons vanilla extract

½ cup peeled and chopped tart apple

12 caramels, chopped

Topping Ingredients:

½ cup packed brown sugar

¼ cup quick-cooking oats

3 tablespoons butter, melted

1 teaspoon ground cinnamon

Directions:

In a large bowl, combine flour, sugar, baking powder, cinnamon, and salt. In another bowl, whisk egg, milk, butter, and vanilla. Stir into dry ingredients just until moistened. Fold in apple and caramels.

Fill 12 paper-lined muffin cups three-fourths full. Combine topping ingredients; sprinkle over batter.

Bake at 350° for 20 to 25 minutes or until toothpick inserted in cake portion comes out clean. Cool for 5 minutes before removing from pan to wire rack. Serve warm.

Read on for a sneak peek of another exciting book
in the Mysteries of Lancaster County series!

The Ties That Bind
by Janice Thompson

An early-morning breeze whipped through the trees outside of Secondhand Blessings. Elizabeth stood in the
open doorway of the shop and took it all in. Her breath caught
in her throat as she watched the first colorful leaves of the season float through the air and then tumble to the ground in a
crisp, dazzling display of red, gold, and orange. Was there anything finer than October in Lancaster County?

"You might want to close that door before those leaves blow
inside." Her younger sister Martha's voice sounded from behind
her. "Then we'll have a mess to clean up."

"Sorry." Elizabeth stepped inside, and the door closed.
"Just couldn't help myself. I feel like it's been years since I witnessed anything this exquisite. God is on full display during
harvest season, wouldn't you say?"

"Yes, and the leaves are beautiful," Martha agreed. "I'll
give you that. But they're hard enough to rake up outside, let
alone inside. The last thing we need is another mess to pick up
in here. Those kids yesterday practically tore the place apart. I
thought I'd never get the shelves reorganized." She tended to a
lantern that was sitting too close to the end of a shelf. "Folks

need to keep a closer eye on their kids. That's all I've got to say about that."

"True." Elizabeth walked behind the front counter and tucked her purse on the shelf below the cash register. She couldn't help but smile as her youngest sister, Mary, entered the shop and stood in the open doorway, gushing over the leaves.

"Have you ever?" Mary clasped her hands to her chest. "Oh, they're glorious! And that breeze just takes my breath away. I feel like God just allowed me to glimpse a little foretaste of what heaven's going to be like."

"I, for one, am praying there are no rakes in heaven." Martha clucked her tongue as she walked their way, broom in hand. "Now close that door, Mary. You're letting leaves in. And it's chilly out there."

"Oh, who cares?" Mary giggled and spread her arms wide as a delicious breeze whipped the leaves into a dance that landed several of them squarely inside the shop. "Oops." She looked at Martha. "Don't worry, I'll take care of those." She took the broom from her sister's hand and began to sweep, humming "All Things Bright and Beautiful" as she worked.

Martha brushed a loose strand of hair behind her ear and turned toward the back of the store. "If anyone needs me, I'll be in the stockroom. I've got to catch up on inventory."

Elizabeth arranged several items on the front shelf then paused to watch Mary sweep leaves. Her sister continued to hum as she worked. After a moment, Mary stopped sweeping, and a dreamy look came over her. She glanced Elizabeth's way.

"I think Anna picked the perfect season to get married. I just love autumn weddings."

"Me too." Elizabeth thought about their old friend's upcoming nuptials. "And I'm sure you and Martha will do a fine job coordinating everything for her. I'm just glad she asked the two of you and not me. I don't think I would have the time or the inclination."

"I plan to make the time. Anna deserves the very best." Mary released a sigh. "She's waited so long for Mr. Right. When you've held on until your midfifties to get married for the first time, you deserve the full regalia."

Elizabeth did her best not to read too much into her sister's words or to let sad memories overtake her. She'd come pretty close to having a wedding herself. Only, her story had taken a turn in the end, one that did not land her at the altar. Shaking off her ponderings, she responded to Mary's comment. "I'm not so sure I'd go all out, even if I'd waited for years. I'd probably go for simple and sweet."

Simple and sweet suited her, she had to admit. Not her sisters, though. Mary and Martha were birds of a different feather, more prone to contemporary dress and style. Mary, especially, kept up to date on the latest fashions and trends. They were certainly the best ones to help Anna prepare for her big day.

"I think Anna's going to ask for the moon, and I'll do my best to give it to her." The edges of Mary's lips tipped up in a comfortable smile. "If you'd told me a year ago I'd be coordinating a wedding, I would've said you were crazy."

Just as quickly, her smile faded, and Elizabeth wondered if Mary was revisiting her broken heart. She wouldn't blame her.

"If you'd told me a year ago we'd be running this shop together, I would've said you were crazy," Elizabeth countered. "But here we are, doing all of the above."

"And loving every minute of it." Mary went back to work, her humming now in full force. "Life has given me lemons, but I've made lemonade."

Elizabeth couldn't help but agree. The rustic old barn had been transformed into a thing of beauty—a shop where people came from far and wide to purchase quaint items. Many items, like the Amish quilts and other hand-sewn crafts, were one of a kind. Their Amish friends and neighbors also supplied them with canned jellies and jams, honey, furniture, and other woodcrafts to sell on consignment. Then there were the secondhand items, the eclectic estate and garage sale gems that kept some customers browsing for hours.

Elizabeth spent the next few minutes prepping the store for customers. Things were in full swing at Secondhand Blessings now that autumn was upon them. More and more folks were coming to their little village of Bird-in-Hand in hopes of finding the perfect Christmas gift. Many, like yesterday's big group, arrived at the remodeled barn with small children in tow. Even though there was a children's area in the center of the shop, complete with small tables and chairs, books, toys, wooden puzzles, and coloring books and crayons, the children ran through the aisles pulling toys off the shelves. The parents didn't seem to mind, but Elizabeth certainly did. So did Martha, apparently. Hopefully, today would prove to be calmer.

Elizabeth walked the aisles and straightened the shelves, taking note of their lower-than-usual inventory. Thank goodness they still had an ample supply of handcrafted Amish quilts and crafts. Otherwise she might be a bit concerned, what with Christmas coming and all.

"It's five till ten." Martha's voice rang out from the back of the shop. "Don't forget to flip the sign, Elizabeth."

"Got it." Elizabeth walked to the front door and turned the sign to OPEN. Her gaze landed on a red truck pulling into the parking lot, a Ford F-150 with mud flaps. Something about it seemed familiar. The owner backed the vehicle into a nearby space with ease, giving Elizabeth a clear view of its bumper. A sticker of an American flag caught her attention, along with the words SEMPER FI. This truck must belong to a marine.

Just as she was about to turn back to tidying work, a beautiful black and tan boxer leaped out of the back of the truck and landed on the gravel below. He stood erect, ears pricked and hind legs extended, as if waiting a judge's approval at a dog show. He had one of those scrunchy faces that only a mother could love. And the white paws and underbelly were a stunning contrast to the black and tan. He wore a dark green collar, a broad one, suited to his larger physique, but wasn't leashed. Hopefully that wouldn't turn out to be a problem.

Elizabeth stepped outside and took a couple of tentative steps toward the handsome boxer, hoping he was safe to approach. The pooch seemed fine. His docked tail wagged in anticipation, and he let out a couple of hearty yips as she moved his way.

"Rocky, wait for me." Elizabeth glanced up to see the owner of the voice, probably in his midthirties, exiting the cab of the truck. The man pulled off his tattered baseball cap and ran his fingers through his messy brown hair then stuck the cap back on...backward. Only then did Elizabeth notice his golden tan. Interesting, considering the time of year. Maybe he worked outside, in construction or something like that. Or perhaps he was a farmer.

He reached inside the truck and grabbed a leash, which he clipped to the dog's collar. He squatted in front of the dog and rubbed its ears for a minute before standing and closing the door of the cab.

Not wanting to appear nosy, Elizabeth walked back into the store. She fought the temptation to peek over her shoulder. Instead, she tended to some crumbs on the countertop, brushing them into her open palm and dumping them into the trash can. The bell above the door jingled as the man entered the shop with the dog beside him. In his arms he carried a package of some sort, wrapped in brown paper.

"Okay to bring Rocky inside?" the man called out before taking a step in Elizabeth's direction.

"Um, sure." Her gaze shot to the back of the store. Likely Martha would have a fit, but she hated to shoo this man off. Besides, the dog seemed to be friendly enough. Boxers were known to be great with people and nonaggressive, most of the time, anyway.

A broad smile stretched across the man's face as he took a couple of steps in her direction. "Thanks. He might look tough, but Rocky's gentle as a lamb. He won't hurt anything."

No sooner had he spoken the words than the dog attempted a getaway. The feisty canine pulled hard against the leash, nearly causing the man to drop the package in his arms. He managed to hold on to both the package and the dog, but Rocky's yelps must have caught the attention of Mary, who came bolting their way.

Her eyes widened when she saw the dog. "Everything okay up here?"

"Yes, ma'am." The man shifted the package in his arms. "Rocky's just testing my patience today. That's not like him, but he's been through a rough time lately."

"Want me to watch him while you shop?" Mary's eyes sparkled as she knelt down to scratch the pooch behind the ears. "Dogs just love me, and the feeling's mutual."

"Sure, if you don't mind." He set the package down on the counter and held the leash out to her.

"I don't mind a bit." Mary took the leash and clucked her tongue. "C'mon, boy. Let's go outside for a walk." She stepped outside just in time for a breeze to blow in another round of leaves. "It's beautiful out today!" Mary disappeared into the parking lot, the door closing behind her.

Elizabeth turned her attention to the man across the counter. For the first time she noticed that his hat wasn't the only thing that was tattered. The plaid shirt had seen better days and so had the jeans, with their frayed knees. She did her best to focus on his face, but the frown lines and wrinkled forehead made her even more curious than before. This poor fellow wore the exhaustion of life on his face, especially around the eyes. Strange for one so young.

"How can I help you?" Elizabeth pasted on a bright smile.

"Well, I saw the sign out front, that you take items on consignment. I was hoping I could place this piece right here. I've had it for years." He pulled back the brown wrapping paper to reveal a gorgeous antique pitcher—ivory with lovely rose-colored flowers etched in gold.

Elizabeth ran her finger along the scalloped porcelain, mesmerized by its beauty. "It's lovely," she said after a moment.

"Vintage," he repeated. "We've had it for years."

"And you're sure you want to sell it?" Elizabeth asked.

He nodded.

She knew better than to argue with a customer over such things. Many times she'd wondered how people could part with items they'd owned for years, but it wasn't hers to question.

"Do you have the washbasin?" she asked. "It will fetch a better price with both pieces."

For a moment the man didn't respond. He seemed to lose himself to his thoughts. He finally shrugged. "Nope. Sorry. This is all I've got. But I figure someone will want it."

"Right." She lifted the pitcher and gave it a closer look. Goodness. This would bring in a pretty penny with its basin, but without it…she couldn't be sure. After pondering the issue for a moment, Elizabeth offered a compromise. "Tell you what. Instead of taking it on consignment, why don't I just purchase it from you outright? That way you won't have to wait for your money. I'm sure the right buyer will come along." And even if they didn't, she would still purchase the pitcher from this man as a thank-you for his service to their country.

"Sure, sounds good." A hint of a smile tipped up the edges of the man's lips, and relief flooded his eyes. "I appreciate it."

"No worries."

They settled on a price just as Mary came bolting back through the automatic door with the dog leading the way. "He's very—" The dog ran down the center aisle, nearly knocking over a holiday display. "Fast!" Mary called out from the back of the store.

A crash sounded just as Elizabeth pulled money from the register to hand to the man. He took the bills then sprang into action to fetch the dog. Moments later he returned, the dog in tow. "Looks like I owe you for a farmhouse cookie jar that Rocky knocked over."

"Nah." With the wave of a hand, Elizabeth dismissed that idea. "It was chipped anyway. Been on the shelf for ages, in fact."

"If you're sure." He thanked her and headed toward the door. The dog continued to wag his tail as his owner gave a little tug on the leash. "Let's go, Rocky. Atta boy." Seconds later the door swung open, and they disappeared into the parking lot.

Elizabeth reached for the broom and dustpan then walked to the back of the store to sweep up whatever mess the dog had made. She found Mary kneeling, picking up the larger pieces of glass and depositing them into a small trash can.

"I can help you with that," Elizabeth said. She gestured to the broom. "Thought we might need this."

"Sure." Mary groaned as she stood. "Well, he sure was a handsome dog."

"That's a good word for a boxer...handsome," Elizabeth agreed. "He had beautiful markings."

"True." Mary nodded. "He was a little rowdy, though." She paused. "What did his owner want?"

Before Elizabeth could explain, she noticed Martha heading their way from the office in the back.

"I just had a phone call from—" Martha didn't finish her sentence. Instead, she gazed down at the shattered cookie jar. "What in the world? What did I miss?"

"Oh, just a dog running amok and knocking things over." Elizabeth swept up the remaining bits of glass. "I was getting tired of looking at that old thing anyway. No one was ever going to buy it." She paused. "Now, who was on the phone?"

"Oh right. Phone." Martha's worry lines deepened. "I'm afraid it was sad news. Bishop Jacob Wittmer has passed away. That was his daughter, Susanna, on the phone. She's asked us to help spread the word to our customers."

"I'm so sorry to hear that." Elizabeth stopped sweeping to acknowledge her sister's announcement. Bishop Wittmer was one of the oldest of all the Amish in their community and well loved by those he served. "I knew he was ill, of course, but certainly didn't expect him to pass away this quickly."

"No one did." Martha placed her hands on her hips. "I've volunteered to take a meal over tomorrow. The extended family will be coming in from all over, and I'm sure they could use something before the day of the service."

"That's nice of you." Elizabeth nodded. "And I'll be happy to help." Anything for a respected member of their tight-knit community.

"Susanna also mentioned an auction this Saturday," Martha added. "She wanted me to know there should be a lot of great pieces we might want for the shop."

"Right." Still, Elizabeth didn't feel like focusing on that at the moment, not with the bishop's passing so fresh in her mind. His death was a great loss to the community. So many loved him dearly.

As she walked to the front of the store, Elizabeth found her thoughts drifting back to the man with the porcelain pitcher. She pondered the creases in his brow, the circles under his eyes. The sadness on his face now matched the feelings in her heart as she pondered the death of one of the community's finest men. Strange how the words on that bumper sticker now seemed to fit the somber news she had just received about a beloved member of their community.

"Semper fi, Bishop Wittmer," Elizabeth whispered. "Always faithful."

A NOTE FROM THE EDITORS

We hope you enjoyed this volume of the Mysteries of Lancaster County series, created by the Books and Inspirational Media Division of Guideposts. We are a nonprofit organization that touches millions of lives every day through products and services that inspire, encourage, help you grow in your faith, and celebrate God's love in every aspect of your daily life.

Thank you for making a difference with your purchase of this book, which helps fund our many outreach programs to military personnel, prisons, hospitals, nursing homes, and educational institutions. To learn more, visit GuidepostsFoundation.org.

We also maintain many useful and uplifting online resources. Visit Guideposts.org to read true stories of hope and inspiration, access OurPrayer network, sign up for free news-letters, download free e-books, join our Facebook community, and follow our stimulating blogs.

To learn about other Guideposts publications, including the best selling devotional *Daily Guideposts*, go to ShopGuideposts .org, call (800) 932-2145, or write to Guideposts, PO Box 5815, Harlan, Iowa 51593.

Find more inspiring fiction in these best-loved Guideposts series!

Secrets of Wayfarers Inn
Fall back in history with three retired schoolteachers who find themselves owners of an old warehouse-turned-inn that is filled with hidden passages, buried secrets and stunning surprises that will set them on a course to puzzling mysteries from the Underground Railroad.

Sugarcreek Amish Mysteries
Be intrigued by the suspense and joyful "aha" moments in these delightful stories. Each book in the series brings together two women of vastly different backgrounds and traditions, who realize there's much more to the "simple life" than meets the eye.

Mysteries of Martha's Vineyard
Come to the shores of this quaint and historic island and dig in to a cozy mystery. When a recent widow inherits a lighthouse just off the coast of Massachusetts, she finds exciting adventures, new friends, and renewed hope.

Patchwork Mysteries
Discover that life's little mysteries often have a common thread in a series where every novel contains an intriguing mystery centered around a quilt located in a beautiful New England town.

Mysteries of Silver Peak
Escape to the historic mining town of Silver Peak, Colorado, and discover how one woman's love of antiques helps her solve mysteries buried deep in the town's checkered past.

To learn more about these books, visit Guideposts.org/Shop